Luck's Tether

by Billy Walker

Proofread by Thomas Mayo

Typeset by Your eBook Partners

Published by Billy Walker Publishing

Printed by Createspace – an Amazon Company

First paperback edition printed 2014 in the United Kingdom

ISBN: 978-0-9928907-0-4

Thanks go to…

Rory Dobner for the illustration of India House Hostel.
www.rorydobner.com/

Jon Gilbert of Angelfire Creative for his work on the front cover.
www.angelfirecreative.com/

Thomas Mayo for proofreading and the blurb.

Andy Marsh - A true friend without whom this story wouldn't
have been possible.

Contents

Crystal Clear

First, the old, fat paedo was trying to get me out for breakfast, and now this weirdo? I'm actually hungry though, so I agree to go. Maybe I can get to the bottom of this and find out a bit more about him. I haven't eaten anything since yesterday evening and it's five o'clock in the afternoon. I don't reckon this guy's dangerous; I'll smash his face in if he tries anything.

"Alright, gimme five minutes and I'll meet you back out here."

This bloke obviously knows his way around Atlanta. If he knows the place so well, why the fuck's he staying at the hostel? He must be over sixty! I haven't got a clue where we're going but he's walking like a man possessed. It's fucking raining too; that's the last thing I need. Throughout the journey, I'm trying to start conversations with this grumpy old git, but he's not talking; I don't even know his name. There's nothing coming back and it's putting me on edge. I'm getting frustrated. Say something, you fucking waste of space! It's one big uncomfortable silence the whole time, even in the restaurant whilst we're eating our food; I'm not enjoying this at all. Is he doing this on purpose? Is he playing some kind of game with me? He's trying to make me lose it; waiting for me to react. Fuck this. He's not bothered by it all. Why come all the way up here? We could've gone anywhere in the centre of town. Is he some kind of lunatic? Does he want me out with him so he can pretend I'm his son? Maybe someone's employed this guy as a spy. Everything that's happened since we arrived at the hostel in Atlanta has been fucking weird; and Marshy isn't here, so I can't tell if I'm being paranoid.

We finish our food, pay, and go back to the hostel the same way we came. We're the only people walking the streets, but the roads are packed with traffic, and it's still raining. I'm getting soaked whilst the cars roll past slowly, spitting water into the air. Still no chat. I've given up trying to make conversation. When we get back to the hostel, I breathe a sigh of relief 'cause I finally get away from the fucking nutjob.

Marshy's lying down on his bed. He catches me by surprise, just when I'm hoping to relax.

"Where the fuck have you been, man?"

"I went to get some food. You'll never fuckin' guess who with."

"Why? Who'd you go with?"

"You know that weird old geezer that was in the bar last night?"

"Which one? That American paedo or the English bloke?"

"The English one. Well, guess what…he's only showed up here, at this hostel!"

"No way, mate! You're fuckin' kiddin'!"

"Yeah, well he says he's stayin' here but it's fuckin' weird, mate, 'cause he must be at least sixty. What's he doing here at that age?"

"Mate, that's fucked up. Why did you go with him?"

"I was hungry and I wanted to try to suss him out. It was proper fuckin' weird though, mate; he barely said two words to me the whole time. He's fuckin' sketched me out. How you feelin'?"

"Bill. This place is fuckin' weird, man."

"You what? What are you on about? Somethin' happen whilst I was out?"

"It's fucked up in here, man, they've got little robotic cameras hidden in here, in this room; they're fuckin' watchin' us mate."

I'm laughing at Marshy. "Naahhhh. Don't be silly, man!"

"No, I'm being serious, mate. And earlier, right, I tried to have a chat with one of the guys stayin' here. He was all fuckin' lairy with me, sayin' when we came in this mornin' and played pool, we woke everyone up. I apologised to him but he got up and fucked off without sayin' anythin' to me."

"Have you been outside yet, mate?"

"No man, I didn't wanna go outside on my own 'cause they've been watchin' me. This is seriously fucked up, mate!"

I'm concerned about Marshy's mental state, 'cause usually, he's level-headed and on the ball. I haven't had a great deal of sleep so I get into my bed and lay down to rest my eyes for a bit.

I'm really fucking tired but I can't switch off. I hear a noise. The door's closed. The sound definitely came from inside the room – an electronic movement like a CCTV camera, like Marshy said. I get out of bed and start looking around the room – under the bed, in the drawers, and along the sides of the walls.

"There it was. Did you hear that, Bill?" asks Marshy.

"Yeah I heard it. Fuckin' hell, mate, that's weird...I've never heard that sound in a hotel room before. Maybe it's somethin' in the wiring?"

"If you say so, man, but I'm sure we're being watched. I think they've got some kind of little gadget out there that they can control."

"What? You reckon it's the people stayin' here?"

"I don't know, man. Maybe they're tryin' to fuck with our heads."

"You need to get up and get some food. Come on, mate, I'll

go with you."

I'm becoming wary of the other people in the hostel now, which is putting me on edge even more. What if they're all out to get us? We're totally outnumbered.

Marshy gets his clothes on and we go for a walk to find the nearest place that sells food. It's too far to go back to where I've just been, so we stay local. We walk away from the city centre, along 'Ponce De Leon', the street the hostel's on. The sun's gone down and it's about nine pm.

"Bill, walk with me down here; I wanna check somethin'."

We cross the road.

"Don't look back right now, but did you see that black four--by-four with the tinted windows, outside the petrol station?"

I'm looking straight ahead, but I remember. "Oh yeah, the one parked up against the wall? What about it?"

"Yeah, well the same fuckin' four-by-four was parked outside the hostel when we walked out, half an hour ago. No shit, Bill, I swear. The engine was runnin' when we walked out. It followed us and turned around in the car park and now it's followed us here. We're being followed."

"Are you serious? Marshy, you better not be fuckin' jokin'. That's some mad shit if it's true."

"Look, I'll prove it you. Let's go down here and see if it follows us again."

We take a left turn, which leads us down a slope and into a large, half-full supermarket car park. As we walk down the steps, towards the entrance of the supermarket, the same black four-by-four takes a left turn, from the main road, and enters the car park.

"Fuck!"

"What are we gonna do?"

"We need to get back to the hostel. Let's keep calm and act as if nothin's wrong."

By the time we're back at the hostel, and in our room, we're both starting to panic. I'm trying to figure out who is following us and why. We can hear people talking in the living room again and we're both silent, listening intently to what's being said.

"Can you hear them out there?" asks Marshy.

"Yeah, I can hear them talkin' about us. They're plannin' on comin' after us."

"They must be workin' with the people followin' us and watchin' us on those cameras; they're all workin' together."

We're sat down on the bottom bunk beds, looking at each other. There's an awkward tension between us; we both know we're in deep shit and we're stranded. It's the people in this hostel; they're trying to get rid of us. It's like some kind of psychological game they're playing to toy with us; the fucking sick cunts. We must have done something to piss them off, but what was it? And how long have we been followed for? Just here, in Atlanta? Since we got here, even? Was it something we did in one of the other cities?

I feel threatened. I can't think straight. We're pacing around the room. We need to get out straight away, in case something bad happens during the night.

I go to the receptionist and ask her to call us a taxi; she's sorted one to arrive in fifteen minutes.

We walk out the exit door and into the taxi. Thank fuck that's over; now we can relax.

"D'you know any other hostels around here, mate?" I ask the driver.

"Errr, there aren't any other hostels but I know a place you can go…"

Marshy's checking behind the taxi to see if anyone's following us. We're speaking under our breath to each other, trying not to alarm the taxi driver.

"D'you see anyone?" I ask.

"I dunno; I can't tell from here."

We must be on the outskirts of the city; the space around us has become darker; fewer street lights and buildings. We approach a turning for a hotel and the taxi driver tells us it's at the top of the hill. I can see it in the distance.

"Shit! Marshy, can you see that up there?"

"What?"

"Look at all those black four-by-fours blockin' the entrance…"

Miami, Florida

2 months earlier...

Welcome to America!

Ahhhhhh Yeeeahhhh! We've landed in Miami and we're getting off the plane. I'm fucking knackered 'cause the jet lag's screwed with my body clock, but on the plus side, I'm hammered already from all the 'complimentary' booze we've caned on our Virgin Atlantic flight. The air stewardesses got fed up bringing us drinks, so they showed us where to get them from. That was a mistake!

"Right, help yourselves from now on," they'd said, "but please don't take more than two drinks at a time."

Not a problem, we thought; we'll have to keep getting up, that's all! But I'm feeling it now.

The adrenaline in my veins is keeping me going. We've got three months of non-stop partying ahead of us, no need for sleeping. I'm battling on; no pussying out for me. I'm swaying whilst I wait in this line of people, following them all from the plane into the airport. Most of these boring bastards have been asleep the whole way, but not me and Marshy; we've been up the whole time, pissing around, laughing and giggling like little kids. That's what happens when we get together – I feel sorry for you, America!

Since leaving Pompey to go to university at Sheffield Hallam, I haven't had much time to get leathered with Marshy, so we've got loads to catch up on, and plenty of new memories to make; hundreds of people to abuse and birds to pull. We're going to show these yanks how to party!

The flight's taken nine hours and I'm guessing we probably don't look or smell particularly respectable. I've deteriorated pretty badly, like the end of a night out on the town, a shadow of the figure that stood in front of the mirror before I left the house. Eyes half-cut, faces dropped, slurring words, and drinks spilt over my clothes.

I'm getting bored of waiting in line now. We're in a massive queue at the international arrivals area, waiting to have our passports checked. This fat, middle-aged, white American bloke is sitting behind his desk, taking forever to let people through. Get on with it, lard-arse! As we both step forward at the same time, he's quick to bark orders at us.

"Stop right there! Only one person at a time. Get back behind the line and wait until you're called!"

Well, ooooooo! Sorrrrrrrry! Fucking hell, mate, no need to get so lairy. He's got this serious, angry look on his face, no joy in his life. He reminds me of one of my old schoolteachers. At first, I'm thinking this guy must be having a bad day, but looking down the row at all the other passport officers, all sat behind thick, transparent Perspex, I realise they're all miserable-looking bastards with the same lifeless expression on their faces. Cheer up for fuck's sake. Maybe they're told to look like that, to try to make you nervous or something.

It's around midday here, so it must be seven in the evening back in England. It'll be dark back home, but we've got another few hours added on to the day.

I'm stood in line, in my own pissed-up world, my head rocking, trying not to fall over; I'm not paying any attention to what's going on around me. After Marshy's been waved through, he's looking back from the other side with this puzzled look on his face. This fat, grumpy old git is interrogating me with all these questions. It must be 'cause of nine-eleven. They've tightened up all their security now. Not surprising really, but this prick's making out like I'm some kind of terrorist. It's like he's already decided I'm going to be on some kind of crime spree whilst I'm here, assumed I'm already guilty of something. He wants answers to all these fucking stupid personal questions – He's going on like:

"How long are you here for? Why are you here? Haven't you got a job? What? You quit your job to come here? That doesn't make sense, why would you do that? Who are you stayin' with? How do you know them? Have you ever been involved in any terrorist activities?"

Faaaarkin' hell! I've never had this at an airport before. It's like they're trying to catch you out; put you under pressure; make you panic. What the fuck do they expect – someone to go 'Okay, it's me, I did it, I surrender!' He's fucking paranoid. I thought we're supposed to be allies! Right now, I'm a big, guilty motherfucker for some crime I haven't committed, until I prove my innocence. I'm not happy with bloke's tone, but under the circumstances of the terrorism a few years back, I'm just going to accept it and answer this guy, without kicking off.

"We're here for three months. Tourism. No, I quit my job. It was a part-time job after university. I wanted to go travellin' and my employer wouldn't let me have a three-month holiday. I'm stayin' at hotels and a friend's house. I found the hotel online and I know my friend from school; he's at university out here. No, I haven't been involved in any terrorist activities."

He's staring me in the eyes, looking all suspicious as if to say 'we're watching you', before giving a nonchalant wave, signalling me to move on. I take my passport from him and walk over to Marshy.

"What the fuck was that all about?" he asks.

As we start discussing the interrogation a few metres away from the desk, I clock the passport officer looking back at us with this deadpan, angry glare. He's speaking into his walky-talky, but I can't hear what's he's saying. We move on quickly, before they change their minds and escort us away for an internal cavity examination. Welcome to America!

Most people from back home who decide to go travelling after university go to places like Thailand, Vietnam, Australia, New Zealand, and that part of the world. Me and Marshy wanted to do something different. Hardly anyone I know has been to the States, unless it was for a week in New York or a family holiday in Florida. We don't really know much about the cities in this country so it's time to explore. Forgetting about the twat at the passport checks, we head towards the baggage reclaim, and I'm buzzing again now 'cause I've remembered we're on holiday!

It's mid-December and twenty degrees Celsius in Miami. When we step out of the airport, the sun's shining and I'm looking at the clear, blue skies; barely a cloud in sight. Can't get much better than this, especially when it's fucking baltic back home in England – it's the middle of the winter over there right now – suckers!

There's a slight breeze and it's blowing the warm air over me; I fucking love this feeling. The air smells fresh and clean. My lungs are filling up and I'm exhaling each deep breath with a sigh of pleasure. It was five degrees and raining at Heathrow, this morning. You fucking beauty!

We're walking along the front of the airport, looking for a

taxi. That must be them over there on the left – that big row of yellow cars.

"South Beach please, mate!"

Even saying the words 'South Beach' is giving me goose-bumps. It's supposed to be one of the main beaches in Miami, on the east coast of Florida. I know a little bit about the area 'cause I've been here before, on a family holiday when I was twelve. It's all about the beaches, sun, theme parks, and the Everglades where all the alligators, crocodiles, and snakes hang out. I remember watching the TV show 'Flipper' as a kid, in the eighties, and they were always going through the Everglades on one of those boats with the big fans on the back. Maybe we'll give that a go whilst we're here.

We're driving through the outskirts of the city, towards our hotel, and I'm noticing all the differences from home – the flat landscape, the Art Deco buildings, the green and yellow road signs, vehicles driving on the other side of the road; and the cars – they're so much bigger here – they're like fucking houses on wheels! The biggest difference though is the accents. All my mates from university are Scousers, Geordies, Mancs, or they're locals from Yorkshire, with their strong northern accents. The Yanks' accents are totally different, stringing out their syllables for an eternity. I only usually hear it on the TV, so the fact I'm miles away from home is really sinking in. I'm used to travelling around; I lived in Scotland a few times and Pompey, Ipswich, and Sheffield too, so it's not a complete novelty.

I'm looking out of the window at the open road, on our way into the city; I feel a sense of independence – no plans or commitments to consider; no kids or girlfriend to worry about; no job to go back to. I've got no idea what to expect – I may have been to Florida, on holiday with my family, but that was when I was a kid and we were only here to go to Disneyland; I had to do whatever my parents told me. Now, I can do whatever the fuck I want to – We'll be shooting off all over the place – towns and cities I've never even heard of. The only thing we have to do is make it from Miami to Los Angeles, where we fly back from. We've got to make it there in one piece and we've got three months to do it. Piece of piss.

South Beach

The roads in South Beach are lined with palm trees. There's a row of large, modern, multi-storey hotels which run along the beach. On the other side of the road, there are shopping malls and smaller Art Deco hotels, painted in bright colours – pale greens, yellows, blues, and whites; they give the place a happy vibe. It's all specially designed for tourists – most of the shops lining the roads are selling souvenirs and 'South Beach' t-shirts on rails outside the stores.

The taxi drops us off at the entrance of our first hotel, 'The San Juan'. Marshy found it on the internet, before we left, and booked us in for three nights. That's very organised for him and I was surprised when he had the idea, 'cause normally, he's pretty useless at being responsible. It was probably his mum's idea. I'm glad; I'd rather book something in advance than trawl the streets, looking for accommodation and getting ripped off 'cause they think we're desperate. And in any case, the last thing we want to be doing after a nine hour flight is walk around the streets with massive rucksacks, looking for somewhere to stay.

The 'San Juan' is no more than a two star hotel; it's no fucking luxury pad. Outside, there's a porch with a few tables and chairs that look out onto the street. There's a couple outside chatting, smoking fags and drinking beer, but they don't acknowledge us.

We walk into the lobby to check in. The receptionist is a large, Hispanic, friendly-looking bloke, and we're chatting shit with him whilst we check in. He gives us our keys and directs us up to our room on the second floor.

It's a large room with two double beds, a TV, and an en-suite bathroom. There are two large windows that look out onto the main road and the large multi-storey hotels. We're not far from the beach at all – just cross the road and we're there. The décor's dated and the room smells musky; you can tell people have been smoking in this room for years 'cause there's a hint of rotten fag ash and old nicotine in the air. The sheets on the bed are ancient; I can see fag burns on the surface – they've probably been there for years too. We're not fussy though; all we need's a roof over our heads.

We take a stroll out to the shops to get our bearings. We need to get some beers in, quick time, 'cause the booze from the plane's starting to wear off. If we stop drinking now, the jet lag will kick in and we'll fall asleep and wake up, full of beans, at three in the morning.

The main pedestrian area isn't as plush as I imagined it to be; it's all pretty old and some of it's starting to crumble – cracks are starting to appear in the walls of buildings and paving slabs. South Beach's been popular for ages, but looking around, I get the feeling it's already had its heyday a decade or three ago, and it's still living off the success and reputation of its past. Faded elegance perhaps; but it's still a pretty cool place. There's a mixture of cultures here – Black, White, and Hispanic. There are loads of Cuban restaurants around, maybe 'cause they can't run their own businesses in communist Cuba, and they can over here? We walk back to the hotel and sit down at one of the tables outside, with our beers.

Later – It's early evening and it's starting to get dark. We've showered, to freshen up after the flight, and we're off out to the bars. We quiz a stranger to give us some ideas of where to go; we're told the place to be is Ocean Drive – even the names of the roads are pretty cool. Everyone we speak to here is sound, which is handy 'cause we need assistance getting used to the way the roads are laid out. It's all one big grid and all the people we speak to talk about 'blocks'.

"Go three blocks, headin' south on Main Avenue, and make a right on Fifth."

At first, it sounded like they're talking in riddles, but I reckon I've sussed it out. Main roads have names and the roads coming off them are all numbered – you have to figure out if the numbers are increasing or decreasing, depending on which way you're walking. Each number signifies the next block.

We follow the stranger's directions to Ocean Drive and it's only a five minute walk from our hotel. As we turn in, I see the lights and I know immediately that this is where we need to be. It's lined with expensive bars, hotels, and restaurants. Walking down the street, all the bars are on our right and the promenade that runs along the beach is on our left. The streets are packed with people walking in both directions, so everyone's reduced to a slow pace, to constantly dodge the oncoming traffic. This area's high class, and it's been specially designed and modernised to attract the wealthiest people. You can tell from all the classy, expensive cars parked on the road.

There are policemen patrolling the promenades on these weird, two-wheeled contraptions that move when you lean forwards and stop when you lean back – we've asked someone and they're called 'Segways'. The pigs look funny standing upright on their little platform between the two wheels. I've never seen these Segways before, but they look like a proper buzz. They don't exactly look any good for chasing criminals though – all you need to do is jump over a wall and the pigs are stumped! This isn't really the type of area where much crime happens anyway – it's pretty obvious the people here are minted, so having the police around is more of a deterrent than anything – making sure the 'riff-raff' aren't sniffing around the posh fuckers!

We look up and down the strip so we can see what's on offer before we decide which bar to go into. There are some shit-hot places around here. One place in particular has a large, open entrance with expensive furnishings and a long pool dissecting the bar, right down the middle. From the street outside, you can see the type of clientele it attracts – well-dressed, wealthy, good-looking people. The blokes are suited and booted and the women all look hot, showing off their figures, all dolled up in their designer dresses; even the barmaids look like models. There's a stylish band with a piano and a double bass, playing jazz music. It's fucking cool. We try to get in but we're knocked back 'cause we're not well-dressed. They say we can come back if we get changed into more appropriate clothes, and they warn us there's an entrance fee or 'cover charge', as they call it, of twenty dollars. We sack it off and continue down the street, looking for bars that are free to get in. We can't justify paying twenty bucks to get into a bar, for fuck's sake. Piss-takers! I suppose they do this so the wealthy, posh cunts can enjoy their money in peace!

We're in one of the bog-standard bars, having a beer and a game of pool. Even this place, which was free to get in, has a large patio at the front with a huge wooden beamed structure above us, draped with palms. The birds in here are all incredible – they're all slim with big tits. They've obviously spent a long time pampering themselves and working on their looks; and the end result is impressive. It's like they've set a standard here which they all aspire to; they've got every aspect of their look down to a tee – shoes, dress, tan, tits, hair, make-up, handbag. You can tell a lot of the birds have had a boob-job and god knows what else. They're all young as well; at least, they look it. I'm trying to avoid being caught perving, but it's hard not to look – my brain's programmed to stare at fit birds! This place is all about money and showing it off.

I see this bloke approach the bar; he's nothing special in terms of looks, but he makes a blatant point of getting his wallet out and offering drinks around. A group of birds, standing nearby, have clocked this guy and move closer to him, like it's all part of the mating process here, and they'll stick around him for the rest of the night, if he pays for their drinks. So he's seen them and he's offering them all a drink, opening up his wallet. Even I can see the thick wad of notes he's got, lucky bastard; he's making sure all the birds can see it too. You can see people targeting each other purely based on appearances – what clothes, shoes, watch they're wearing, what they're drinking. There's no more obvious place to see blokes using money to get the good-looking birds; and the birds going for the rich blokes. I'm probably jealous but there's no doubt in my mind, seeing all this in action, this is a place where money talks. It's going to take some getting used to; after all, I've just come out of Sheffield Hallam University where you could get a double Vodka Red Bull for ninety-nine pence or a blue WKD for a quid! You could get half-pissed for a tenner and pull a bird at the university club night by buying her a bottle of Reef for one-pound-fifty; and that was only if you felt like treating her! Those lucky girls.

The drinks aren't cheap here. As two young travellers on a budget, I'm thinking we'll have to change our strategy for pulling birds 'cause we can't afford to be plying them with drinks at ten or twenty dollars a time. I'm not going to worry about money too much on the first night though.

We continue on a bar crawl down Ocean Drive and stop in a quirky bar serving alcoholic slush puppies. The people in here are closer to our age, but we're not making any inroads meeting people, probably 'cause we're both knackered from the jet lag and not exactly the life and soul of the party. We've spent a load of money on booze but spent the whole night by ourselves; we definitely need to find a better way of meeting more people and I reckon staying in hotels, and going to expensive bars, where the other clientele are all several times richer than us, isn't where we're going to do it.

Holidaymakers go to lavish bars, not travellers. Holidaymakers save their cash all year to go somewhere for two weeks – they don't worry about what things cost so much – they eat in nice restaurants, drink in nice bars, stay in nice hotels. Travellers, on the other hand, go away for a lot longer and need to find the cheapest way of doing things – stay at a hostel, get booze from a supermarket and get pissed before going out – we can't be paying cover charges to eat and drink, that's a waste of valuable cash we can spend on beer! Marshy's shit with money though, and he'll just spend, spend, spend till it's all gone. If we carry on like this, we'll cane all our money in the first few weeks. We need to change our tactics and find a hostel; find some other travellers. Fuck wasting time at these posh joints.

After a good sleep and a lie-in, we spend our first full day in Miami looking around, exploring the 'downtown' area – the city centre. We walk over the large MacArthur Causeway Bridge. On our left is the port where the cruise ships and cargo ships dock. On the other side is an estuary, where the river meets the Atlantic Ocean. The river banks are lined with huge mansions, each one with its own multi-million pound yacht, moored on its own private berth. This is where the filthy rich and the celebrities live – and it's right in front of my eyes. Each mansion has got its own unique design, creating an eclectic mix of awe-inspiring architecture; it's completely exclusive.

At the end of the bridge, we come to a shopping quay called 'Bayside Marketplace', where there are more boats and yachts. It's getting close to Christmas and all the decorations are up. Children are chaotically running around, screaming on fairground rides, causing havoc, and enjoying themselves. It's strange being in the sun at this time of year, as we're used to being in cold England with the frost, clouds, rain, and snow, but I'm certainly not complaining.

Downtown Miami is a short walk from Bayside, and I'm surprised how run down and dirty the city centre is. I've always imagined Miami to be a glamorous city, from the TV programmes and films I've seen, but in reality, the old city centre is nothing like that. It seems the newer, more glamorous shopping malls, on the outskirts, have become the places where the Americans go, and the centre has been left to rot. The streets are quiet and the grey concrete buildings look worn out and neglected. You can tell that the people walking around the city centre aren't particularly wealthy from the clothes they're wearing and their general health. It's a bit of a shock. The gap between rich and poor is becoming more and more obvious.

Here's a tip for you…

We take a different route back to the hotel and stumble across a row of bars and clubs, with promoters standing outside, handing out flyers. We're talking to them and Marshy's found a place that's got an offer on tonight: 'Drink as much as you want for twenty dollars!' This is more like it.

It about nine in the evening, we're at the all-you-can-drink bar, just as it's opening, and we're straight onto the booze. There are only two other people in here but fuck it; we're nailing the drinks 'cause we're on a mission to get leathered. Once it passes eleven pm, the place starts to fill up. We're already on our sixth round and starting to get pissed, dancing round like idiots on the half-full dance floor.

We both go up to the bar to order our next round. This time, we're ordering three drinks each to get the binge into full flow, and so we don't have to keep going up to the bar every ten minutes. The barman obliges, and we're about to walk away, but he kicks-off at us, throwing his cloth on the bar.

"That's it! I'm not servin' you guys anymore."

He turns his back to us and he's properly pissed off. We're not sure what's going on, so we call him over, both leaning over the bar towards him, so we can hear what he's saying over the loud music.

"Excuse me, mate, what d'ya mean when you say 'that's it'? It's free drinks all night, isn't it?"

"I've served you guys seven times now and you haven't tipped me once."

"Tipped you? Oh! We thought, as the flyer said, it's twenty dollars all-you-can-drink? That's what we were told."

"You're supposed to tip every time you get served. I have to live off my tips and you haven't tipped me once. Fuck you guys."

"Okay mate, we were gonna tip you at the end. There's no need to be so rude though, mate."

"All you British guys say that, then you get drunk, walk straight out, and go home."

What a fucking mardy bastard. I've heard you need to tip over here but it didn't cross my mind to be tipping for every fucking drink! Especially when it's an all-you-can-drink night! To me, that's a green light to drink as much as I possibly can. And maybe we should've tipped him but who the fuck does this guy think he is, speaking to us like that? The cunt. We probably would've tipped him at the end as well, but he'll get fuck all now! Once we've finished our round, we go back up to the bar. There's a second barman there so we get another three drinks each, and Marshy gives him a twenty dollar tip, making sure the lairy twat sees him hand it over. He makes a point of complimenting him.

"Thanks for the great service, mate!" He's got a massive smile on his face and the other bartender's absolutely fuming. Me and Marshy are cracking up 'cause the miserable bell-end deserves the wind-up.

Outside, at the end of the night, we're talking to people we've met in the club and looking for birds to chat up. I look around to see Marshy chatting to a bird and her friend, and they're both fit. I go over and start chatting to the other girl. They're both from Miami and we're getting a lot of attention. They're laughing at all our jokes and we're all going for another drink, in a different bar they know. Marshy's run out of money so he stops at a cash point. Me and the birds are waiting for him. He gets his cash out of the 'ATM', as they call it here, and we carry on walking.

Fifty metres down the road, Marshy puts his hands on his head.

"Shit!" He's getting his wallet out of his pocket and panicking. He's checking all his pockets. "I've lost my card."

"What d'ya mean? You just used it a minute ago."

"It must be back at the cash-point. It's probably fuckin' gone by now."

"Go and check."

He runs back up the road and I go with him, but the card's not there.

"Bollocks! The machine must have swallowed it."

"You fuckin' bell-end!"

"Oh for fuck's sake, man," he says, "I hope someone hasn't nicked it."

"The machine probably swallowed it, mate. Nothin' you can do about it now. You won't be able to get that back, mate; once they're inside, they get sent back to the bank."

"Twat!"

In England, the cash-points give you your card back first then the money. Here, they give you the money first then your card afterwards. Being programmed, as you are from habit, Marshy had taken the cash and walked away, presumably thinking he's already put his card back in his wallet. Being absolutely caned from the booze probably didn't help either. Whatever's happened, he's fucked now, he'll have to get a new one sent over from England, which will take weeks, and we don't even know where we're going to be, let alone if we'll be there long enough to wait for it to arrive. Well, fuck it – we'll have to forget about it now and concentrate on the task in hand – trying to pull these birds.

There's a bar, a few hundred metres down the road, that's still open. So we head there, and soon we're all sat round a table and I've bought the birds a drink. It's getting pretty late and the bar's about to kick out. Marshy's trying to seal the deal.

"D'ya wanna come back to our hotel room then?"

"Yeah, sure, but it depends on what you want."

Initially fazed by her reply, Marshy replies, "Err, sorry, what d'ya mean?"

"Well, how much money have you guys got?"

The reality sets in. Although they're posing as hookers, they really don't look like it; they look like students. Maybe these birds think they can make a quick buck? We're not having it though and we turn them away. The atmosphere changes immediately and we go home by ourselves to get some sleep. Crash and burn.

Wait a Minute...

It's pure blue skies and we're on the beach to help nurse our hangovers. The coast runs for miles – a long flat strip of golden sand, clean water, and hardly anyone else around. It's not exactly boiling but it's still around twenty degrees and that means one thing – anyone else on the beach right now is probably British!

We fancy getting stoned so we're figuring out how we're going to get some weed. I had my first joint with Marshy and we've been smoking hash and skunk ever since we were thirteen. At university, I'd get through at least five joints a day, shared with mates. I'm a little bit nervous about trying to get something illegal in another country, 'cause we don't know anyone here and we've got no idea who to approach; if we get caught, we could end up in prison. There's no-one at the hotel and people will probably be on their guard 'cause they don't know us and can't trust us.

We're in the centre of South Beach looking for a suitable character to approach, being careful to keep our eye out for the pigs. After we've both failed a few times, Marshy finds this scruffy-looking bloke who says he can sort us out. He's mixed race, in his thirties, quite skinny, with a dirty t-shirt and torn-up jeans.

"Yeah, man, I can get you guys some chronic but you'll have to walk with me a few blocks up the way."

"How far d'ya reckon, mate?"

"It's just around dis corner, man, like a five minute walk'n'shit. We gotta get away from the city, yo, case the cops be 'round."

So we're all walking up the road away from the beach. After fifteen minutes, I'm starting to wonder where the fuck this guy's taking us but we're going with it – he's being polite and asking us questions, making conversation; he seems like an alright bloke.

"So, where you guys from?"

"England, mate." I answer.

"And what about y'self?" he asks Marshy. "You from England too?"

"Yeah, England as well."

"England, hey? Whereabouts in England?"

"Portsmouth."

"You like soccer?"

"You mean football, right?"

"Football's a different game over here. understand what I'm sayin'? It's just on the left down here, man."

We follow him down a large alleyway, off one of the main roads. We're walking past all the entrances to the gardens and garages at the back of the buildings. It's pretty seedy and there isn't a soul in sight. Anything could happen to us down here and no-one would see it. We stop at a doorway in a brick wall, outside the garden of what looks like an old, run-down hotel. There's a long concrete pathway that leads to the back door of a multi-storey building, which is open. The garden's overgrown and in need of some serious attention – I can't imagine too many people would want to stay in this place; it looks ropey as fuck.

"Hey, yo, this is the place, man. Pass me forty bucks and I'll be back in like, five minutes'n'shit."

Marshy hands me twenty bucks and I put it with twenty of mine.

"Here ya go, mate."

"You guys hold tight till I get back."

We watch him disappear through the back door of the building. We can't see which room he's gone to, so we'll have to wait and see what he comes back with.

Forty minutes pass, which feels like hours, and he still hasn't come back. We're pretty sure he isn't coming back either. We walk through the garden gate, towards the back door of the hotel and realise it leads straight through to the other side. There's no-one around. It looks like this place isn't even a hotel anymore – it's probably been sold off for studio flats or something similar to council houses. He must have walked straight out the other side and legged it, leaving us standing there like muppets. The fucking bastard has hustled us good and proper – that was probably the easiest forty dollars he'll ever make.

In hindsight, we should've made him bring the weed to us first before we handed the cash over, but it's too fucking late for that now. I'm fucking gutted. We've lost twenty bucks each and this place seems to be full of people trying to scam you, or get money out of you any way they can!

The first few nights have been a bit of a learning curve for us; we seriously need to wisen up. Our three nights at the hotel are up; it's time to move on and find somewhere with other people our age. We need to find a hostel.

Party People

We've checked out of the hotel and we're in an internet cafe, looking for hostels in South Beach. To our surprise there's one about three hundred metres down the road from the 'San Juan' called 'Tropics'. It's fifteen dollars a night in a shared room, with bunk beds. This place looks sweet though, 'cause there's a big swimming pool, a bar outside the rooms, and a screen for watching films in the evening. All the guests are travellers, roughly our age, give or take a few years, and there's a pool table too – It's is exactly what we're looking for. Everyone's on the same level there – they all want to meet other people.

We fetch our bags from the hotel and get our room at the hostel sorted. As soon as we step into the room, we meet our roommates and we've got instant drinking partners. This is what I imagined the trip to be like – meeting people from different countries, drinking together, going on spontaneous adventures. And plus, I know Marshy's my best mate, but there's only so much of one person you can take! I can see him irritating the fuck out of me at some point and I'll likely do the same to him. I'm sure we'll probably meet the occasional mentalist in the hostels, but at this price, we'll take our chances.

As we've cut our budget right down, our diet has had to change dramatically too. We started off eating in restaurants but we can't afford to keep doing that, so instead, we've found vouchers for Subway in these coupon books you get, all over South Beach. We've got a stack of these buy-one-get-one-free twelve-inch sub vouchers and we've worked out it'll cost us three dollars each for a full twelve-inch sandwich. Each morning, we're buying a foot long Subway – we eat half of it in the morning for breakfast and save the other half until evening time, for dinner. We would've bought one at breakfast and one at dinnertime but we can't agree on toppings; and I'm a fussy git when it comes to food – Marshy wants a load of stuff on his sub that I'm not happy with. It's pretty minging, 'cause by the time we're ready for the second half, it's been sweating away in our rooms for six or seven hours! But saving on food means more money for beer so fuck it – we're not arsed.

This is the fucking life. We're sitting around the swimming pool, having a few beers from the bar. As the alcohol starts to take effect, our laughing's becoming louder, so other people are looking over and coming to join in. They're all on the beers too. Some of them are on their own so we're calling them over; others are in small groups. By the time the sun's going down, there's around twenty of us on the lash. As the drinking pace picks up and the group becomes more comfortable with each other, the tone of the conversation soon deteriorates to filth. We've got an ongoing joke where everyone's given a nickname as they join the group. As me and Marshy started it all off we 'came first'. One other bloke gets up to get a drink from the bar and runs back – he's 'came quick'; a bird who only stops for one drink is labelled 'come and go'; a person we invite over but doesn't want to join us we call 'couldn't come'; a bloke who's moving between a few different seats is called 'came all over the place', and so on. We're all pissed as arseholes and cracking up every time someone 'comes up' with a new one. I'm loving this now.

The following morning, we're woken up by this Australian bloke called Paul. He reminds me and Marshy that we've agreed to go on a mission with him, and this Dutch bird, to Key West, in his hire car. I don't remember having the conversation to organise this but I'm game anyway. We're setting off early doors, and as we wait for Paul to bring his car round we're laughing and joking by the bar. I'm still pissed from last night. This thirty--something German bird's walking by and she stops to have a go at Marshy in an angry, harsh tone.

"It is you that was laughing last night. Why do you laugh all the time?"

Me and Marshy burst out laughing.

"Why not laugh? It's good for you!"

"Yes, but you laugh at nothing!" She's all serious and Marshy's waving her off.

"See you later!" he says. "Have a GREAT time whatever you're doing! Don't laugh too much; you might get a life!"

What a moody cow!

Being in the car with Paul is a nightmare. The poor bloke couldn't figure out how to start the engine – it's an automatic and you have to keep your foot on the brakes when you turn the ignition. Then he hits someone in front of us whilst we're in a traffic jam. Me and Marshy abusing him the whole time probably didn't help.

We stop off on the way for a boat trip in the Everglades – I'm sat on the edge of the boat, shitting myself as I watch the alligators crawling into the river and swimming over towards the boat. That's enough sightseeing for one day; take me back to the bar!

We're back in South Beach playing some pool, in a bar a few streets down from the hostel, and we've agreed it's time to move on from Miami so we're considering what to do next. We go to buy some more cigarettes and we spark up outside the shop. An Irish geezer comes over to us. He's a rugged-looking character, with a dark beard and a weathered face. You can about tell he's

Irish but his accent's faded 'cause he's been away from his homeland for a while.

"How's it goin' dere, lads? I hope you don't mind; I overheard yous talkin'. Yous English?"

"Yeah, mate, we are."

"Have yous ghat a lioght for mi rollie?"

"Of course. Here you go, mate."

"So what're yous doin' over here, den?"

"Just travellin' mate. We're on our way to LA and we're gonna stop off at places on the way. You travellin' too?"

"Ah no. I've lived out here a while, the last eight years. Where yous going next, den?"

"Dunno. We're not really sure where we're gonna go next or how we're gonna get there."

"Have you heard of a company called Autodriveaway?"

"No, why's that?"

"Well they've ghat an office somewhere not too far from here, it might be Fort Lauderdale I tink. Have you ghat a drivin' licence wit ya?"

"Yeah, I've got mine. What's the deal with them?"

"Well, you should have a look, so you should. People leave dere cars wit 'em, so they can be delivered somewhere else, ya know. So…you pick a car going somewhere and you take it there for 'em…an' you get to use de car for free."

"For free? That can't be right. Sounds too good to be true. What's the catch? You must have to pay somethin'?"

"No, 'onestly, I use 'em all de time; it's how I get around de place. It's pretty simple really – the charge you would usually pay to rent de car, well, dat's your labour cost for taking de car for 'em. So it's not actually free, but no money changes hands."

"I see – you scratch their back, they scratch yours, yeah?"

"You got it, kid."

"Where did you say their offices are?"

"I think der's one in Fort Lauderdale, look 'em up – Autodriveaway, dey're called."

"Alright, well, thanks for that, mate, we'll have a look at that!"

"No bother. Have a good trip, lads."

Sounds a bit odd – I've never heard of anything like that but it's worth checking out anyway. We head to our usual internet café, a place in the lobby of a big hotel, to check the company out, and sure enough it's there – Autodriveaway in Fort Lauderdale. We check out the rest of their website and they've got offices all over the country. For each office there's a list of cars that need to be delivered to different cities all over the USA – just as the Irish dude said. We've got to get to Fort Lauderdale first but it's not far from South Beach. Paul's still got his hire car so we ask him to give us a lift.

Fort Lauderdale, Florida

Used & Abused

I've never heard of Fort Lauderdale before so I've got no idea what to expect. The thirty-five mile journey, north of South Beach, takes us forty-five minutes. I noticed a bunch of leaflets in the lobby at the hostel in Miami, advertising all the different hostels of the cities around the States – they must have some sort of agreement to advertise for each other.

We've taken a handful of these leaflets for different cities that we like the sound of, in case we end up going there and need to find a place to stay. The hostels are definitely where to find all the birds and the parties so we're sticking to them from now on. One of the leaflets is advertising a hostel in Fort Lauderdale so we head there, to see what the craic is. It's called 'The Backpackers Beach Hostel' and it's on North Ocean Boulevard.

Fort Lauderdale looks very similar to Miami in places, at least the rich parts anyway – there's some serious money around here. The hotels look plush, the houses are all huge and detached; most of them have got a yacht or a boat in the driveway – you can see the tops of the masts pointing up from behind the tall perimeter fences, hedges, and walls that surround the grounds of the houses. It looks like a sailing town, so no wonder it's full of rich bastards. Each plot of land looks as if it's been expertly landscape gardened; it's a very clean place too – not a piece of litter in sight.

With the help of a road map, the hostel's easy to find. Our Aussie mate, Paul, drops us off, comes in for a look around, and shoots off. It's on the corner of a T-junction off the main road, which is a wide dual carriageway. On the other side of the road's a large hotel that looks over the beach; I can see the sand and sea through the gaps between the palm trees. There's a long concrete wall surrounding the hostel, with a set of gates in the middle that lead into a courtyard, with trees and plants dotted around. There are several stone tables and benches decorated with mosaic tiles, filled with people drinking, chatting, and laughing. They acknowledge us with a collective nod of their heads as we enter, and we're nodding back. The owner comes out to greet us and show us around. She's asking us questions and she seems pretty laid back – it's all very welcoming and I like the vibe here. The building is shaped like a 'U', and we're standing in the middle of it. There are two floors – the bottom floor is where all the bedrooms are and the top floor is the communal areas. There are stairs on each side, leading up to the first floor. On one side, there's a games room with a pool table and some computers, on the other side is the kitchen. There's a roof terrace on each side, with sun loungers. It's a pretty fucking smart place for a traveller. It doesn't have a bar but everyone's drinking, so there must be a shop close by. It's cheap to stay – only fifteen dollars a night. We pay up and the hostess shows us to our rooms.

We're greeted by two Scandinavians – Jasper from Norway and Isak from Sweden; we're sharing the room with them. They're chatting away in near-perfect English and they're cool as fuck. They've got their own boat and they've sailed across the Atlantic Ocean together. They learnt how to sail at a young age, worked for a few years to save up the money to buy a boat, and quit their jobs to sail around the world. What a pair of legends! When I hear their stories, I'm thinking how some people choose to live their lives, completely different to everyone else. I grew up on the south coast of England in Lee-on-the-Solent near Pompey. There was a sailing club there but the thought of learning how to sail never even crossed my mind; maybe that could've been me and Marshy sailing across the Atlantic.

Isak's just finished rolling a fresh joint, which he's pretty open about, and he asks us if we want to join them in smoking it on the roof terrace; we're already on a high with this place. There's a cool, laid-back atmosphere; everyone knows each other; they're all joking and having a good time, including us in their banter and interested to hear our stories. Sometimes the places you go or things you do when you haven't got any expectations are the best – the only reason we've come here is 'cause of a chance meeting with an Irish geezer in the street, who wanted a lighter for his rollie.

We're smoking the joint and watching the sunset – it's that commercial weed, the type with a few seeds in it. Only American weed is this strong – I don't know exactly what they do to it to get it this strong – genetically modify it? Or lace it with something? Whatever it is, I'm pretty fucked after a few tokes. We ask the Scandinavians if they know where we can get some for ourselves and they're happy to sort it out for us. Let's hope they don't leave tomorrow and fuck off with our money, like that twat did in Miami. It'll be sweet if they can get it for us – we won't have to go anywhere; it'll be delivered straight to us. We're told it's twenty dollars for a decent-sized bag. I reckon it'll be roughly an eighth but we'll see when we get it. Maybe our luck's turning now? This place's definitely going some way to burying the disappointment of being hustled before – the good ol' U S of A is definitely going up in my opinion. We're chilling for the first night, with some beers and spliffs, getting to know some of the other people staying here.

I wake up late the following day, and when I check the time on my mobile, it's afternoon before we've even surfaced. Smoking weed tends to do that to me – I hardly ever got up before midday when I was at university. We've missed half of the day but we're not in a rush for anything in particular, so fuck it. Some of the others have organised a night out, which we've been invited to, so it's probably a good idea we get some rest; we can go on boozing for longer into the night. There's a group of about fifteen people going out and most of them have been in Fort Lauderdale a while, so they know all the best places to go – we're tagging along and hoping to find some fit birds.

We start the night off with a few beers, bought from the local convenience store, to save on paying bar prices. The taxi's come to collect us. Me and Marshy end up in different cars but we're all going to the same place, so it shouldn't matter. In my taxi, which is only meant for four people, we've got seven. The taxi driver's alright about it too – what a lad! The blokes are sitting on the seats, one bird's sat on the lap of the guy in the passenger seat, and there are two more birds lying across the top of the people in the back. We're all pissed and laughing about it – it's pretty surreal having fun with all these relative strangers, crammed in a small taxi – everyone's alright with it though. Me and Marshy have fitted in, sweet as a nut, in this place.

When we get to the main strip of bars in the centre of Fort Lauderdale, I can't see the other taxi, Marshy's one. They set off before us, so they've either been held up somewhere or the driver's dropped them off at a different bar. I follow my group to a bar and make sure they're staying put, whilst I go and look for Marshy and the others.

We're on Hollywood Boulevard – a long road full of bars and

restaurants, all lit up. Every place's packed with people, spilling outside onto the pavement – I'm having difficulty finding the other group or recognising any faces. I go into a few bars, have a scout around, but can't find them anywhere so I give up and go back to the group I arrived with. Maybe they'll come and find us. For now, I'm going to crack on with the task at hand – getting pissed.

This bar's awesome and there are some proper fit birds in here. It's not a large place but it's full of people and the birds are all dolled up for the occasion; As I'm chatting away to my new friends, they're telling me that Fort Lauderdale is full of wealthy 'daddy's girls' who go to the college nearby. As I stand chatting in a circle of people from the hostel, a fit blonde bird, with nice eyes, is standing next to us, listening to our conversation. I can tell she's had a few drinks already; she butts in, totally uninvited, and joins our group. I'm loving her confidence – she's not shy in the slightest.

"Um, excuse me, are you English?" She's looking at me with delight in her eyes.

"Why, yes I am."

"Oh my gahd that's so cool, you sound like Prince William!"

Even though I don't sound anything like him, I'm taking that as a chat-up line and flirting back with her.

"Why thank you, that's a very nice compliment coming from such a beautiful girl. You look like Shakira!"

"Well don't we make the famous couple!"

I turn towards her to give my full attention, whilst the rest of the crew carry on chatting amongst themselves. Straight away, she's putting her hand on my arm as she speaks. I'm taking this as a definite sign of interest and I'm going to try my luck.

She's with a group of girls so I ignore her for a while, and turn back to talk with my friends; I want to see if she'll react to this and try to get my attention again. We're back-to-back, briefly brushing against each other, talking to the others in our groups. I feel a hand work its way to the top of my jeans. I'm pretty sure it's hers but I subtly turn around to check. Thankfully, it's her hand! She doesn't react to me turning around so I leave her to it; I want to see what happens next! I've got quite loose jeans on which allows her to get her hand down between my jeans and boxer shorts. She reaches further down and starts to rub my balls. I'm pretty sure no-one else is seeing what's happening and I'm smiling, trying to concentrate on the conversation with my friends. After a few minutes, I'm getting turned on and it's too much of a distraction so I pull her hand out and turn round to her. I'm chatting to her again and I'm totally intrigued by her sheer audacity; to do this when she's only just met me! We don't even know each other's names yet! On top of this, she's hot as well; I can't believe my luck. She's got perfect blonde hair, no roots, sexy eyes with full lashes curled at the end – they look so sharp they could slice you open. She flirting with me outrageously; smiling and laughing at my jokes. I'm trying to maintain eye contact with her and stop myself from looking at her cleavage; I want to focus on what she's saying but it's fucking difficult because she's got great tits. I can't find fault with her. I'm starting to think this could be too good to be true; is she going to end up being another whore? Or just a dick tease? I'm trying to play it cool, flirting back with her, touching the small of her back. There's a slight pause in the conversation and she's staring at me with those sexy eyes, biting her lip. She moves in, closer to me, and whispers in my ear whilst gesturing suggestively with a movement of her head towards the back of the bar.

"D'ya wanna go for a little walk?"

"Sure, let's go." I've got a smug grin on my face. I've got to be in here – don't fuck this one up now!

She leads me by the hand into the men's toilets, and into a cubicle. I lock the door behind us. As I press her against the door and start kissing her, she halts me.

"Stop, stop."

"What's up?" I'm impatient and kissing her neck.

"This isn't dangerous enough for me." She opens the door of the cubicle and walks out by the sinks. There's no-one else in here. I hesitate for a second. Fuck, I was just getting into that! I can feel this chance slipping away.

I've got to come up with something. I follow her out of the cubicle to see if I can think of anything, off the top of my head, to make this situation more dangerous. I notice that the main door to the toilets is only held open by a doorstop, so I kick it away and hold the door closed by pushing my back against it. I beckon her over.

"Is this dangerous enough for you?"

"That's more like it." She walks over to me with this seductive look in her eyes. We're kissing again now and I'm really enjoying this. She's getting excited and her hands are all over me, but she won't let me touch her; she wants to be in control. She pushes my chest back against the door and slowly goes down onto her knees. She's a fucking expert. She's looking up at me, with smoky eyes, and I know she's teasing me. I'm praying she carries on and no-one comes in. She undoes my belt and slowly pulls my boxers down and takes a hold of my cock with her hand and starts sucking. It feels amazing and she's keeping eye contact the whole time and moaning, like she's loving every second. I want this to go on forever; I'm trying to control myself, to stop myself from cumming, but she's too good. She's licking the underside of my cock and all the muscles in my body are tensing up. She's sucking faster and faster; I can't control myself; I'm lost in the excitement of the naughtiness of where we are and what we're doing. I'm pressing back hard against the door as I cum in her mouth. She keeps her mouth over my cock as my body relaxes and I'm jolting slightly, with pure pleasure, as I try to get my breath back. Suddenly, there's a heavy banging on the toilet door and a loud man's voice shouting.

"Who's in there? Open the door right now!" He's pushing the door, trying to get in, and I'm stopping him by leaning back against it with all my weight, whilst I do my trousers up. There's another forceful shove, which I absorb, before moving right out of the way; then the door flies open. Two bouncers are standing in front of us and there's a queue of about five blokes outside waiting to get in!

Luckily for me, the bouncers are alright – they could chuck me out, but instead they see the funny side of it – they're smiling, but one of them orders us not to do that sort of thing in their bar again. We both offer a feigned apology to them as we walk out of the toilets; they blatantly know what we've been up to. We're doing the walk of shame past all the blokes queuing up outside. When they see me, they look annoyed initially and they're giving me angry looks, probably 'cause they really need a piss. When they see the bird walk out after me though they all start laughing! And I feel like the dog's bollocks now, walking around this bar like I'm Tony Montana at his peak.

I'm fascinated by this bird for being so daring and making me so daring – she's brought out a side in me I didn't know existed!

So now, I'm interested and I'm trying to talk to her some more, but as quickly as she became interested, she becomes distant and cold; and now she doesn't want to know me! She goes and sits on her own. I'm trying to make conversation with her but she's acting like we've never met each other! I'm totally confused. I'm not getting anything back from her so I leave her to it and go back to my mates. By this point they've all figured out where I've been, so they're patting me on the back and quizzing me about it.

It isn't long before the bar starts closing and they're kicking everyone out. The girl, whose name I still don't even know, is sitting on her own on a stool outside the front window. Her friends must have left and she doesn't look too happy. I go over to talk to her but she's completely unresponsive and says she's going home to sleep. I'm trying to invite myself round to her place, so I can get a shag, but she's having none of it so I leave her there and that's the end of it. Oh well, easy cum, easy go!

There's still no sign of Marshy, and I've got no way of getting in touch with him – our phones don't work over here. I look around the bars, but the streets are packed and there are too many people to sift through, especially when I'm this drunk. The guys are shouting over to me to get in the taxi with them, back to the hostel.

In the taxi, everyone's carrying on about the bird in the bar, and I'm telling them what happened and how crazy the whole situation was, and they're all laughing about it, but they're pleased for me. I'm in a bit of shock but in a good way – I've got a massive grin on my face, in my happy daze.

When we get back, we're continuing the session up in the pool-room, on the first floor of the hostel. I go down to my room to get some weed, thinking Marshy might be in bed, but he isn't.

Where the fuck are all the others? I hope I'm not missing out on some cool party! I roll up a joint and take it upstairs to pass it round. As we're smoking on the roof terrace, the others arrive back in a taxi outside the front of the hostel. I'm expecting to see Marshy with them but he isn't there, so I call down to them.

"Alright guys, is Marshy with you lot?"

One of them replies. "Your friend? No, he was with us all night then we lost him at the end. He walked off to go and find you but didn't come back."

Another one of them says: "Yeah, we waited for him but he didn't come back so we thought he must have found you."

"Alright man, cheers for that, maybe he pulled or something. Was he wasted?"

"Yeah, he's pretty smashed, dude, that guy's fuckin' crazy!"

I would've been surprised if he wasn't absolutely tailed! Marshy's always been like this. I go on nights out with him, back in England, and lose him all the time; well it's more like he loses himself or gets hammered and lost, on purpose. Sometimes he'll get lucky and go back with a bird; or he'll get really drunk and end up being kicked out of the club; or he'll be talking to a random group of people in a corner somewhere. I reckon he's pulled a bird and gone back to her house.

I'm stoned and pissed now, playing pool in the games room with this American bloke called Ben. He's a good lad. We're giggling away at how shit we are at pool, 'cause of the state we're in. A few of the others are still up and joining in, having a beer and a smoke. We've been back for an hour so I've just about given up worrying about Marshy when I see a nice BMW pull up outside the hostel, and what looks like Marshy getting out of it. He's pissed and staggering all over the place – yep that's definitely

Marshy. I'm thinking, 'fair play, mate!' He's obviously pulled a posh bird and got a lift home from her too! He walks up the stairs and I'm smashed, smiling and laughing, eager to find out about this bird, so I'm asking him all the questions.

"Hello, mate, where the fuck have you been then? Who's the bird with the nice Beamer? Did you shag her? Wait till you hear about what happened to me!"

I realise, as I'm talking, something isn't quite right with him. He's not returning the vibes and looks shaken up by something, like he's seen a ghost. He's seriously on edge.

"Everythin' okay, mate?" I ask.

He answers tentatively and slowly. "Yeah, I'm alright, but you're not gonna believe what's just happened to me."

"What? Nothin' bad is it, mate?"

"Well, sort of. I'm alright but I've just had the scariest and weirdest experience of my life."

"What? What is it? Come on!"

"I'll tell you in a minute, mate, but is there any weed left? I need to calm down a bit first."

"Yeah, we've got a bit left in our room. I'll roll you one, mate. Hang on a sec." I rush down to the room to get some more skins, and run straight back up the stairs. I don't want to miss any of the story; I'm rolling the joint as he talks. We light up the spliff outside, on the roof terrace.

"So, we lost you lot in the taxis and then I got leathered in the bar with them lot," he says.

"Yeah, I saw them come in without you and thought you'd pulled."

"Yeah, well, when it all kicked out and we all went outside, I went lookin' for you for about half an hour."

"Right…"

"I couldn't find you and when I went back, they'd all gone, so I thought, bollocks, and started walkin' back to the hostel 'cause I was pretty sure I knew the way."

"You fuckin' nutcase, you should've just got in a taxi."

"Well I haven't got any money on me, Bill, and I didn't think it was that far. Anyway, after a while I realised I was completely lost."

"No shit! Where were you then? Anywhere near the bars?"

"I dunno, man, don't think I was near the bars, but I was on a main road somewhere. Then I saw a police car so I went over to ask them if they'd give me directions to the hostel, and I thought I'd be cheeky and ask them for a lift."

"Alright, what did they say?"

"He just fuckin' laughed at me and said it would cost me twenty dollars for a ride back. Cheeky prick."

"The pigs tried to charge you twenty dollars for a lift! You're fuckin' kiddin' me!"

"Well anyway, I haven't got any money on me 'cause my card was swallowed in that ATM in Miami, and I spent what I had in the bar, so I started walkin' again."

"What, so you've been walkin' around all this time, tryin' to find the hostel?"

"Well hang on, mate, and I'll get to that. Anyway, I got lost on the way back and as I was walkin' along the main road, this sports car pulled up alongside me and the windows came down."

"Was that the one you pulled up in just now then?"

"Yeah."

"Who was in it then?"

"This Colombian bloke called Juan."

"A Colombian bloke called Juan?!"

"Yeah, you really couldn't make this shit up, man. Anyway, right, he asks me where I'm going, in English, and I tell him I'm tryin' to get back to my hostel and he offers me a lift, so I took him up on it."

"Fuck! I thought you'd pulled some nice rich bird, mate!"

"Couldn't be further from the truth. Wait till you hear this. This guy, right, starts drivin' along the road. Then he takes a turning off, away from where I thought the hostel was, so I say to him 'I think the hostel's that way', you know, correctin' him. Then he says in his Columbian-English accent, 'Don't worry, man, we just gotta make a stop somewhere first'. I say, 'Er, sorry, man, but I need to get back to the hostel'. Next thing, he pulls up on the side of the road in this little lay-by, hidden away, and turns his lights off. He turns around to me, reaches in between my legs and pulls the lever and my seat goes flyin' backwards, you know, so I'm almost layin' down, facing the roof of the car, and he says, 'You ever felt another man's lips on your dick, man?'."

"You're fuckin' kiddin' me! Ahahahaha! What the fuck did you do then?"

"Well, I told him in no uncertain terms. 'No way, mate!' And at this point I just shit myself and froze. I'm thinkin' I'm gonna be anally intruded."

"Mate, that's fucked up!"

"I kept tellin' him I'm not interested and I like women."

"What did he do then?"

"He moved back into his seat and I said to him, 'Can you take me back to the hostel now, please? I wanna go back!' So he brought me back."

"That's when I seen you getting out of the car. Fuckin' brilliant! At least you're alright though, mate. Are you walkin' funny at all?!"

"Yeah, fuck off. I'm not religious by any stretch, but fuckin' hell, someone's answered my prayers tonight!"

When he finishes the story, me and Ben look at each other and burst out laughing. Marshy's a bit shellshocked by the whole experience and he's looking a bit pale, but the spliff has helped him calm down. This is the perfect time to take the piss, so me and Ben are ripping into Marshy at every opportunity. Playing pool was a perfect chance to throw in the puns.

"D'ya wanna game of pool, Marshy? Oh, actually, sorry mate, you probably don't wanna be playin' with balls and a big stick right now, eh?!" It's great to be abusing Marshy 'cause for all the years I've known him, he's usually been the one slating everyone else! Although Marshy looks pale as fuck, he's probably enjoying having the piss ripped out of him, rather than being thrown in a lay-by after being butt-raped. I'm sure he'll be waiting to get me back for this, so I'm enjoying it whilst it lasts.

"Do you want this shot, Marshy? Or don't you want to think about pottin' the brown right now?"

We've had a few nights in Fort Lauderdale and it's been a right laugh. but it's time for us to move on; we've got so many places to get around. I'd love to come back here again, sometime. It's getting pretty close to Christmas now so we figure it's a good time to move on. We go onto the 'Autodriveaway' website to check the list of cars and where they're going. We've got no idea where to go next but there's a car on there that needs delivering to New Orleans. I don't know anything about the place but if it's anywhere near as good as it's been here, we'll be sorted. It's across the country towards Los Angeles, so it seems like as good a place as any; and there's a free tank of petrol with the car so it'll cost us practically nothing to go.

We take down the address of the office and find it on the map. It's a ten minute walk down the road, from the hostel, and the car's available to take. I have to register with the company, give them some copies of my driver's licence, fill out some forms, and hand over a deposit of a hundred and fifty dollars. Now, we can use cars from any of the Autodriveaway offices in the USA for free, as long as we deliver them to the correct address within the time limits we're given. Sweet as a nut.

We negotiate with the manager of the office to give us a bit more time to deliver the car, so we can make an additional stop near Tampa Bay. The owner of the car is flexible with the dates so we've got three days to get the car from Fort Lauderdale to New Orleans. Perfect.

We're given the address we need to deliver the car to, in New Orleans, and they hand me the keys. We've got a Ford Ranger, a pick-up truck. They explain to us how it works – the hire cost of the car's covered by the labour costs I'm paid for moving it from one city to the other; we don't need to pay anything else. It's just as the Irish bloke said it would be. I drive back to the hostel so we can get our bags, ready to leave. It's weird driving an automatic pick-up truck, with the driving wheel on the other side of the vehicle, as well as driving on the other side of the road, but the more I drive it, the more I get used to it. I've got to figure out how the crossroads work 'cause some people are going round the corners, even when the lights are red.

We're all set and we've got a mission to complete. First, I want to stop in Clearwater near Tampa Bay – a place I remember going with my parents when I was a child. We say our goodbyes to our new friends from the hostel and set off on our next adventure. I'm starting to get into this now – if the rest of the cities around the States are like this, it's going to be fucking awesome!

Clearwater, Florida

Something I said?

We're heading west across Florida to Tampa Bay, along the 'I-75'. The roads are pretty much straight the whole way so you've got to keep your concentration; your brain doesn't really need to work very hard on a straight road, in a car with an automatic gearbox. It's easy to switch off, especially considering I've been getting pissed pretty much every day for the last two weeks. I'm not exactly hitting my peak performance right now. Having weed in my system tends to make me stare into thin air quite a lot too; I drift off and start daydreaming. It's quite easy to go ten or twenty miles on this road and suddenly come round and realise "Fuck! I'm drivin' a fuckin' car!"

I'm supposed to be concentrating on the road, but instead, I'm choosing my starting eleven for the England football team. We're smoking loads more than we normally do back home. Usually I smoke weed during the day and I don't need any fags, but I'm on a pack a day out here, at least; and fuck it, why not? We're on holiday; we can do what we want now. It's not a problem – me and Marshy are fucking hardcore; always the last ones to bed; always drink everyone else under the table.

Once we reach the western edge of the state and start heading north, the journey becomes a bit more interesting. There isn't a great deal of scenery between the cities, just a lot of barren land. I went to Clearwater with my parents, when I was a kid, and I remember it being a nice place so I figure it's a good place to stop, en route to New Orleans. It's a small, quaint village by the beach on the outskirts of Tampa Bay. The majority of buildings don't get above two or three stories and the pace of life is slow and relaxed. It's on a small strip of land facing the Gulf of Mexico. All the houses are set in big plots of land and the streets are wide and lined with palm trees. It's quite similar to Fort Lauderdale. From my first visit here, as a child, I remember the white sand on the beach and the water being warm. There's a big theme park nearby, on the outskirts of Tampa, called Busch Gardens, so I tell Marshy we need to go there and he's up for it.

We've done three hundred miles and it's taken us four hours. We arrive in the evening and drive around Tampa to see if we can find any hidden gems. Our strategy isn't really working though. We haven't got a clue where we're going and we end up cruising down the back streets through some old, run-down factory buildings. It's starting to get dark and there's no-one around; it all looks a bit dodgy. I've heard stories of people holding you up in your car if you get stopped at a red light. I make a quick U-turn and head back onto the main roads. I don't want to be held at gun-point and have the truck robbed off us; we'll be stuck in the middle of nowhere! So much for being adventurous.

We need to find the hostel. I stop at a supermarket so we can get directions and stock up on food. The two hostels we've been to so far have both had cooking facilities and I'm sick of the sight of Subway sandwiches. We've found a deal on frozen pizzas – three for ten bucks – a bargain! That'll be our diet now, until we get bored of them. There's only one hostel around here so it should be easy to find. We're staying at the 'Clearwater Beach Hostel'.

It's situated on a quiet residential street, a few minutes' walk from the beach. It's very quiet around here; no-one on the streets and no noise besides the occasional car rolling past. We park our pick-up outside and walk up the pathway to the entrance; it's covered with bushes and trees. Outside, there's a communal area, but the tables and chairs are empty. There's a swimming pool here but it's got a cover over it; they aren't using it 'cause we're bang in the middle of the low season. There are a couple of separate buildings surrounding the reception, which are the bedrooms. The hostel isn't busy so we get a four-person room to ourselves.

There isn't much going on here – there's no big strip of bars – we'd have to venture into Tampa for that but it's a bit too far and we don't know anything about the place. We're not staying long so we might as well hang out round here. We settle in and get talking to the owner. He seems happy for the male company 'cause most of the other guests are birds. There are no more than ten people here. We meet two English birds, Angie and Briony, in the garden, and we all – owner included – go to the main bar in Clearwater, a few minutes' walk down the road. There are only two people in it – it's dead. The hostel owner, Keith, knows the owner of the bar; it's such a small place, I imagine everyone knows each other.

After beer number five, the conversation's flowing nicely and we're getting on with Angie & Briony. They're telling us some mad tales of their trips to Ibiza, and clubbing nights during their university days. They're pretty cool and we're exchanging stories of how wrecked we used to get. The owner of the bar's been sitting with us, talking to Keith. I go up to the bar to buy another round and the bar owner walks over. He must have taken offence to something I said 'cause he refuses to serve me, tells me I've had enough, and orders me to leave. He's worked up and angry. What the fuck did I say? Is this 'cause we didn't tip again? He isn't happy about it, whatever it is. I really don't know what's got his tail up but he's fucking raging. Fucking bell-end, I'm only just getting warmed up as well! What the fuck is this bloke's problem? The others turn around to see me being ushered towards the door by the bar owner, but he won't tell them what I've done and he's not changing his mind; I walk out, dumbfounded. I try to reason with him but he's adamant I have to leave. Marshy follows me out.

"What have you done, Bill?"

"I dunno. I was about to get a round and he told me I had to leave."

"Come on, what have you done, Bill?"

"Nothin', he's sayin' I'm too drunk. Look at me. You know when I'm drunk!"

"Well fuck it, time to go anyway, let's just leave it."

This dickhead's standing at the door, staring at me, waiting for me to walk off. I'm staring back at him, puzzled, waiting for everyone else, shrugging my shoulders at him. They're all leaving with me. You just lost yourself a load of business, you donut. This is the second time a barman's kicked off. What's this all about? I'm leaving it and walking away – it's really not worth getting wound up over and causing a scene; you never know who you could be messing with. Maybe I said something he didn't like?

We're up at eight o'clock in the morning. It's Christmas Eve and we've agreed to go to Busch Gardens, with Angie and Briony, in the pick-up truck; if we can fit them both in there. There's a bit of rain but hopefully that'll work in our favour 'cause less people will turn up. Our Ford Ranger has only got a single bench in the front cabin; it can fit three normal-sized people comfortably; but there are four of us. As I'm driving, I've got plenty of room. Marshy's sitting in the middle and Angie and Briony are on the right. They can't sit on each other's laps, in case the pigs see us – if we get stopped and reported, we won't be able to use the Autodriveaway cars anymore. Well, that, and the possibility I might get arrested! Angie is sat on the seat with her feet up and Briony is on the floor, in the passenger seat footwell, with her head below window level. The truck's pretty high up so we'll take our chances.

The drive to Busch Gardens takes forty-five minutes. Fair play to Briony for sitting in the footwell for so long – that would do my nut in.

As it's Christmas Eve and it's raining, there's hardly anyone around. The longest it takes us to queue for a ride is ten minutes; it's a giant playground. There are some great rides here and it's well worth the effort. I've swapped my hangover for an adrenaline rush. By the time we're done, I'm ready for more booze.

Back at the hostel, everyone's preparing for Christmas. Drinks are flowing, food's being made, and presents are being wrapped. Me and Marshy don't usually bother with presents, but as it's our first Christmas away from our families, we wrap up a couple of beers and give them to each other.

Christmas Day in the sun is odd, but I'm loving it all the same. All the birds have been cooking all morning, whilst we've been in bed. When we surface, at midday, we head to the communal area and there's a huge table of food. Everyone chips in five dollars to cover the costs and we all help ourselves. It smells and tastes amazing. Me and Marshy are enjoying this ten times more than everyone else 'cause all we've been eating for the past few weeks is Subway sandwiches and pizza. There are five different types of vegetable, roast potatoes, mash potatoes, beef that's pink in the middle, and a big joint of ham that falls off the bone – perfectly cooked. The birds have done us proud here so we do our bit by washing the dishes and tidying up.

We can't drink today as we have to leave for New Orleans in the evening. I've had one glass of wine all day and it's been tough to abstain 'cause I've had to watch everyone else get pissed; I've had a real hankering for some beers but I've had to show some restraint for once. As soon as we get to New Orleans, I'm going to make up for missing out today.

There isn't much point in staying around here – we've done the activities and I've already been kicked out of the only bar.

Late in the evening, we set off to New Orleans in the Ford Ranger. We're quite weary of our time limitations with the pick-up, as we've already stayed in Clearwater two nights and we have to deliver it within three. Our plan is to drive through the night to save on the cost of a night's accommodation. The longest I've driven before this journey is two hundred and fifty miles. From Clearwater to New Orleans is about seven hundred miles – this is going to be a proper mission, in the dark, with a couple of weeks' hangover kicking in. I can't wait.

We're taking the I-75 again, going north out of Florida. Then we pick up the I-10, which leads us directly across to Louisiana, and down into New Orleans from there. We're getting into the unknown now – long roads in the middle of nowhere, without a person in sight, miles away from home. I've been to Florida before – I knew what to expect. I don't know anything about New Orleans and no-one I know has been there, either. It could be rubbish. Clearwater certainly wasn't up to much; well, not for drinking anyway.

I'm driving out of Florida and it's taking forever. As it turns two o'clock in the morning, I'm starting to get really knackered. I'm so tired, I'm seeing things crossing the road; my mind's starting to wander off like it does when you're falling asleep. Maybe I'm dreaming whilst I'm awake? I'm seeing illusions of chickens and other animals running out into the road; I keep thinking I'm about to run something over but there's nothing there. I need to rest my brain so we pull over at the next service station, fill the tank up, and Marshy takes over. He isn't authorised to drive the vehicle, 'cause he didn't bring his licence with him, but there aren't any other cars around and we've got a long way to go, so he takes the risk. We're chatting about all the girls we've pulled since we were teenagers but after a while my eyes start closing and I'm drifting off.

New Orleans, Louisiana

The House of the Rising Sun

I must have been sleeping for quite a while 'cause when I wake up, we're in the centre of New Orleans. Marshy's driven the whole way through the night without sleeping. I'm rubbing my eyes and stretching my neck out 'cause I've been lying, in a fucking awkward position, with my head leaning towards the floor, against the passenger side door. It's lucky the roads are so straight 'cause I'm pretty sure otherwise Marshy would be turning into corners, as hard as he could, so my head would smash on the door. I open my eyes and they're stinging from the brightness of the daylight.

"Fuckin' hell, mate, what time's it?"

"It's about eight-thirty."

"Fuck! You been awake all this time?"

"Yeah, man, I drove straight through. No problem. Hasn't been too bad, actually."

Marshy's looking straight ahead, focused on the road. His eyes are half-cut and from his expressionless face, I can tell he's knackered.

"Fuckin' nice one, mate. How long have I been asleep for?"

"About three hours, four hours, somethin' like that."

"Aren't you tired? I'll take over if you want?!" I'm pissing myself laughing.

"Well we're here now, you fuckin' penis."

"Where we going now then?"

"To a tourist information shop to get a map and ask some questions."

"Fuckin' hell. That's quite a good idea for you, mate."

"They probably won't open till nine o'clock though."

"Yeah, we'll just wait outside until it opens, then you can take over and I'm gonna kip 'cause I'm completely fucked."

"Don't blame you, mate."

After driving around the centre of the city for twenty minutes, we find a tourist information shop, so we pull in a lay-by, opposite. The one-way roads and tram-lines make this place difficult to navigate; all we've got to go by is a large map of America that shows the main interstate roads on it; we haven't got a town map with all of its main roads. We also haven't any idea how to get around New Orleans or where anything is. I've heard the city's built on a swamp and it's actually below sea level. We've also been told it's a major party city and we're right in the middle of one of the biggest weeks of the year for getting smashed – the week between Christmas and New Year. If that's true then we're going to be right in our element. Let the parties commence.

After waiting half an hour for the shop to open, I get out and run across the road; Marshy's minding the pick-up truck. We've got to complete our mission now – find a hostel, get a bed, drop our bags off, and find the office block, in the centre of the city, where the car has to be delivered to. I get a map, from a helpful fella in the tourist information shop, and he tells me there are two main hostels in New Orleans – India House and Marquette House. He shows me where they are and marks the address where we need to hand the vehicle over. I ask him which hostel is the better out of the two. He says the India House is more popular with tourists, 'cause it doesn't have any restrictions on what time you can stay out till, whereas Marquette house does and you're not allowed booze there. Plus, they also turn all the lights out at midnight. Well they can shove that up their arses – we won't be going there! The India House is about two miles away from the city centre and it's got a reputation for being a party house, so it's an easy decision.

I'm also warned, very stringently, about a couple of areas on the map to stay away from, at all costs. There are two large estates the Yanks call 'The Projects', which are nicknamed 'The Hood'. They're like massive council estates where mostly poorer people live and, he says, we won't be welcome there. He circles these areas on the map in thick marker pen. One of the estates is on the other side of a main road from where the India House is, so I make a mental note to stay clear.

I walk out of the shop and run back over to the truck, showing Marshy the map straight away and making a particular effort to tell him about 'The Projects'. I get the impression he's not really paying attention as he's sitting in the passenger seat, practically falling asleep. I take over the driving, trying to get him to direct me to the hostel, but his eyes are closing uncontrollably. After twenty minutes, I stumble across it.

This city is amazing. You can see the clash of nature and man everywhere you look.

We're heading up Canal Street – a large access road that leads you directly in and out of the city centre. The roads are wide, with three lanes of cars going each way, as well as a tramline in the centre of the road with plenty of space, either side, for people to get on and off. The pavements at the sides of the roads are lined with gigantic trees, so big and powerful, the roots have forced their way up through the paving slabs, making them crack and rise up. People walking down the road have to climb over the roots like it's some kind of obstacle course, using the trees to help them balance.

The population here is different to the other cities we've been to – Miami's got an even mixture of all races; Fort Lauderdale is pretty much all white; New Orleans is mostly black. The accent is different too – people from the South have a certain twang in the way they pronounce their words – even longer, drawn out words, like they aren't in a rush for anything. It's very different from anywhere else I've ever been – it's got its own vibe, the people are friendly, there's a nice smokey wood scent in the air, the same scent you get from flavouring food. I like this place already; I've got a gut feeling, I can't quite put my finger on it, but I just know I'm going to have a fucking good time here.

Driving away from the city, I take a left turn into South Lopez Street. The India House isn't far down the road, on my left. At the start of the road, there's a huge church on the corner; me and Marshy agree it's a good landmark to remember the road by. The rest of the street is lined with family houses, most of them detached, and built in a similar but quirky style. They've all got big porchways, supported by pillars, and stairs leading up to the front doors.

And there it is, like some kind of Mecca – the building's got an aura around it. You can tell just from looking at it – things are happening here. There are a shitload of cars parked up outside, only no-one's paid attention to the lines of the parking spaces; there are cars sprayed all over the place – it's a fucking free-for-all. There aren't any rules here – you come and go as you please; you drink and sleep when you want; you govern yourself…well, you're supposed to.

It's an old but well-maintained Creole townhouse. Although there are only two storeys, it stretches back quite far. It's fully detached and looks like it's been there for a long time. It's painted sea green, with white windows and pillars on the porch that hold up a balcony above it, which is surrounded with a cast iron fence. Flags of different countries hang from poles sticking out of the balcony, welcoming everyone.

Walking up a small set of stairs at the centre front of the building, to the entrance, I can hear the atmosphere intensify. The noise of people talking, laughing, and enjoying themselves gets louder – this place is oozing fun from its seams. There's a constant stream of people going in and out; some others sat on chairs, under the porch, and they greet us as we walk in. It's a popular place – somewhere a certain type of person knows about – like a place you only hear about through the grapevine. Only sound people are here, no twats or boring fuckers.

Immediately through the entrance is the reception desk. The walls all around the desk are covered with photos of previous guests; smiling, making funny faces, and posing in fancy dress outfits. I'm transfixed on the pictures but snap out of it as the female manager gets my attention.

"Hello there, sir, have you made a reservation?"

"Oh err, no we haven't, but we were told about this place by the tourist information shop, downtown. I don't suppose you've got any beds going, have you?"

"Errrm. Not sure if we do. How many of you?"

"Just two people."

"Let me check what we've got left."

I'm starting to worry now, thinking we might miss out on all this fun. The place looks packed and I've already got my heart set on staying here.

"I think you're in luck, there's still a few places left, in the shared dormitories?"

"That's fine, that's just what we're lookin' for. How much per night?"

"It's twelve dollars a night, sir."

Marshy and I look at each other in amazement; it's less than we've paid in the other cities.

"Can we pay for two nights now and then go from there?"

"Sure, that's fine. That'll be…forty-eight dollars then, please."

Sweet as a nut. We're in. She disappears behind the desk for a moment and then returns with some bed sheets.

"If you follow me, I'll show you to your beds – they're just out the back here."

We walk through the main living room – the walls have been knocked through to make one large space but they're still used as separate areas. At the front of the house is a communal area where people are sitting on cushions on the wooden floorboards, talking, playing cards and board games. There are weird and wonderful paintings on the walls and hundreds more photos of guests. We're nodding to everyone as we walk through and they're all returning the greeting. They can see new people arriving and we're getting inquisitive looks; they're sizing us up. Towards the back of the open plan room, the curtains are drawn and the space becomes noticeably darker. This is the TV area. It's much quieter and the TV's in the far corner, on the right. There's three rows of old tatty sofas surrounding the TV; the fabric's ripped on most of them.

The spaces in this house make it easy for people to chat to each other. It's completely different from the other hostels we've stayed in. Comparing the merits of the hostels we've been to so far – this one wins by a mile.

As we walk through, the receptionist's telling us what we need to know.

"The hostel's open twenty-four hours so you can come and go as you please, but just make sure if you've been out drinkin', that you're respectful of the other people stayin' here. The dormitories where you're stayin' are out the back in the garden."

Through a door at the back of the TV room, on the left, are the toilets and a stairway leading to some private rooms on the first floor. Past that is another door leading into a large, well-fitted, but old-skool kitchen. The owners cook and sell meals for the guests but you can also buy your own food and cook it. There's a large square wooden table on my right, with long benches on all four sides; you can fit fifteen to twenty people around it. This table's not just used for eating at but also for playing drinking games, out of the way of the people chilling in the TV room, so you didn't disturb them. You can meet new people easily here. Everyone talks to each other – it's that kind of atmosphere; I can't feel any tension in this place. Everyone's having fun and they're all walking around with smiles on their faces.

A door at the back of the kitchen leads into a big courtyard. We walk down a shallow set of steps onto a paved floor. There are tables and chairs at the bottom of the stairs with more people drinking, smoking, and laughing. Tall fences protect the sides of the premises so the courtyard is completely closed off to the outside world. On my left, there's a swimming pool with wooden side panels, resting on the surface of the concrete. At the back of the courtyard, there are three large blocks in a row. The one in the middle is a shower / toilet block and the two either side are dormitories, both of them full of bunk beds. We're taken into the one on the left. It's dark inside and some people are still in bed, nursing their hangovers.

"There's only a few bunks left so you can either have this one...or that one over there."

We choose our beds. I've got the top bunk and Marshy's on the bottom one. The mattresses are old and worn with all kinds of different stains over them. The dormitory is made out of wood; it looks flimsy as fuck. The bunk beds are lined up, one after the other, against the walls, and in the middle of the room too; there's just enough space to walk around. It stinks of body odour, cheesy socks, and old rotten furniture in here. The mattresses probably haven't been changed for decades. It's a fucking skank-pit. I know some snotty, posh birds that would run a mile if they saw it. Everyone's crammed in here like livestock. At night, when everyone's lying on their bunk beds, you either have someone else's feet or someone's head thirty centimetres away from you, depending on which way you're lying; unless you're at the end of the row or by a wall. It isn't everyone's cup of tea but I'm not really arsed; all we need's a roof over our heads for a few hours each night. This hostel may be low budget and a couple of miles away from the action, but it isn't difficult to get to the centre of town from here.

To add to all that, the dormitories are unisex too. We're chatting to some people and they're telling us to be prepared for people shagging in the dorms at night. Apparently, if people fancy a quick shag, they take the white sheet from their mattress and tuck it into the base of the top bunk so it drapes over the bottom bunk, for some privacy! Then they'll go at it like rabbits and go to sleep. Does anyone ever kick off? No! Why would you want to piss on somebody's fire? No-one wants to be a killjoy. Go for it! Although I don't imagine people will be gathered round shouting them on, either.

Once we've put our sheets on our beds, we place our bags on top to show the bunks are taken. There's nowhere to lock anything up but we're not bothered; it seems to be the way of the place.

Have you heard about Bourbon Street?

We go to the TV room. Marshy's got a face like a slapped arse 'cause he hasn't had any sleep and needs to rest before we go and deliver the car. He tries to watch TV but within two minutes he's out cold and snoring, so I'm leaving him to have a power nap for an hour. There's a guy sat on one of the sofas and I get chatting to him. He's a tall American called John, with long, brown hair tied in a ponytail. He's not a traveller, he's come to New Orleans to work on the oil rigs and ships, off the coast in the Gulf of Mexico; apparently the money's really good. On his time out, between shifts, he stays at the hostel so he can meet people and go out partying. He's from a small town in Texas but there's no work there. I'm quizzing him to find out what we should be doing and where we should be going.

"So you've never heard of this place, at all?"

"No, not heard anythin' about it really, apart from Mardi Gras. You never really see anythin' on TV back home about New Orleans. Maybe Florida or LA or New York, but not here."

"Really? It's a big party town, man. Mardis Gras is a big thing round here, but you won't see it – unless you're here till February?"

"Oh shit, man, that's a shame, we haven't got that long."

"Okay, well you're here for New Year, right?"

"We might be. Not sure. We're gonna see if we like the place."

"Oh, come on, man, what's not to like? There's no way you guys are gonna go now – there's only a few days to go and plus, you got a bed now. This is one of the greatest places to spend New Year's, man, Bourbon Street will be awesome!"

"Where's Bourbon Street?"

"What? You guys dunno about Bourbon Street?"

"No, man."

"You're kiddin' me! That's the reason most people come here! You guys never heard of Bourbon Street?! Ah, man! That's fuckin' crazy, man."

"Seriously, is it that good? Where is it then?"

"Ah, no shit, man. Seriously. Look uhhh, we're goin' down tonight if you guys wanna come?"

"Sweet, for sure, we'll be up for that. You up for that, Marshy?" I look at Marshy but he's asleep. "Right, well, we need to go drop this truck off and get some sleep, but what time you headin' out?"

"Be here around nine o'clock, dude. We'll have a few drinks here first then head down."

"Okay, cheers, John, see you then."

I'm waking Marshy up by slapping him round the face, and he's not happy, but it's got to be done. He's a grumpy twat right now. We get back in the truck and use our map to find the offices. I drop the keys off inside a big office block, sign a form and that's it – done. All we have to do is go to the Autodriveaway office in New Orleans, wherever that is, and choose another car. Our problem now, though, is that we haven't got a car anymore, so we've got to find our way back to the hostel on foot, or get the tram.

Even though it's the end of December, it's still fairly warm in New Orleans – around fifteen degrees Celsius, so we can handle being outside without a car. Neither of us can be arsed to walk so we find the tram stop and jump on, checking with the conductor to make sure we can get back to Canal Street. The trams are still used a lot and they're cheap too. They're ancient but well-maintained; getting on one is like stepping back in time. Most of them are made out of wood – the varnished seats are ridged, like the seats in a church; you sit bolt upright. They're busy with locals, mostly black people, and they're all talking to each other; even random people that have never met each other start talking away – you rarely see that in Pompey or anywhere else I've been, unless it's on a night bus back from a club and everyone's pissed; when all their inhibitions have gone. The people of New Orleans are happy and friendly with each other. I like it but I'm not confident enough to start chatting to people just yet. I've got this thing inside my head – I reckon people will think I'm crazy if I start talking to someone I don't know. Is this an English thing? Once we get back to the hostel, me and Marshy go to our bunks to get some sleep.

I'm up and I'm asking Marshy if he wants anything from the shop 'cause I'm getting hungry and we need some booze for tonight. He's staying in his bed for a bit longer. I walk out, down the side of the hostel, through a gate in the fence, out to where the cars are parked. I need to find a shop so I'm looking for someone to ask them for directions. The first person I see is this American dude wearing a tartan kilt, massive moon boots, and a black, heavy metal t-shirt.

"Excuse me mate, d'ya know where there's a shop around here so I can get some booze and food?"

This guy's pissed already and it must only be four o'clock right now. What a fucking legend. He's tall and skinny with spiky, dyed red hair. He gives me directions to the supermarket around the corner and gives me ten bucks to get him a bottle of bourbon, before he stumbles back into the hostel garden. This guy sounds like a fucking right laugh and I reckon I'll be having a few drinks with him! He's got this angry demeanour, not like he's pissed off with you, but in a funny way – like an angry stand-up comedian.

I find the supermarket and they've got the same pizzas we've had for the last few days. I get some more of them, for our dinner. When I find the booze section, I'm absolutely buzzing – a large bottle of bourbon, which is something of a local speciality in Louisiana, is only seven dollars. At the current exchange rate, that works out at four English pounds for a litre, which is a fucking touch. It isn't a big name brand like Jack Daniels or Jim Beam, but it smells pretty good, nonetheless. It seems like everything unhealthy is cheap in America – fast food, junk food, ciggies, booze, etc. And I'm looking at the cereals and they're eight dollars for a box – all the healthy shit's fucking expensive…I can buy a litre of bourbon for less than a box of cereal – that's fucked up! I've also got some cheap cola and some beers, all set to get smashed before we go out and it's only cost us ten quid. I fucking love this place!

It's easy to meet new friends in the India House; people just sit down and join in your conversations. I'm doing it too; it's so fucking cool – exactly the type of scene me and Marshy revel in.

We're beginning our first night in New Orleans. Marshy's awake and we've eaten our dirty pizzas, again. We're sitting around the table in the kitchen with our bottles of bourbon and a few decks of cards. There are six other people with us and the group's growing in size; every fifteen minutes someone else joins in. There's no small talk, everyone's straight into outlandish, smutty conversations – total filth, including the birds. It's great to finally meet some real Americans from other cities around the States, especially as I don't know much about New Orleans, but they all speak about it like we should. It feels like we've stumbled across a hidden gem here – America's best kept secret.

A few drinks at the hostel has got me in the mood for partying, and it'll set me up for the rest of the night; it's much cheaper to get half-pissed before you go out, rather than buying all your drinks in the bars. We round everyone up and set off on a pissed--up mission to the city centre. We're going back down Canal Street now. Having been along this road a few times today, I'm already becoming familiar with my surroundings. We're on our way to Bourbon Street, which John mentioned to me earlier. Me and Marshy haven't got a clue what it's like or where it is. In order to get there we've got to jump over the roots of the trees pushing their way up through the pavements – everyone's joining arms, running and jumping over them like they're hurdles, then turning round to the rest of group with their arms held up in the air triumphantly, as if they've just accomplished some amazing feat. We're all big kids in a real-life adventure playground.

We're walking past all these local, independent restaurants selling cajun chicken; it's one of the local specialities. As we get closer to the centre, the trees stop and the buildings become taller. We're heading towards the French District – the centre of New Orleans and the beating heart of the city. As we walk further in, the buzz of music and people becomes louder; I can feel us getting closer.

The beginning of Bourbon Street is off the main road on our left. From a distance, you can see people streaming in and out of it. As soon as you get there, you can see why it's so famous. The road is narrow and the streets are packed with people. There's enough room for a single car to fit down it but it closes to traffic in the evenings, due to the sheer volume of people. I get an instant adrenaline rush as I enter the street. It feels like I'm closed in, like Bourbon Street's got me in its grasp. Every single building for a mile is either a bar, club, restaurant, strip bar, hotel, or souvenir shop, all painted in vibrant colours and covered in neon lights. Many of the bars have balconies which are crammed full of revellers, looking out onto the streams of people, most of them carrying a drink in hand. There are hundreds of people in fancy dress, just for the sake of it, for the party, because they can. Animal costumes, cheerleaders, top hats and tails, face paints, hats, wigs, you name it. It's Boxing Day and there's a carnival atmosphere tonight.

Most of the people are wearing bead necklaces. The tradition is to throw a necklace at a girl and she flashes her tits at you; fucking sweet! Most of the birds are walking around with at least ten necklaces. They aren't shy – there are breasts popping out all over the place – all different shapes and sizes – I don't know where to look! There are a lot of people here but it's a tolerant atmosphere, considering most of them are drunk and knocking into each other every couple of seconds. Everyone knows it's party time; there's no stress or aggression. If someone knocks into you, or vice versa, it isn't given a second thought – no-one kicks off, you just move on.

John takes us into a souvenir shop to get some beads to throw to the ladies. I pick up ten necklaces and head over to the counter to pay. As I'm standing in line, I notice there's a couple of beer taps by the till. I need to double take to make sure I'm seeing straight – this is basically like having a bar in a souvenir shop! It doesn't sound right but sure enough, when I get served, I'm asked:

"Would you like a beer with that, sir?"

"Don't mind if I do!"

I then take my beer out onto Bourbon Street, walk along the road drinking it, and it's fine to take it into some of the other bars, no questions asked. Sweet as a fucking nut. Where can you do that in England? No-fucking-where!

Hidden Gems

The music scene is crazy here. Every bar we walk past has got a live band playing jazz, soul, blues, funk, rock, or some other style of music. The best bit – no entrance fees. There are hundreds of other bars coming off the adjoining streets, too. As we walk down the road, taking in the atmosphere, we're swept away by the crowd – the constant waves of people create two currents going in opposite directions. It's difficult to stick together as a group; if I lose concentration for a second, I'll lose everyone. We stay close and shout to each other when we see the bar we want to go to. We're trying to hold hands to keep with the others, but people crossing the road from the other side force us to break the chain; that's all it takes to lose a couple of people for the rest of the night. We've got to know the name of the bar we're going to before we move anywhere, in case we go past it. We can't just turn around and go back, we have to wait until the crowd slows down to get to the other side and catch the current taking us back the other way. It's pandemonium, but everyone's got a smile on their face. Once we get inside the bar, we can relax.

We go up to the balcony. There are people leaning over the sides, looking for a fit girl to throw some beads at. Similarly, there are people throwing beads up to the girls on the balconies. They get the biggest cheers 'cause more people can see them, looking up from the street. There are some real exhibitionists out tonight! Five seconds of fame every time they get their tits out! And why not?! The cheers of the crowd get louder the drunker everyone gets. In the narrow road, the atmosphere has nowhere to escape – it's all around you. The intensity builds through the night, like a kettle boiling water. As the beers go down, people start to lose their balance, so the crowds in the street begin to sway harder and faster; it's like you're on some kind of rollercoaster.

We don't make it very far down the street on our first night; John wants to show us the best bars and he reckons they're all near the beginning of the road. We only make three of the bars, but that's enough. We stay out late, talking to our new friends and other groups of people we've met along the way. Although me and Marshy only planned to stay here a few nights, I'm loving this place so much that I can see us staying longer. This place pisses on everything else we've seen so far. It's the coolest place on earth!

It's four o'clock in the morning and we're heading back to the hostel. Everyone's smashed. We stay up chatting back at the hostel before going to bed.

I'm trying to avoid smashing the head of the person in the bunk next to me with my feet as I get into my bunk bed. I like this place. I've made friends with a few people today and they're friends with others we haven't met yet. We're being introduced to new people all the time, which can only mean potential to pull more birds.

It's early afternoon and I've just got up. I'm sitting in the living room, watching TV, nursing my hangover; this city isn't going to be a place where we do a lot of sightseeing, unless we class all the different bars as 'sights'. If I'm going to be getting absolutely fucking leathered all the time and going to bed at five in the morning, there isn't a snowflake's chance in hell I'll be doing anything during the day, except maybe more drinking. But fuck it – I didn't come on this trip to go sightseeing. There's always someone, somewhere in the hostel who's drinking; if I want to join in, I can clock in and clock out as I please and that's alright with me. I'm caning the ciggies too.

At two o'clock in the afternoon, we decide to start drinking early, under the philosophy: 'The best cure for a hangover is to carry on drinking'. We've still got some bourbon left, so we drink it for breakfast. We're also operating under the motto: 'Eatin's Cheatin', so we can get pissed more easily and make our money go further. New Orleans is a party city and we intend to do it justice.

We're sat at the tables and chairs in the courtyard garden. We're looking for people to recruit into our session when I see the bloke who was wearing the kilt yesterday. He's got all his goth bling on today – piercings in his nose, chin, tongue, ears, and eyebrows. I remember he was drunk about this time yesterday, so I find out if he's up for joining us.

"Hello, mate, how you doing?"

"You guys started already, huh?"

"Yeah, sure, take a seat, man, come and join in. Here, have a swig of this, it's bourbon."

"I can see exactly what it is, man! I'm gonna have to get to the shop, aren't I?"

We get on instantly – this guy's our type of piss-head. His name's Ben and he's from Georgia. He's got a ginger goatee and we're ripping the shit out of him for being ginger, but he's enjoying it, in the same way that some people like being tortured. He's abusing us back for having yellow teeth 'cause apparently, the Yanks all laugh at the Brits for having shit teeth. He's our age and left home after some turbulent times with his parents, who've divorced, so he's decided to travel, and get a job wherever he can find one, to fund it. This guy's quick-witted and he's got a repertoire of 'Yo mama' jokes:

"Yo mama's so fat she had to go to Sea World to get baptized!" and "Yo mama's so fat, she got arrested at the airport for ten pounds of crack!"

He's calling me and Marshy 'England' and we're calling him 'Georgia'; not the most imaginative of nicknames, but they work.

After eating pizza, again, we're invited by the rest of our crew to a bar near the hostel to watch some live music. It's a few blocks away. There are twenty of us walking there and the group's growing as we get closer to New Year's Eve. The bar is in a residential area, which seems a bit strange, initially. I'm used to having bars on residential roads in England, but being tourists, we've only been going to bars in the city centres or specific areas, like Ocean Drive in Miami and Hollywood Boulevard in Fort Lauderdale. We haven't been to any local pubs or bars yet – the places where the tourists don't go. I'm sure the locals won't mind, as long as we behave ourselves!

We walk for five minutes to South Jefferson Davis Parkway, on the corner of a block. The building is an old, empty, run down barber's shop that probably went out of business years ago; someone has got the key and put some tables and chairs in it. There's space for the band and their instruments by the door on the right, as you walk in. It isn't a big place but there are large mirrors on the walls, so it feels bigger. There are six or seven rows of rickety old chairs towards the back of the room, facing the band. It's full and there aren't any seats left, so we all get a drink and stand behind the chairs, with a decent view of the band. The room's dimly lit and I'm getting pretty drunk.

The band comes back from their intermission, to a loud ovation. The lead singer's a large black woman. There's a keyboard player, saxophonist, drummer, bass player, and guitarist. They start playing and I can't believe my ears; they're incredible! The lead singer's got a voice like Aretha Franklin. The band sound so good, they wouldn't look out of place playing in front of fifty thousand fans; yet here they are, playing in some tiny little clapped-out barber shop in a residential street of New Orleans that doesn't hold more than fifty people. We're all looking around at each other, jaws dropping onto the floor. I'm wondering to myself if this is a secret, one-off performance by a professional band, or if this city's actually so full of talent like this that they're left undiscovered and never given the opportunity to make it in the big time. In any case, we've found another hidden gem.

When the show finishes and the band's received their much-deserved applause, we're straight back down to Bourbon Street, arm-in-arm. Alongside our first drink at the next place, someone's ordered a round of shots to go with it; I'm having my first ever shot of Jägermeister. I've never heard of the stuff but apparently it gets you pretty pissed, and everyone drinks it out here. It tastes rancid but twenty minutes after we've downed it, everyone's bouncing off the walls. We're all getting smashed and some of the birds are starting to show their liberal side; two of the them start snogging each other and it's great to watch! They stop and one of them whispers to the other one. Then they each grab a different girl and kiss them. Soon enough, all the girls are kissing each other, full-on tongues. The lads are all spectators on the sidelines, doing fuck all. I fancy a piece of the action, so I wade in and they soon follow.

It's like being back at a school disco, seeing how many birds you can pull. I'm kissing one bird, and another one pulls her away from me and kisses her, then she kisses me, like some kind of snogging Dosey-Doe! I've kissed eight different birds in the space of five minutes – it's like they're under some kind of spell, like something's come over them – they've all let themselves go wild. It's fucking crazy and I can't believe my luck; I'm loving every second of this – outnumbered two to one by sex-crazed women. Then it just stops and we're all snogged out.

I've found my weakness tonight and it's Jägermeister. I'm all over the place. At the peak of being wrecked I was having a fucking blast, but the shots have kicked in now and my head's spinning. It's time to go home; I'm telling myself 'that's it, need to go home now, need to sleep.' I've done a stealth exit from the group and fucked off. I need to get back to the hostel now. I've walked a mile or so up the road, back towards the hostel, stopping off at Maccy D's on the way. I've got two double cheeseburgers. I'm eating them but making sure I take the gherkins out; no matter how pissed I am I'll still take the gherkins out. I've no idea what the time is but I know I need this food. My head won't stop spinning.

Jäeger-Monster

I'm waking up in my bunk bed with a really sore, pulsating headache. At first I think I'm dreaming. I can hear a woman's voice calling out my name and Marshy's name.

"Billy? Where are Billy and Marshy?"

I'm stirring as she repeats the call.

"Where's Billy Walker? Does anyone know which bunk beds Billy Walker and Andrew Marsh are sleepin' on?"

It takes me a while to come round. As I stretch out my contracted muscles, I realise I'm awake and someone's actually looking for me. I've still got my clothes on from the night before; my mouth's bone dry and I'm still drunk as fuck. My brain kicks into gear and I reluctantly groan out.

"Yeah, I'm over here."

My voice is deep and croaky – the result of shouting all night and smoking copious amounts of cigarettes.

"Ah right, there you are. Can you get up and go straight to reception please. And bring your friend with you."

"What? Why?"

"I'll explain when you get there."

I look at the time on my watch. It's early in the morning, eight-thirty; I must have only had a few hours kip. I get out of bed.

"Marshy, you awake?"

He groans pathetically as I shake him. He's in the same state as me.

"Uuuggghhhhhh, yeah, what?"

"Did you hear that?"

"Yeah."

"What d'ya think that's about then? Were we really bad last night?"

"I dunno, mate. I don't think we were that bad. I went straight to bed when I got back."

"Was I with you? What did I do? I can't remember."

"No, you stayed up for a bit. You were completely hammered, Bill."

"Well come on then, mate. We better get up and go find out."

"Oh dear, Bill, what have you done now?" He's not expecting an answer, and in any case, I don't even know what I've done myself. The last thing I can remember is sitting in McDonald's. I don't remember getting back and there's a whole raft of unanswered questions going around my head. I've got a total blackout from McDonald's to waking up just now, in my bunk bed.

We get dressed slowly and saunter through the kitchen and living room, to the reception. I've got a severe headache; I feel a thudding pain in my head with every pulse of my heart. I'm still absolutely fucking smashed. Between the two of us, we look a disgrace; being woken up this early in the morning is the last thing we need. All I want to do is crawl back into my pit and sleep the booze off. The receptionist, who called us from the dormitory, is standing behind the desk and she doesn't look impressed.

"Right, which one's Billy?"

I put my hand up in the air, raising my eyebrows, trying to look sorry even though I don't know why I'm there.

"I am."

"Do you know what you've done?"

"No, I've got no idea." I'm shrugging my shoulders with as much shock and surprise as I can muster. "What did I do?"

"So you don't remember fallin' asleep on that sofa over there?" She points over to the TV room, on the right-hand side against the wall. As I look around, I notice all the people in the room are looking at me, smiling and laughing.

"No. I don't. I woke up in my bunk bed when you came in this mornin'. I didn't mean to-"

"That's not the end of it."

"What d'ya mean? What else did I do?" I'm smiling now but starting to realise that I'm in trouble. She's talking in a pretty serious tone.

"First of all, you fell asleep on the sofa. The night manager tried to wake you up but you kept pushin' him away so he left you for another twenty minutes. You then stood up, walked behind the television and urinated all over the air conditionin' unit."

Marshy bursts out laughing, which probably isn't helping our situation, but he can't help that. And now I'm laughing as well 'cause I can't remember doing it, at all! The receptionist continues.

"You might laugh but it's taken hours to get that fixed and cleared up."

I've still got a smirk on my face, but I'm trying to stop myself laughing and be serious. It isn't working though.

"Oh my god. I'm so sorry; is there anything I can do to make up for it?"

"Well not really, it's been cleared up now. We've decided what we're gonna do…"

I'm standing there with my hand over my mouth in shock. I've got a bit of a history of doing this – it's uncontrollable when I'm that drunk. Never mind sleepwalking, more like sleep-pissing! Marshy's got a history of it too. He used to piss in the corner of his room, in his wardrobe, and in his bath. I'm sure most blokes do it at least once in their life.

But this time round, not only have I pissed in a communal living room but on the air conditioning unit. Apparently a few people were watching TV whilst I was sleeping. When I've gone behind the TV, they've jumped out of their seats and started calling out:

"What's he doing?!" Like they thought I was possessed. Initially, I can't remember this at all, but when I stop to think for a second, after she's told me what I've done, I get a vague recollection of feeling my way around a wall with my hands, whilst my eyes were closed, looking for the door to get out, towards the toilets. Obviously I wasn't anywhere near the door so I must have given up looking and unleashed wherever I was standing. To be fair though, I wasn't actually that far away from the toilets.

My punishment, or should I say, our punishment, as they've decided to impose it on Marshy for being my general partner in crime, isn't as bad as it could've been.

"Both of you are to leave the hostel for at least three nights."

I'm confused in my weary, drunken, sleep-deprived state. Just three nights? Surely if they're going to kick me out, they would kick me out for good, but no – three nights.

"Seriously?"

"Yes. You need to learn your lesson."

"But where else's there to go?"

"You'll have to go and stay at the other hostel, where you aren't allowed to drink on the premises. I can give you the address if you like? And show you where it is on the map?"

I'm powerless to do anything; I've just got to accept my punishment. Gutted.

"Okay then, where is it, please?"

She marks out the location of the other hostel on a map and passes it to me.

"So you'll need to get a tram into the centre of town and then another one, going west. Can you get your bags and go now, please?"

"Okay, but can we please come back in three nights time?"

"I'll think about it – we'll make our decision if you come back. There may not be any beds left by that point."

And we leave it there. As Marshy and I walk back to the dormitory, I can see the mixture of amusement and annoyance on his face. I try to apologise.

"Fuckin' hell. I'm sorry, mate! I had no idea that I'd done that, at all."

"Don't worry about it, man. it's pretty funny. But I can't believe they've kicked me out as well. Obviously I'd still go with you, mate, but for fuck's sake, the cheeky bastards! It's not as if I'm your fuckin' carer or somethin', although you do need one, you fuckin' disgrace!"

"You can't talk. I've had to look after you in a fuckin' state several times."

"Fair enough, can't argue with that."

"What date is it today? Will we be back in time for New Year's?"

Today is the twenty-eighth of December, so three nights away means we could potentially come back on the thirty-first, for New Year's Eve, if they let us back in! And I hope they do let us back, 'cause I really fucking like this place.

Walk of Shame

The reality of the situation starts to sink in. We're packing our clothes and we've got an absolute mission to get to the other hostel, especially at this time in the morning, in the state we're in. The last thing I want to be doing right now is hauling a big rucksack around, but I've got to take it on the chin and accept the punishment. We don't want to be spending too much money on tram fares, so we walk to the centre of the city.

Everyone we walk past is shocked, almost offended. We must look a train wreck. But maybe we'll make them feel better about themselves in an 'Oh my god, I'm glad I don't look like that!' kind of way. I'm getting some of the strangest looks I've ever had as we stagger over the pavement, with messy hair and bloodshot eyes, squinting in reluctance to accept being awake. This is a real walk of shame. No time to shower, still drunk from the previous night's antics. We're both carrying large, heavy rucksacks; we must look like tramps. I look at Marshy and see the grumpy look on his face, as he looks down towards the floor.

He isn't pissed off with me, more the situation. It feels like we're back at school again, being punished – what a fucking load of bollocks!

The other hostel, Marquette House, is just as far away from the action as the India House, in a completely different direction. We walk into the centre of town and get a tram going west which can drop us off close by. The funny looks continue on the tram – we stick out like a sore thumb – we look like something out of Halloween with our pale hangover skin. I take a guess at the stop we need and alight from the tram. We're on another large main road called St. Charles Avenue; the hostel's on a parallel road behind it so it's got to be around here somewhere. The area looks okay; there are more restaurants, bars, and shops here. We find Carondelet Street and the hostel a few yards around the corner.

The cost per night is much higher than at the India House – twenty bucks a night here. You can tell by the size of the houses surrounding the hostel that it's a more expensive area. Like the India House, this hostel is also situated in the middle of a residential street. There's a large reception area, where you check in, and the wall behind the desk is lined with small lockers for guests to keep their valuables secure. You have to pay for the privilege, but it's differences like this that set the two hostels apart. There's nowhere to lock up your belongings at the India House; you have to trust everyone, regardless of whether you actually do or not, but it seems to work with everyone there.

Here, they also separate the men's and women's sleeping quarters. There are several large wooden huts, raised up on brick berths for the blokes. Each hut is filled with bunk beds but there's ample space between each one. There are six bunk beds in each hut. The birds' accommodation is totally separated, in a much larger building; their rooms are up on the first floor of the main block, above the reception. It's obvious they've designed the place like this, maybe for the birds to feel safer but more likely to stop people shagging.

It's about ten o'clock in the morning and we're checking in. We're assigned a bed, rather than being able to choose one ourselves. I'm on a top bunk, right by the door. The bottom bunk is already occupied by a stranger. He's hanging around the communal area, outside the cabins, and sees us go into the hut. He follows us in and starts chatting away. He's six foot four, broad, and doesn't have any front teeth, just a big gap where they used to be. He's from New York and I can tell there's a difference from the other American accents I've heard, but I haven't studied them enough to know exactly what they are. It must be the same for a Yank listening to Scousers and Mancs. He's got long, messy, curly hair that hasn't been cut for some time. He's telling us how he doesn't have a home and makes a living from busking on the streets, getting anything up to a hundred bucks a day. He says he's homeless, like a hobo, but he can't be doing too bad if he can afford to stay at a hostel.

Now he's taking on the role of tour guide, showing us where the toilets are and telling us the rules of the place. He's pretty much following us wherever we go, like he wants to be our friend. He seems alright so I take him at face value and have a chat.

We've dropped our bags off in the hut and we're looking around the grounds. There isn't much to it besides the sleeping quarters and the reception. Outside, in the space between the huts and the main building, there's a small patio area with two tables and some chairs – that's the only place any kind of social interaction can take place – it's fucking soulless. I can't help but think it's designed this way, to stop people from talking to each other, so you can't get noisy; it's so fucking quiet and boring. It's not a popular place either – there are probably ten people staying here and most of them are blokes. There's no buzz, no atmosphere, no laughing, no drinking. After having such a mad time in the other hostel and down Bourbon Street; I didn't think anywhere this shit existed in New Orleans, but this is worse than any of the other places I've stayed at – and not just in America, anywhere I've ever fucking been! There are two Irish birds and two American birds here but if you were to do a worldwide competition to find the most square and dull birds on the face of the planet, we've won it. This place couldn't be more different to the India House if it tried. I'm concerned we might be wasting three days of our time if we stay here. Maybe we should fuck this place off and go somewhere else.

Hair of the Dog

The hobo's chatting away to us, non-stop; all sorts of bullshit about his busking days in New York and places he goes to play around here, to get the maximum flow of tourists. Although he's friendly and pretty much harmless, I'm still massively hungover and he's starting to get on my tits. Me and Marshy agree to try and get rid of him by going to do a clothes wash. We pack our dirty clothes in some plastic carrier bags and head out to look for a laundrette. It's been nearly two weeks since we washed our clothes so they're probably starting to smell. In the haze of drunken stupors, followed by hangovers, neither of us have really noticed. Plus, it costs money to clean your clothes so we're waiting until we absolutely have to wash them before using up valuable beer tokens; I've run out of clean boxers so it's got to be done. We don't know where we're going but it's a chance to have a general wander and see what's nearby. Just as we set off to leave, the hobo runs out from the hut.

"Hey, you guys, do you need a laundrette?"

"Yeah, d'ya know somewhere?"

"There's a place round the corner, man, I'll show you."

Fuck. All we wanted was directions, but now he's tagging along like a right cling-on. Me and Marshy exchange a quick look, raising our eyebrows and rolling our eyes. The hobo takes us back to the main road, where we got off the tram, round the corner from the hostel. He walks straight into a bar and I stop him.

"No we don't want a bar, we want a laundrette, man!"

"I know; chill, dude, the launderette's in here!"

"Oh! Really?!"

What a fucking cool idea – a bar in a laundrette! This is another novelty for us; I can see a pattern starting to emerge in New Orleans – they seem to put bars everywhere – souvenir shops, old barber shops, launderettes. Where the fuck next? At work?!

As we enter, the bar's on the right and there are three pool tables on the left. Towards the very back of the room, there's a row of washing machines along the wall, on the right, with a row of tumble dryers on top. We put our coins in the machines, start the spin and realise we've got an hour or two to kill, whilst waiting for the machines to finish. Hmmm...I wonder what we can do whilst we're waiting? Have a couple of beers and a few games of pool I guess! I fucking love this place! What a great idea. In the launderettes in England, there's absolutely nothing to do besides sit on a bench, read a newspaper, or watch a TV screen that you probably can't hear 'cause of the noise of the machines. But in New Orleans, you've got special offers on jugs of draught beer! It's obviously a good idea for the owners too though – they've got you right where they want you, at your most vulnerable. We're still hungover so we figure the best way to sort it out is to get boozy again.

Me and Marshy buy a jug to share but the hobo's making out like he hasn't got any money. This coming from a guy that's been banging on about making a hundred bucks a day from busking. We don't bother making a song and dance about it; we give him some beer out of our jug, which is pretty cheap anyway. At the same time, the cheeky fucker takes advantage of our generous nature and successfully manages to scrounge five cigarettes from us, one after the other. After a while, it's clear he's not going to buy any fags or booze so we stop giving him handouts; funnily enough, when we don't offer him any more beer, he soon fucks

93

off to go and earn some money. The fucking tight cunt doesn't even offer to buy us a beer in return.

We're starting to get pissed now, and I know 'cause I can't pot anything on the pool table. The hangover's long gone. We're chatting to other people in the bar – they're locals, as opposed to tourists, and this sound black guy is teaching us how to say 'New Orleans' properly.

"What d'ya say there, boy? New Or-leeeens?" he asks, mimicking an English accent. "Y'all got it wrong there, boy. Y'say it like dis – N'Or-lans."

Marshy's taking his shot. There's a man and woman playing on the table next to us and she's standing in Marshy's way, but he needs some room to take his shot.

"Excuse me, my lovely."

She's alerted and intrigued by his accent.

"Sure. Where you from?"

"England." And he's hit it off with her straight away; they've both completely forgotten they're in the middle of their games. Unfortunately for me, there are no other birds around so I'm on wingman duties, keeping her male friend occupied. I'm guessing this bloke is her friend, otherwise he probably would've said something by now; Marshy and this bird may as well be banging each other senseless on the pool table right now. I'm getting bored of chatting to this lad 'cause he's got no personality. I go over to Marshy and introduce myself to the bird, have a brief chat, and finish potting the rest of the balls. Her friend soon fucks off so I'm a bit of a third wheel. Her name's Melissa and she invites us back to her flat, for a drink.

It's only a few minutes down the road from the hostel. I don't want to be cock-blocking so I won't stay long. We pick up our washing, dropping most of it on the floor, having lost the powers of coordination; maybe that's their trick – get you so pissed, you drop your newly clean clothes on the beer-sodden floor and they need washing again!

We're at Melissa's first floor flat and I'm pretty sure they'll be wanting to get it on soon so I'll stay for a drink, to be polite, and then I'll fuck off. She seems like a cool bird – she's an artist, living on her own, using her flat as a studio. I have a look around. The walls are covered with her paintings and there are more resting on the floor against the walls; they're all pretty good. Looks like Marshy's done well here, she's pretty fit as well. Lucky bastard's getting some pussy tonight, whilst I'm going back to that fucking morgue that calls itself a hostel. Looks like we might be staying the three nights after all – fuck their rules anyway; we'll find a way of having a laugh, wherever we are.

I'm sorting my washing out, back at the cabin, packing all my clothes into separate plastic bags – one for socks, one for t-shirts, one for boxers, etc. I'm pretty smashed and it's well into the evening, around nine o'clock. I'm tired but not quite ready to go to bed; I've got a buzz from the booze and I'm up for some more. I'm not used to being on my own though – I'm usually getting leathered with Marshy or some other poor bastard. Surely I can find someone else to bring down to my level; I'm going on the hunt to see if I can rope anyone else into a session. As I walk out of the cabin, I can hear a few people chatting in the communal area, in the garden. Sweet, let's see what the craic is here. There are three blokes sitting around the tables – this is the peak of this place's socialising capacity, so I guess I should consider myself lucky. They're all sat there reading, not even talking to each other. I walk over and introduce myself. Two of the lads aren't interested in talking; they say 'hi' and bury their heads back into their books. The other one seems grateful for the company, so we're having some banter. Fuck those two with their books, they're going to have to listen to us, so they may as well join in. This fella's name is Matt. He's slim built and average height with short dark hair, spiked up. He's well-presented, wearing some kind of work uniform. He's the only normal person I've met at this hostel, the only one who isn't either socially retarded or trying to scrounge off us.

So, now I've got a new pal for the evening and he's a fucking sound bloke with good stories; we're chatting around this table. He's an Italian American, the same age as me, and he works at a posh Italian restaurant, in the centre of New Orleans, or N'orlans, as I'm calling it now. It's a proper high-class joint where celebrities and the rich go to eat. The restaurant is owned by his uncle. The cover charge alone, just to sit at the table, is a hundred bucks, and that's before paying for food, drinks, and tips. Apparently, the tips are insane and he can earn over five hundred bucks a night. Matt's got a large extended family, who all go to eat there, and they sort him out with cash tips. He's also a weed smoker and I'm happy as larry when he gets this really strong weed out, and asks if I fancy rolling a joint. I gladly do the honours. Looks like this place might not be too bad after all!

Now we're both high, giggling away, and he's showing me this photo album that's filled with pictures of him and his friends. In some of the pictures, they're all holding guns; they must be teenagers, probably eighteen. I've seen news programmes reporting shootings in America and I always see people being shot in American films and TV programmes, but I haven't seen a handgun in real life. I know a lot of people have got guns in this country but I've not actually seen anyone, besides police, holding one yet. I mean, it's not like citizens walk around holding them like a mobile phone! I ask Matt about guns in America and he tells me that tourists won't really see people with them 'cause most shootings happen away from the heavily policed areas, where tourists go. Before I came here, I was a bit worried that if we got into an argument with someone, they might shoot us, but Matt's laughing this off and assuring me that you'd have to do something really bad for someone to want to shoot you, unless they're totally fucked up in the head.

Initially, I thought that all Americans carried guns around with them everywhere they go, but apparently it's not like that at all. Some do and keep them concealed, like in the glove compartment of their cars, but the majority keep theirs at home. It's weird seeing pictures of normal everyday people holding guns – I can't imagine Matt as an aggressive kind of guy – he's making jokes, seems laid back and relaxed, but you never know what might happen if you piss someone off – they could turn on you. I remember Joe Pesci's character in the film 'Casino'. He's all jokes and smiles, taking the piss out of people, until someone cracks a joke back at him; he can't take it and batters the guy to death. Matt doesn't give off any kind of vibe that he'll cause any trouble but now I've seen the pictures, of him and his mates with guns, it's kind of making me worried, especially 'cause I'm stoned after that joint. I need to make sure I keep on the right side of this guy! I'm pretty sure we're pals now!

Matt's also part of the 'Sons of Italy', which, until now, I've never heard of. He tells me it's an Italian American fraternity, founded about a hundred years ago to help Italians settle into American society. He's telling me what it's there for – to teach people of Italian descent, who live in America, the traditions, culture, and language so they don't forget their roots, basically. He knows his stuff – he seems to be on a different level to all the other Americans I've met so far. I'm wondering if it's all Mafia-related – surely it must be somewhere along the line. I don't want be too nosy, in case I come across ignorant and offensive, and he ends up wanting to shoot me. Shit, I really am a bit paranoid right now. I tell him about what happened to me and Marshy, in Fort Lauderdale, and he's laughing his ass off. I'm pretty sure he's a good lad.

Matt has to go to work and I can't believe he's going after smoking that weed, 'cause I'm totally fucked. Good job he's going now, too, 'cause my heads spinning out and I can't take any more of that weed. Looks like Marshy's staying at that bird's house tonight too so I'm going to bed. The first day at the boring hostel wasn't much of a punishment really – I've actually really enjoyed myself.

Mugged Off

I've had a good twelve hour sleep and I've woken up, still feeling stoned. Fuck me, the weed's strong out here. There isn't much going on today, which is probably just as well 'cause I can't be arsed to do anything. Marshy comes back in the afternoon and I'm glad 'cause I'm bored out of my brains. We round up a few of the others to go down to Bourbon Street but they aren't much company; they don't really want to get drunk 'cause they want to be fresh so they can go sightseeing the following morning. How fucking boring. You're in one of the greatest party cities in the world but you don't want to party? It's starting to seem more like a sentence now – punished with boredom. I'm hoping and praying the India House will take us back.

It's the end of our stay now and the morning of New Year's Eve. I've woken up and I'm packing my bag. I can't find my mobile phone though, which is annoying 'cause I've been using it as a clock and an address book, to take people's contact details. Fuck, it must be here somewhere. Fuck it, I'll look for my camera – it's got some really cool photos on it from India House and the guys in Fort Lauderdale and Miami. Bollocks, that's not there either. I'm starting to panic now, checking all my stuff faster, over and over, emptying my bag out onto the bed.

"Mate, I can't find all my stuff."

"What stuff, mate?"

"All my fuckin' phone and camera and shit. It's all gone from my rucksack."

"What? You sure? You checked under the bed?"

I rummage all around the area, looking everywhere twice, but I can't find anything.

"No fuckin' way, man. I only just got that camera. It's definitely gone, it was right down the bottom of my bag and I haven't taken it out since we arrived at this hostel. Some cunt's fuckin' robbed it."

"Seriously? Fuckin' hell, man. What're you missin'?"

"My digital camera, my mobile phone, and even my fuckin' half empty bottle of aftershave! Who the fuck would rob half a bottle of aftershave? Is anythin' gone from yours?"

"No, mate. I didn't bring anythin' valuable anyway 'cause I know I'd lose it."

I'm fucking furious and I've only just woken up. The mobile phone was an old piece of junk that didn't even work in America; the aftershave, I couldn't give a fuck about; but the camera… man, that's got all the fucking good photos on it, of all the people we've met and the places we've been to; and it was an early Christmas present from my old man. Which fucking cunt has stolen it? My bag was lodged all the way under the bottom bunk bed the whole time we've been here so it would've taken someone who knew the bag was there. I know for a fact it isn't Marshy, so it must be one of the other people who's got access to our block, and there are only three other people staying here. There's two shy, timid, geeky looking blokes who don't say a word to anyone. I'm pretty sure they wouldn't even consider it; they wouldn't have it in them. I can't be a hundred percent certain but I'm pretty damn sure it was that fucking scrounging hobo cunt. We've hardly seen him around since we first got here, but all his stuff's still here. He's a scheming bastard – it must be him.

I report the theft to the pigs, without pointing the finger at anyone in particular. They don't come down; instead they make a report over the phone and give me a crime number, which I'll need to make a claim on the insurance. Fucking typical – the first place we stay in, with lockers for your valuables, my shit gets stolen. Fucking twat. The hobo returns – he's probably been out, selling all my shit to people for fuck all. I see him lurking around the bunk beds; I go over and tell him what's happened so I can look him in the eye and see if he's guilty.

"Oh, no way, man, that sucks. I'm sorry to hear that, bro."

I know it's him, it's written all over his face, but I can't prove anything so I've just got to forget about it. Twat. This is making me want to get back to the India House even more. I've had it with this place – I'm glad we're going on a mission to the other hostel, so I haven't got to hang around feeling bitter, frustrated, and suspicious of the hobo. Maybe he'll steal the whole fucking bag next time. He must have known we were leaving, so he robbed all my shit whilst he still had the chance.

We pack up and make our way back to the India House – our sentence is over. Leaving Marquette House is like the gloomy clouds parting, to make way for the sun to come out.

NYE, Two Thousand & Three

It's such a relief to return to the India House; I'm just praying they've got space left for us and more importantly, that they'll let us back in. Marquette house was an experience in itself – on the plus side we did meet a couple of cool people and Marshy got laid. We're also a lot healthier than we would've been if we stayed at India House the whole time, as we would've been getting shit-faced every day. It's good we've actually had a bit of a break.

As soon as we step through the door, we're instantly recognised by the receptionist.

"Oh, it's you two. Wait there a second."

One of the blokes that was in the TV room when I pissed on the air conditioning unit is there again. He sees me walk in and he's grinning from ear-to-ear as he recalls the incident in his head. Most of the people who were here when we were kicked out, still are. We're stood at the desk, waiting to see if we can get a bed, just as we did first time round.

"Is it okay for us to get a bed for the next few nights?" I've got a repenting look on my face. "Please let us back in! The Marquette House is soooo boring! I hate it there AND someone stole my camera and my phone."

"Oh really? I'm sorry to hear that. Don't they have safes there?"

"I didn't lock my stuff up."

"I'm sorry to hear that. Okay, let me check with the owners. Has it been three days already?"

"Yeah, it's been exactly three days and three nights."

"Okay, one minute."

She calls the owners, using a landline, and we're standing

there, waiting in anticipation, hoping for a positive outcome. This decision will decide the fate of our New Year's Eve. If we don't get let in we're fucked. We'll either have to go all the way back to the shit hostel or try to find somewhere else, which will be fucking expensive. Please, please let us back in! She puts the phone down.

"Okay, you're good to stay but you're very lucky 'cause there's only three beds left in the whole place."

"Thank you sooo much."

"And, guys, I've been told to tell you two to go behave yourselves this time; this is your last chance." She pauses to fill in some forms and take our money. "Okay, you're in the block on the right this time. The other one's full up now. Whichever beds are free you can have."

The hostel has filled up to its capacity now. There are people walking around everywhere; the TV room is full; all the seats on the sofas are taken. When we walk in to the hut to find our beds, there are people, bags, and clothes all over the place. This block has much less space than the other one. There's one empty bunk left, in the middle of a row, on the left-hand side of the room. I take the bottom bunk and Marshy takes the top one. We're so lucky to get these beds, I can't believe how jammy we've been. It's a good job we got up so early – a few hours more and we would've been fucked. The extra people have added to the atmosphere; there's an anticipation in the air, like a car revving up at the start of a race before the light turns green. Everyone knows something big is going to happen tonight. We're back.

Neither of us can be arsed to cook, so we treat ourselves to the hostel meal. We'll need this to line our stomachs for all the booze we're going to cane tonight. The session begins right after dinner. We're all sat in the kitchen, around the table, with four sets of cards mixed together, playing the largest drinking game I've ever been involved in – it's 'The Ring of Fire'. All the cards are placed face down in a big circle, in the centre of the table. This is a perfect game for stitching people up – if you get a two, you make someone down two fingers of their drink. I'm getting made to drink quite a lot for pissing on the air con unit. They probably want to get me drunk again, to see what I'll do this time! Bastards. By the end of the game, most people are half-cut and ready to party. I've downed a shitload of shots and beer; I'm well on my way. I know it hasn't hit me yet but I can feel it coming – I'm going to be annihilated in twenty minutes and we haven't even left the hostel yet! It's only ten o'clock and my head's starting to spin. I'll sober up on the way down there; it'll be fine.

We're walking down to Bourbon Street; well, I'm trying to walk but I'm stumbling all over the place, bouncing off people. As expected in a place that's as popular as Bourbon Street, which is busy at the quietest of times, New Year's Eve is pandemonium. You can barely move; the street is clogged up like a fat cunt's arteries. It's chaos in the main part of the road, where all the best bars are. We're forced in one direction; it's best to go with the flow. I love the madness. Navigating this whilst being smashed is pretty difficult; I'm trying to keep up with everyone but I keep losing them. I have to wait for my vision to stop spinning around so I can focus for a second. I catch a glimpse of someone I know and follow them into a bar.

Within the first thirty minutes, we've lost half the group to the crowds and there's no chance of catching them. We might bump into them somewhere, later on. Every bar we go to, we lose a few more people. Fuck it, let's gets some more drinks in. John and Marshy are with me and that's all that matters. There isn't long to go until midnight; it must be around eleven o'clock now. Most of the people here are already wired. I've already drunk a shitload back at the hostel and I'm carrying on down here – I want to be in a complete state tonight – I'm really fucking going for it. I'm going to get completely trashed; yeah, that's what I'm going to do. Oh wait, fuck, my head's spinning too much now, I think I need to put my head down, close my eyes for a few minutes.

New Year's Day, Two Thousand & Four

I'm waking up; it's midday. All the people around me, in the bunk beds, are in the same state – hungover, bloodshot eyes, messy hair, wearing the same dirty clothes from the night before 'cause they fell asleep in them. Broken, croaky voices are speaking quietly. The room stinks of booze, farts, and sweat. I don't even remember the New Year countdown; in fact, I don't know if I even made it to midnight. What the fuck happened last night? The last thing I remember is being in a bar and shutting my eyes for a few seconds. I need to find out what happened; I need to speak to Marshy. My hangover isn't too bad, which is weird; usually, I feel a whole lot worse than this. I must still be pissed. I kick the underside of Marshy's bed – on the top bunk – to get his attention.

"Marshy!"

No response, so I get up and stand next to the bunk bed waiting for him to stir.

"Marshy, you awake? What happened last night?"

"Mate," he says, waking, "you were an absolute disgrace last night. D'ya remember any of it?"

"No mate, why? What did I do?"

"You don't remember the bouncer kickin' you out? Fuckin' hell, Bill!" He's sitting up to tell me the rest of the story. I'm finding it all quite funny. I've had another black-out from caning it so hard.

"Right, well, we were in one of the bars, just about to leave, to go somewhere else, and I've looked around to find you and you're still at the bar, but you were asleep."

"Oh yeah, I remember that place, I remember my head spinning so I had to shut my eyes."

"You don't remember after that?"

"No, why?"

Marshy's giggling to himself. "Right, we're standin' at the door, waiting for you, and this fuckin' massive bouncer's walked up to you, to tell you to wake up and get out of the bar."

"Yeah, go on…"

"He was tappin' you lightly on the shoulder, so you'd wake up, but you've…hahaha…you've just pushed him away!"

"What?!"

"He's not happy with you at this point, so he grabs you by the arm, pulls you off the chair onto your feet, and then you smacked him, right in the face!"

"No way, man, you're fuckin' kiddin'. Did he beat me up? Have I got any marks on my face?"

"You're fuckin' lucky, man! I reckon he was about to, but me and John were watchin' all this happenin', from the doorway. The bouncer was about to lay into you, but John, who's obviously pretty big himself, jumps on his back to stop him from knockin' ten barrels of shit out of you. Then there was this massive melee, and this other midget bouncer comes runnin' over to help the other bouncer out."

"A fuckin' midget bouncer?! Did I get abused by a midget bouncer?!"

"Nearly, mate. John was shoutin' in the ear of the massive bouncer to calm down, and I dragged you away to the outside of the bar, onto the street. But you were a fuckin' mess, Bill."

"Noooooo! You're fuckin' kiddin' me. How did I get home?"

"You don't remember that either?"

"No, not at all."

"You went back with those two English birds. You owe

them, mate, they were going back to the hostel 'cause they'd had enough, so they took you back with them. That's the last I saw of you."

I've just had a vague flashback of gibbering to some birds in the back of a taxi. I think I'd better find them and say thanks.

It's a schoolboy error – too much booze, in a short space of time. I don't remember any of the night, not even the count-down. And I've had to cut short one of the best nights of the year. In hindsight, I should've had a tactical spew, to get rid of some of the alcohol and empty my stomach out. Gutted.

Marshy's telling me about the rest of his night. Luckily for him, the birds were looking after me, so he didn't have to. He's saying how amazing his night was, just to rub it in and wind me up. But then again, he nearly got killed. He lost everyone and wound up with a French bird. He was having pissed-up rants, drinking Guinness with some random strangers, at a lock-in, in a bar on one of the roads coming off Bourbon Street. He's still out in the early hours of the morning and it's starting to get light. Once he's spent all his money, and the French bird has gone home, he's getting drinks bought for him by this old fella, at the bar. Once the old timer's left, he walks back to the hostel. Not learning from his Fort Lauderdale experience, he attempts to find his way back using the 'homing legs' method. Instead of ask-ing people for directions, he gets lost again. I don't quite under-stand how he's managed this, 'cause the route back to the hostel is two straight roads, Bourbon Street and Canal Street, and we've walked it several times already. Marshy's walked across wasteland, a railway track and a quarry and then into 'The Projects' – the no-go areas – 'The Hood'. They were labelled no-go areas for a reason. Marshy's swaying around, looking at the ground, thinking he's going the right way, but then he realises where he is. He's wearing a bright red t-shirt with beads around his neck, looking like a typical tourist. A car drives over and slows down to a curb crawl, alongside him, as he stumbles down the road. Someone in the car winds their window down halfway, and he sees the top of a gun pointing out towards him. He hears a voice saying 'get out' repeatedly, so he makes a swift turn to try and find his way out, and luckily he goes the right way. We really have been so lucky on this holiday; sometimes I wonder how we get away with so much!

All Apologies

I need to find John, to have a word with him. I need to make an apology and thank him for saving my ass. He's sat in TV room again, so I sit down next to him. He's surprisingly laid back about what happened, but he does make his feelings clear.

"I've just heard from Marshy," I say, "about what happened last night."

"Man, that was some pretty fucked up shit that went down last night."

"I know, mate. All I can say is that I'm sorry for puttin' you in that position. I was so hammered, I didn't even know what I was doing. I don't even remember doing it."

"You guys are fuckin' crazy. You gotta be careful about shit like that. If we weren't there to jump in, man, he could've really fucked you up, man."

"I know, it's not good."

"Man, I'm not tellin' you how you should be, but you really gotta calm down, man. People in the city, man, don't fuck around. You dunno who you're fuckin' with, man."

"I hear what you're sayin'. Look, I'm not usually like that, I don't get violent. But thanks for helpin' out, I owe you a beer or two, mate."

"Alright man, no sweat."

I know I've been a bit stupid but it's only 'cause I was so pissed. It was just too much alcohol. I think he's okay about it now. Whilst I was speaking to John, Marshy came into the TV room and he's chatting to the two English birds. They're the birds that took me back in the taxi, last night. I walk over to join in and Marshy's looking at me disapprovingly, shaking his head.

"Bill, I think you owe these two birds an apology as well."

"Really? What for?"

"Well, apparently you were being a bit touchy feely in the taxi on the way back."

I'm standing there in shock, with my jaw on the floor, holding the back of my head with both my hands.

"No way. Are you serious?"

I look at the birds and they both look appalled with me. They're looking away from me, towards the floor, shaking their heads, refusing to make eye contact with me. Things are going from bad to worse. I apologise to them repeatedly.

"Did I really? I am so, so, so, sooooo sorry. That was completely out of order. Did I really do that? That's not like me at all. I've never done anythin' like that before, I can't believe I would…"

Marshy keeps on ripping into me, embarrassing me in front of these birds.

"Got ya! Only kiddin', mate!"

The fucking bastard! He got the girls to play along with it and he's got me good and proper. Fair play. I knew something would be coming, after ripping him for what happened in Fort Lauderdale; he's seen his opportunity and taken it with both hands. He's got this smug grin now, 'cause he's really happy with himself for winding me up. I shat myself when he first told me, too!

Clippers

It's the second of January and we've pretty much recovered from the New Year's party. We're back on form and ready to get smashed again. There are still plenty of people at the hostel for a good piss up, although some of them left straight after New Year's Eve. We've had some more pizza and we're in the courtyard, at the tables, hanging out with some of the others, telling stories and drinking bourbon. An American bloke comes outside and stands nearby, listening in to our conversation. He's young, probably about eighteen, five foot ten, and skinny. He introduces himself as Sean. He's fairly well-groomed and he's got expensive clothes on – not your typical traveller.

There are a mixture of birds and lads at the table. We're talking about whether or not to bother cutting your hair, whilst travelling – it can be an added expense, after all. One of the guys says he always brings a pair of clippers with him to cut his own hair, 'cause it's cheaper than paying for a hairdresser. Sean wants to get involved in the conversation, so he's butting in.

"I could really do with a haircut right now, does anyone know how to cut hair properly?"

Marshy volunteers. "Yeah, I'll do it for you, mate, I cut my friend's hair all the time, and my own."

"Do you really? You're not just sayin' that?"

"Yeah, of course. Look at my hair. I did my own. Take a seat and I'll do it for you."

"Alright, but don't take too much off."

"Of course I won't!"

Marshy had his hair cut in a hairdresser's in Fort Lauderdale a few weeks ago and the only haircut he's ever done, besides giving himself a skinhead, is to give one of our mates a skinhead, on a rugby tour we went on four years ago. Skinhead is the only haircut he can do. Sean really doesn't know what he's letting himself in for. The lad with the clippers runs off to get them. I'm sitting back and watching the show with a nice bourbon and cola. Sean sits down on a chair and gives Marshy instructions of what he wants done. You can hear the nerves in his voice.

"Can you make the back and sides a bit shorter please? I usually get the same person to do my hair every time back home and she's done it for the last ten years."

"Don't worry, mate. This won't take long."

With the clippers in hand, Marshy gets to work. He starts at the back of Sean's neck and shaves one big straight line, right up the back, finishing on the top of his head. He shaves a few selected parts of his head, around the back and sides. I'm trying not to laugh the whole way through, as Sean keeps asking questions.

"How's it lookin'? Is it good?"

Marshy's replying back sarcastically. "Yeah, yeah it looks brilliant. Wait till you see it!"

Sean looks fucking ridiculous – like one of the characters from 'Dumb and Dumber'. Everyone's laughing. He goes to look at himself in the mirror and comes running back.

"No way, man! It's totally fucked up! You fuckin' asshole, man!"

One of the birds shaves the rest of his hair off, to save him the embarrassment. He's taking the joke quite well to be fair, but you can tell he's properly fucked off.

Hot Sauce

We're still in the courtyard, carrying on our session and laughing at how gullible the American kid was to let Marshy shave his hair. People are coming and going but no-one's really staying for more than a couple of drinks. Two Irish guys come out of the kitchen door and down the steps towards us. We haven't met them before; they've just arrived after staying in a hotel, closer to Bourbon Street, for New Year's Eve. Me and Marshy are already well on our way to being pissed, again. They look like a laugh, so we invite the Irish lads to join us, and they're more than happy to oblige. They're called Greg and Muzza.

Greg is stocky with dark hair and a smiley face; Muzza is taller with ginger hair and a fair-sized beer gut. They look like people you wouldn't want to mess with. They're straight on to the booze with us, and I can tell instantly that these guys are on our wavelength. They look like they're in need of a good shower, just like me and Marshy did when we got kicked out of the hostel. I'm wondering what they've been doing to get so scruffy, and they're keen to tell the story. The previous night, after drinking around Bourbon Street, Muzza was arrested for being 'drunk and disorderly' and locked up for the night. He was told to sleep off the booze, in the cells. Greg didn't want to leave him there by himself, in case someone tried to tamper with his arse, so he asked to be thrown into the cells with Muzza, so they could look after each other. That's friendship for you! Hearing this makes me feel better about myself; it's not just us causing trouble! They're great guys, these Irish blokes. We sit and drink with them all afternoon swapping stories – they might just be worse than us!

Greg's got this idea. He stands up, gets everyone's attention, and pulls out this bottle from his trouser pocket. It's a very small bottle and I can't see what's in it, 'cause his hand is covering the label. He passes it around and I read the label: 'The World's Hottest Sauce'.

It's a little red glass bottle with about fifty millilitres of sauce in it, and there's a pretend, miniplastic fire extinguisher as a little gimmick to go with it; it hasn't been opened and it's still wrapped in the packaging. Muzza is telling us, if we have one drop of this stuff, we'll be in absolutely agony. And now, Greg's dared us all to have a drop of the sauce together. We're getting drunk now so the inhibitions are gone, and they've been replaced by bravado. I'm not into hot food really; I like a bit of spice, but at most, I'll order a medium curry in an Indian Restaurant; that's as far as my body can take before I start sweating. This bottle claims to be the 'world's hottest sauce', but I reckon one drop can't do too much harm, so the challenge doesn't seem to be a bad one. It'll be uncomfortable for a few minutes and then it'll be fine. But then again, by the looks on the faces of the Irish guys, I'm not so sure. As people walk past, they hear what's going on and they're stopping to watch us. We've got a crowd of six or seven people, and one of them is Sean, fresh from his haircut. Greg places one drop of the sauce on our index fingers, and one for himself.

"Okay, I'm gonna countdown from tree, den we all do it at de same time. Ready, tree, two, one, go!"

We all lick the sauce off our fingers and react the same to the bitter, foul taste of the sauce, by screwing our faces up. Greg's preparing us for the worst.

"Just wait a few seconds."

The first ten seconds are fine, this isn't going be too bad. But hang on. Here it comes – it's starting to kick in now. The heat's growing progressively hotter and hotter. I'm salivating constantly and swallowing it every few seconds. I'm getting restless. We're all moving around to try to distract ourselves from the heat burning our mouths. I keep rubbing my face and I'm starting to sweat; I have to take my jumper off. I've forgotten about having the sauce on my finger, and my eyes are hurting, where I've been rubbing my face. The skin on my nose and my eyes feels like it's burning. Within a minute, all four of us on the floor, spitting saliva out. I crawl over to the table to get my drink to try and cool the heat down. We're all making stupid noises whilst sticking our tongues out, we're all looking at each other, reduced to dribbling wrecks and it's making us laugh – it's a strange mix of pain and amusement. I've got a runny nose and tears are streaming from my eyes. Everyone's laughing at us being idiots. After five minutes, the worst of the heat has gone and we're back onto our chairs. I can still feel the tingling on my tongue. Fuck! I can't believe such a small dose of something could be so powerful and cause so much agony. We're still giggling and coughing, till we fully recover another five minutes later.

Sean, the American bloke with his new haircut, has something to say about all this.

"Oh my gahd, you British dudes really can't take your hot food! You have one drop of that stuff and you're all rollin' around the floor, like, 'oh help me, help me!' You British dudes are pussies!"

We're all looking at each other in amazement, laughing at what he's said. Muzza has something to say back.

"Well first of all, we're naht British, we're Irish." Pointing at himself and Greg. "An' second of all, do ya tink you could do it?"

"Hot food seriously doesn't bother me, man, I can eat any hot food. I eat chillies all the time."

Marshy's stoking the fire.

"I think we've got ourselves another challenger!"

"No problem, man, I love hot food, I eat it all the time. It's no big deal to me." Sean starts feeling around his pockets and pulls his wallet out. "Okay, look, I'm a bit short on gas at the moment, and I need to fill my car up, so I can get back home. How about you guys give me forty bucks, if I down a shot of that sauce?"

All four of us at the table are looking at each other. Muzza's looking at me and Marshy.

"How much have yous got?"

We're all frantically scratching around, checking our pockets, to see what money we've got. Marshy's got two dollars, I've got five, Muzza puts a ten down, and Greg picks it all up and replaces what's there with forty dollars, from his wallet.

"Now dis, I gotta see!" Greg runs into the kitchen, asking if anyone's got a shot glass, and the excitement's building in the courtyard. He comes back briskly, with a wide grin across his face. Muzza screws the cap off the top of the bottle and fills the shot glass, to the line – twenty-five millilitres of the world's hottest sauce. More people, from inside the hostel, have heard what's going on and they've come outside to watch. The American is fearless. We brace ourselves and count him down.

"Three, two, one, go!"

And down it goes – all of it!

Bearing in mind what one drop did to all four of us, Sean's doing okay, to begin with, standing there all proud, looking around everyone.

"You see?" He's poking his tongue out, to show us he's drunk it all, "No problem!"

After fifteen seconds, the effects start to kick in. He realises the pain's coming, so he walks over towards the swimming pool, and sits on one of the steps. He starts taking deep breaths and sighing very loudly.

"Arrrrrrgggggghhhhhh, arrrggggghhhhhhhh." He starts talking us through his actions like a commentator, which makes the whole thing really comical. "I can feel it burnin' in my stomach…oh my gahd, I can't feel my throat, it's numb…I don't feel so good…I think I need to be sick."

He spews all the sauce back up but it's too late 'cause it's already taken effect. He's rolling around the floor then standing up, bouncing off the fences all over the courtyard. Someone shouts out.

"Get a photo of him, quick!"

This sets everyone off laughing. A few people run in to get their cameras and they're taking photos of him. We're all in stitches, keeled over with that uncontrollable belly laugh. Every time he says something, we all laugh harder.

"Oooohhhh gahd, I need some water." Then he shouts at everyone. "GET ME SOME WATER!"

Now we're all laughing even harder. He's using his fingers to scratch the sauce off his tongue and then he's rubbing his face. The potent red colour of the sauce has spread around his mouth like a clown's make-up. He's got perfectly formed red hand marks on his neck, where he's been holding his throat. He's cowered away by the swimming pool.

"I can't breathe, I can't breathe, call an ambulance!"

One of the spectators is worried. She walks over to him.

"Do you honestly need an ambulance?"

"Yes, yes, I need one, call one now! NOW!"

"Okay, okay, I'll call one for you."

He's hyperventilating and we realise the situation might be more serious than we first thought.

Five minutes later, an ambulance arrives. I didn't know this before, but whenever an ambulance is called, in America, a police car is alerted at the same time, so they can assess the situation and see if a crime has been committed. The police car arrives a few minutes after the ambulance. Events have escalated from a dare to a neighbourhood scandal, like a scene out of 'There's Something About Mary', where Ben Stiller traps his ball-sack in his zip.

The doctors put a bag-valve-mask resuscitator over Sean's face, and he starts to calm down. The police are asking questions to find out what happened. We explain the story to them, as it happened, and everyone else backs us up. Whilst we're telling the pigs what happened, the hostel owner comes out the back. He sees we're involved and he's standing there, angry, shaking his head at us in disapproval. The bad news isn't over for Sean though. Of course, hospitals and medical assistance are private in the USA, so when you call an ambulance out, they charge you for it – sixty dollars! He pays with his credit card.

Doing the maths, he earned forty dollars but had to pay sixty, so it's actually cost him twenty bucks to do that shot of the world's hottest sauce. Good value!

We've been in New Orleans for eight days now; we had only planned to stay for three. It's so good we couldn't resist staying longer. Me and Marshy agree that it's about time we move on. The hostel is starting to empty out, as the New Year festivities wind down. People are going back to work and travellers going somewhere else. We haven't got a clue where we're going next, so we go to an internet café to check out the Autodriveaway website. We check the New Orleans branch to see what cars are available and where they are going. There's only one that's reasonably close and it's going to Memphis. The only other cars are going right up to the north-east corner, by Washington, or all the way to Los Angeles; they're too far away. I have a friend that lives in Nashville, which isn't far from Memphis, so it makes sense to head up that way. According to the website, the car is available tomorrow, so we've got one final night in New Orleans. We better make it a big one, then!

There are far fewer people here at the hostel now, so everyone has calmed down. Most of the people remaining have been here since we arrived, so it feels like we really know them. There are still plenty of familiar faces to muster up a good-sized group for a party. There's a bird I've noticed around but not had the chance to talk to. Funnily enough, she arrived with Sean, and I'm not sure if they're together or not; I haven't had the chance to ask, but if she's single, I definitely fancy a go at pulling her.

A group of us head out to Bourbon Street; it's the final night for me and Marshy. The drinks are flowing. There's a lack of females out with us tonight; the birds that are around are getting a lot of attention from the blokes. Marshy's strolled off down the street with a couple of the others, and I've stayed with Sean and his fit mate. Her name is Lisa and I've found out they aren't together, they're just school friends from the same town – sweet. We head back to the hostel and stop off for some food in a restaurant on Canal Street. It's pretty late, about three in the morning. Some of the guys from the hostel are in the restaurant and they come and sit with us, which isn't helpful to my cause – they're cock-blocking. I try to ignore them, as I focus my efforts on the girl, but they don't take the hint. I reckon they're hoping I'll get bored and leave, so they can swoop in. It's a standoff but I reckon I can sit this out. One by one, they get bored and leave. We're left with one guy sitting there with us so I start kissing Lisa in front of him. Soon enough, he gets uncomfortable and goes back to the hostel on his own.

When we get back to the hostel, I'm thinking of places to take her, where we can have some privacy. It's cold outside and there's nowhere else to go, besides my bunk bed in the dormitory.

I pull my bed sheet off, tuck it into the side of Marshy's bunk so it drapes down, covering the entrance to my bed. Marshy's snoring heavily, on the top bunk. Lisa lays down on my bed. We're both leathered, trying to be quiet, but it's impossible. I take her trousers and knickers off clumsily; she doesn't seem to be bothered by my carelessness; I'm too pissed to care anyway. I leave her blouse on.

The bed's creaking every time we move. It takes a while for us to manoeuvre into a comfortable position. There are people sleeping in the bunks next to us, centimetres away from our feet and our heads; it's pretty weird to be doing this when they're that close. I'm kissing her whilst searching my bag, in the dark, to find a condom. I can't find one. Shit! For fuck's sake, where is it? I'm feeling around the pockets, making a right racket. It takes me five minutes to find one and I'm ecstatic. This girl is pretty hot. I put it down on the bed, whilst I try to get my clothes off. I feel myself hit something with my left foot as I slip whilst trying to push myself up the bed; I'm pretty sure I've just kicked the bloke's head in the bunk behind me. I've probably woken him up! If we haven't done that already. Fuck it, I'm carrying on. Now I've got my trousers and boxers off, I'm searching for the condom in the dark again, but I can't find it. I must have put it down somewhere around here; I'm sure it was next to her right leg. I'm feeling around everywhere, but still no joy. Jesus fucking Christ man, I just want a fucking shag! I go down on her whilst I try to find the condom. It's lost on the bed somewhere and I'm so pissed I can't find it. I'm rustling around for what seems like an eternity. This is getting embarrassing now. Where the fuck is it? I've got to find it. I've probably woken half of the dormitory up now; I can hear people moving around in their beds. Fuck them. Finally I've got it, that's taken at least fifteen minutes; I'm surprised she's still here. We fuck, but it's not my best ever performance; it's awkward trying to have quiet sex in a room full of people! Afterwards, she goes back to her bunk bed and I fall asleep.

It's morning and we're leaving today. We aren't in a hurry; as long as we get to the Autodriveaway office before five-thirty, we'll be okay. We watch some films and order a taxi to the Autodriveaway office. The car we want is still there, so I sign the forms and drive it back to the hostel. This time we've got a Chevrolet Impala. We throw our bags on the back seats and say our goodbyes. On our way out, we see the owner.

"Thanks for everythin'. I'll be tellin' all my mates about this place, when I get home."

"Well they better not be anything like you two!"

Just as we're leaving, he takes our photo. I hope it'll find its way on to the wall, with the rest of them. I imagine they're happy to see the back of us. Still though, what an amazing place!

Memphis, Tennessee

Detox

It was a monumental ten days in New Orleans and my body is speaking to me, to tell me it's fucked; my health has started to deteriorate. I'm loving every second of this experience but I've been drinking most days for nearly a month now; I'm starting to crave booze to feel normal. All the drinking, added to four years of caning it at university before this trip, is starting to take its toll. I've been smoking heavily without needing to worry about the cost of fags – they're so cheap over here, compared to what you pay in England. If we get a cheap brand, a pack of twenty cigarettes costs the equivalent of one pound, which is fuck all.

We're going through a pack a day, each, and more if we're drinking in the evenings. I can tell my body's suffering from the abuse, 'cause I've started to get this little blister on the roof of my mouth, right in between my two front teeth. It's fucking annoying and I can't stop running my tongue over it, even though it hurts every time I do it. I'm trying to leave it alone 'cause it swells up a bit every time I touch it. I need to give it a chance a heal but every time I smoke another cigarette, I aggravate it. I can't stop myself from smoking 'cause I'm pretty much addicted, especially when I'm drinking. I usually have two per pint – when I hit the half pint mark on my glass, that's the signal for another smoke. The only chance the blister has to heal is when I'm sleeping, but I'm not getting much of that at the moment. I need to give it a chance to sort itself out. Although we're nowhere near finished with our escapades, me and Marshy both agree it's time to give our bodies a break.

We time our drive to go through the night, again, to save on paying for a night's accommodation. The journey from New Orleans to Memphis is about four hundred miles. After our seven hundred mile journey from Clearwater to New Orleans, it's a piece of cake. We take the I-10 out of New Orleans and pick up the I-55 going north, through Mississippi, towards the state of Tennessee. Memphis is situated along the Mississippi river, which acts as a divide between two states – Arkansas is on the other side. We don't think to check how long the journey will take, so there's a problem when we realise it doesn't take as long as we thought it would. We arrive on the outskirts of Memphis at three o'clock in the morning. There's a service station, just before we reach the city limits, so we stop there and try to get some sleep in the car. We find a car park, with a row of trucks parked up. The drivers are sleeping in their cabins, so we figure this is as safe as anywhere else we could go; at least there are other people around us. We've locked the car doors and turned our lights off.

It's early January and deep into winter. The further north we go, the colder it gets. At this time in the morning, the weather is at its coldest. I'm freezing my tits off; I'm so cold I can't smell a thing. After being in Florida and New Orleans, where it's a lot milder, we realise just how unprepared we are, sat here with fucking t-shirts on. The temperature gauge on the electronic dashboard says fourteen degrees Fahrenheit. I don't know what that is in degrees Celsius, but I'm guessing it means 'baltic'; I've never felt cold like this – it goes straight through to the bone, the second it hits my skin. We put some extra layers of clothes on and use more as blankets. We roll the seats down and try to sleep.

An hour passes and it's far too cold to sleep; I'm shivering uncontrollably. Marshy's still awake, so we sit up to have a smoke. We wind the window down to let the smoke out, which makes the inside of the car even colder. I turn the car engine on and put the heating up to full power. I'm going to leave it running whilst we try to sleep.

I wake up to see the sun shining directly through the windscreen, piercing my eyes. I feel like I'm having a hangover that's built up from the day we started drinking at the airport. It takes ten minutes for my eyes to open fully without being in pain. The engine is still running and there's condensation over all the windows. I wipe some of it off with my sleeve to see the service station is set in a huge park, filled with trees and green fields. It's good to see some countryside after spending so much time in different cities.

We set off to complete the rest of the short trip into the city centre; it's less than an hour's drive. We need to look up the address of the company to deliver the car to – it's supposed to be delivered this afternoon before five-thirty, so we've still got a bit of time to drive around and find somewhere to stay.

We've made it to Memphis and we're driving alongside the Mississippi river. I see a car park and pull in, to check out the views of the river and the enormous steel bridge that leads to Arkansas, on the other side. The valley that the river runs through is so deep, the banks are more like cliffs; the river itself is so vast that the land on the other side seems like it's another country. I've never seen anything like it. We've ticked the box for sight-seeing now.

It's getting towards midday. We find the centre of town and park the car on the side of a road. The wind is freezing cold and there's hardly anyone around. It's not a particularly built-up area and I can't believe how barren the streets are; it's like a ghost town. Maybe it's 'cause everyone's at work? I thought there would be a bit more life here considering its mentioned in famous songs like 'Walking in Memphis', or 'cause of its reputation for music from Elvis. I'm looking at this in a positive light though; if it's quiet here then hopefully it'll stop us from going out. Marshy walks over to what looks like a large café on the corner of the street. He looks through the large glass windows.

"There's hardly anyone in here, mate. The place is dead."

"Is it worth stoppin' off for a drink?"

"Nah, although there's a bloke in here who looks exactly like that bar owner from Clearwater."

"What, the one that kicked me out?"

"Yeah."

"Let's have a look."

"At the back in the corner, on his own."

He's in his fifties and has a large beer gut, just like the bar owner from Clearwater. He has the same island of dark hair on his balding head, and thick lines on his forehead that follow the frown of his eyebrows. I'm ninety per cent sure it's him.

"Oh yeah, that does look like him. Shall we go and say hello?"

"Nah, fuck it. We need to get going."

"Alright. That's weird though. I wonder what he's doing all the way up here?"

We move on and find an internet café to look up the nearest hostel and the location of the office where the car needs to be dropped off.

We've got a bit of a problem. The office's blocks are fucking miles away, right out in the suburbs, in some purpose-built business park. We're trying to figure out how we're going to get back into town. There are no trains or buses; it's too far to walk with big rucksacks.

We didn't even think about organising any of this before we set off. That's the way we've ended up doing things – totally off the cuff. I'm sure it'll work out somehow. I look up hostels in Memphis and there's only one, which is quite far out of town, in the opposite direction to the place the car needs to go. It doesn't have a website and I can't find a telephone number for it. Our best idea is to drive to the hostel to see if we can get a room, drop our bags off, then deliver the car, and somehow find our way back to the hostel. We jump back in the car and go to the hostel.

We've found the address, only, where there should be a hostel, there's a record store. We go in and speak to the bloke working there. He's on his own. We ask him if there's a hostel around but he tells us it closed a few years ago. This isn't going well. We're getting fed up of looking for somewhere to stay so we decide it'll be easier to get a motel room for a couple of nights; we can chill in peace for a few days, eat junk food and watch TV. We drive around the interstate roads and turn off at the first motel we see. The only way we can stay here is by keeping the car for an extra day. This is against their rules but we'll just make up an excuse. They won't miss it for one day. I don't want to phone in, just in case they start asking us questions. In any case, we need it to get food and to get about. It's weird being inside a quiet, seedy motel – I don't know if I like this.

It's morning and we're leaving the motel, after some much-needed rest. We throw our bags into the back seats of the car, again, and set off to Graceland, the former home of Elvis Presley. When we arrive and check the entrance prices, we turn around and walk away. I know he's a legend and a musical genius, but we aren't paying thirty-five dollars each to see a house. Instead, we look at the house and the grounds from the outside. Ticked that box – been to Graceland. It's a nice house.

Now, we're on our way to drop the car off and it's a mission and a half. We haven't got a clue where we're going but we've got a fucking gigantic map, which Marshy has unfolded, and he's trying to read it whilst I'm driving. He knows where we need to get to, but he can't figure out where we are on the map in the first place. We stop at a couple of petrol stations on the way, to get some directions, and after a couple of hours, we find the business park. It's at least fifty miles away from the centre of Memphis, in the middle of nowhere.

The grounds are huge and we go to three different buildings before we find the right one. I'm asking random people if anyone knows the person the car belongs to, and where to drop the keys off, but no-one knows. Eventually we're directed to reception, where a nice lady offers to take the keys from us. She puts a call out around the offices, letting everyone know the car keys are on her desk, ready to be collected. It's out of our hands now. On to our next problem – how do we get back? I ask the receptionist how to get to the city centre and she's looking at me, puzzled, like I'm some kind of lunatic, totally perplexed that we've come all the way out here without being able to get back. She's an excitable lady with a strong American accent.

"All people that work here arrive by car, honey. Y'all got no car?"

"No. The one we had is the one we had to drop off here – it's part of a service for a delivery company. We didn't realise we would be so far out of town."

"Good Lord. I ain't never hearda nothin' like that before. Say, where's that accent from – are y'all two Australian?"

"No, we're English, we're here on holiday for a few months. We heard about this company that lets you use people's cars to get places if you deliver it somewhere for them."

"Oh, okay, so that's why you're stranded here then. I understand now. I tell you what. I gotta go pick up my daughter from school in about an hour. If y'all can wait till then, I can give you a lift to the bus station? It ain't in town but you can take the bus from there?"

We both sigh with relief.

"That would be great, thank you ever so much."

"You're welcome. Anyway, my daughter would love to meet you English boys. She's gonna be soooo excited when she sees y'all!"

We wait for the lady to finish her shift, reading magazines in the reception and smoking cigarettes outside. She takes us to her large four-by-four and we get in the back. Her daughter is waiting on the side of the road, outside her school, and she jumps in the front of the car. She can't be much older than thirteen.

"Who are these guys, Mom?"

"These two lovely boys are from England. I'm droppin' them at the bus station 'cause they needed a lift from the offices."

The daughter turns round, excited, and introduces herself straight away.

"Well hey there, my name's Candy, pleased to meet you!"

"Hi, Candy, nice to meet you too."

Her mum interjects straight after.

"What d'yall say 'bout gonna Taco Bell? I dunno about you guys but I could eat a horse!"

"Oh, can we, Mama? Can I have a five-layer burrito? Pleeeee-ase?"

"Of course you can, sweetie. Would you guys like to go to Taco Bell with us?"

"Yeah, that would be nice, we haven't eaten lunch or dinner yet, so yeah, that would be lovely. We don't have a Taco Bell in England though, what do you recommend?"

"Oh, I love their accent, mommy. Don't they talk nice!"

"You don't have Taco Bell in England? Oh my lord, well you've gotta go for the five-layer burrito. That's what I would recommend. You won't turn back after that! You'll be takin' them home with you, all the way back to England!" She's laughing her head off, and me and Marshy are laughing with her. It's really sound of this bird to help us out like this.

We arrive at Taco Bell, in the car park of a large shopping mall, and go inside to get some food. It's not the healthiest food in the world, but it can't be much worse than the cheap pizzas and Subways we've been living on, till this point. We all have the five layer beefy burrito and sit down together in the restaurant, talking away. They're really nice people and I appreciate meeting some more locals.

Once we've finished, we're directed to the bus-stop, across the road from the restaurant. Fair play to this lady – it would've been a hell of a walk, or taxi ride, to get here, so we let her know how much we appreciate her help. It makes a nice change from getting hustled, anyway.

We're waiting at the station, in the cold, for the bus to the centre of town. We've got our bags with us, the sun's setting and we haven't got a plan. The area we're in doesn't look very safe either. I'm hoping we get a bus going the right way. Even when we do get back to Memphis, we don't know anywhere to go and stay. It's freezing again and it's becoming more and more obvious that we haven't got the right clothes for this part of the country, at this time of the year. Everyone around us is wearing big coats with scarves and gloves; I'm standing here in an Adidas tracksuit top with a hood. We thought we were going to be visiting warm places. People must be thinking we're a right pair of muppets.

The bus comes and we jump on. We're sat down on a bench facing inwards and I take out some more clothes from my bag and start building the layers up. I'm getting some funny looks from people, but I couldn't give a fuck what I look like right now, so long as I'm warm. The bus is full of poorer people; you can tell by the way they look and dress; they haven't got the money to look after themselves like the rich do; I suppose they wouldn't be on the bus if they did. It's getting dark now; all I've got to look at are the cars on the roads and the shadows of lampposts, changing angles as we drive past them. It's enough to send my mind into a daze for the long and slow journey back, making stops every couple of minutes. My daze is disturbed when I hear Marshy groaning on his seat. He's curled over, holding his stomach. His Taco Bell Burrito is playing havoc with his digestion and he's struggling to hold it in. When we finally get to the centre of town, he runs off to the bogs straight away and I'm laughing to myself whilst I wait for him, looking like a right freak, all on my Jack Jones.

We need to decide what to do next; we're just standing around. We could stay another night and find another hotel; or we could take a Greyhound coach somewhere. Memphis hasn't got an Autodriveaway office, and even if it did, it's too late for us to get a car as the offices all shut at half five. There's no-one around, even at night-time. As Memphis seems so dead and life-less, we decide it's not worth staying another night. It's been a bit of a letdown; I'm sure this place has a lot more to offer; we were probably here at the wrong time. If anything, maybe it's been a blessing in disguise 'cause at least it's meant we've been able to cut out the booze for a day or two, to recharge the batteries. We find the Greyhound station and look at where the coaches are going on the departures board. There's a coach leaving to Nashville in thirty minutes. That's where Charlie lives. Fuck it – let's go.

Nashville, Tennessee

Local Knowledge

I've heard stories about the 'Greyhounds', particularly how they can be dangerous, if you're sat near an unhinged nutcase. Between cities, you're on long open roads and I'm having images of some mentalist shooting everyone on the bus; or maybe a scene out of a horror movie, where the bus breaks down and you end up with your arms and legs chopped off, and your torso is left hanging on a hook, like in 'Texas Chainsaw Massacre'. A certain type of person travels by coach instead of driving or getting the train, 'cause it's cheaper; they're full of poorer people like students, the unemployed, travellers, and drug addicts. We're crammed onto this coach and I can smell a fucking awful stench around me, like the rotting flesh of a staunch alcoholic – maybe we'll be smelling like this soon, if we carry on going the way we're going; maybe the smell is coming from us! After fifteen minutes pass, I've accepted the potent reek and it's become a background annoyance that I'm putting up with, 'cause I haven't got any other choice. The Greyhounds are fucking cheap though, so I'll live with it and save my money for booze.

We arrive at midnight; the journey takes us four hours, without any delays. My mate from school, Charlie, knows we're planning to visit him in Nashville at some point, but we never agreed a specific date. My last message to him was when we were in New Orleans, a few days ago; I told him we might make it to Nashville in the next few weeks. He's got no idea that we've just turned up. I call his mobile from the payphone at the Greyhound coach station in Nashville, asking him to pick us up. Thankfully he's still awake, although he's a bit shocked, which is understandable; he hasn't had any time to prepare for our visit, but nonetheless, he comes down in his Volkswagen Bora and takes us back to his house. What a fucking legend.

Charlie's a well-built black man, with a goatee beard, which he grooms meticulously. He used to be a lot fatter at school but since he moved to America, for university, he's definitely become more vain. I can tell he's being going down the gym quite a lot 'cause all the fat has disappeared, and it's been replaced with muscle. He's done well to resist the temptations; with all the cheap junk food over here, he could've quite easily gone the other way, into obesity. He always had a skinhead or a squared-off high top at school, 'cause those were the only two hairstyles the school barber knew how to cut on a black man. Now, he's looking pretty cool with short dreadlocks, trailed back over the top of his head; it looks like he's been standing in front of a gigantic fan for a few hours. We used to call him Big Mac at school, mainly 'cause he was fat, but even though he's lost weight, the nickname stays the same.

I've known him since we were thirteen – he joined my school at the same time as Marshy. They're friends, but I wouldn't say they're close. I used to live in the same boarding house as Charlie, so we saw each other all day, every day. They're two of my best mates but there is one fundamental difference in their characters – maturity. Even though we're all the same age, Charlie is supporting his sister and her two kids, working three jobs to help pay for it all. Marshy is an only child, with no responsibilities, drinking every night, and a fucking nuisance when drunk. If you put them both on a scale of maturity, they're at opposite ends; having these two in close proximity to each other could be a recipe for disaster. Charlie is the father figure who craves discipline; Marshy is the outlandish child who does what he wants and thrives in chaos. They don't dislike each other, but Charlie isn't always appreciative of Marshy's anarchy.

On the drive back from the Greyhound station, Big Mac stops at a gas station so he can fill his car up. We all get out. Charlie's at the gas pump, me and Marshy are getting food in the shop. We walk up to the attendant behind the till and put our goods on the desk to pay for them. I'm pointing over towards our adopted, cheap, brand fags. The tobacco in these smokes resembles something closer to tree bark.

"Hello, mate, can I have two packs of those cigarettes in the red box, please?"

He looks shocked when he hears me speak. "Uh, say, I don't recognise that accent, where are you guys from?"

"We're from England."

"Oh wow, that's awesome. What brings you guys to Nashville?"

Charlie walks in behind us, ready to pay for his petrol. I turn round as he approaches.

"Alright, lad. You not getting any food?"

"Nah, I'm alright thanks, mate."

"That's unlike you, Big Mac! You on a diet or somethin', you fat bastard?!"

"Shut up, fat boy."

The attendant butts in. "Uhhhh, do you guys know each other or somethin'?"

"Yeah we went to school together, in England."

The attendant's jaw drops on the floor. "Are you English too?" he asks Charlie.

"Yes, mate, I'm English." Charlie answers him with a quiet frustration. The attendant is shocked and confused and asks:

"They have black people in England?"

Seriously? No fucking way. This is, by a mile, the stupidest thing I've ever heard anyone say. Initially, I'm in shock, then I burst out laughing at the sheer ignorance of this thick cunt. I know this sorry excuse for a human isn't a representation of all the people in the USA, but it's still pretty worrying for the planet as a whole, that this person will potentially reproduce. Is this fucking moron for real? What does he think? That you only get black people in America? Has he spent his whole life thinking that?! How did he possibly come to that conclusion, in this day and age?

We get back in the car. Charlie's not offended by the comment; instead he's laughing at how much of a muppet the bloke is. He's astounded, like me, that someone can be so fucking thick, yet still able to survive. You would think a cunt as thick as that would forget how to breathe! I hope this isn't a sign of things to come in Nashville; I'm pretty sure it won't be.

We pull up to Charlie's driveway. He's living in the suburbs in a rented, detached bungalow, set in a large plot of land with garden all the way around it. There aren't any fences to divide the land. We're right next to a busy interstate road that's raised up on concrete pillars. It's all very grown up – the type of place I'd live in with a family and kids, when I'm older. All the other houses in the area are the same – made from white, painted wood; they don't look stable but they're in good condition. There are two separate apartments in the building – the main two bed flat, where Big Mac and his family are staying, is on the right. There's a small, one bed apartment on the left, with a separate entrance.

This is where me and Marshy are staying. We go in. Through the front door is a large open plan living room / kitchen with a TV on a wooden cabinet, and a sofa bed. There's a small bathroom at the back of the room on the right, and a bedroom next to it, on the left, with a mattress on the floor. No other furniture or bed sheets. This flat hasn't been lived in or used for a long time; it's as basic as it gets but it's free for us to stay in. It's perfect for me and Marshy 'cause we've only planned to stay for a few nights. Charlie tells us he'll introduce us to his mates and makes it clear he'll be working most nights, so he might not be able to come out with us as much as he'd like to. He's finishing off his degree, whilst working in the medical school, and waiting tables in a couple of restaurants. He's earning good money through the tips he gets at the restaurants – that's how he's able to support his sister and nieces. The introductions to his friends will go a long way, as there aren't any other travellers to meet, like there would be if we were staying at a hostel. This suits us – it's different. Instead of hanging around with travellers, we'll be hanging around with his workmates and students of the university – locals and residents that know the area and the people. They can introduce us to birds and the best places to go. I'm looking forward to this.

Charlie's got a rare night off work, so he takes us out. We go to a bar called the 'Broadway Brewhouse'. It's a large, modern bar packed out with people. On the wall behind the bar is a huge selection of draught beers from all around the world. Each one has its own tap; some of the taps are so high up the wall, the barman has to climb up a ladder to reach them. I like the quirkiness – you don't get this sort of place in England. Charlie introduces us to some birds he knows from university; they're all in their early twenties and every one of them is smoking hot. Nice one, Big

Mac! We drink and talk with them all night and they invite us back to their house.

It's nothing like the scummy, rat-infested places I lived in during my first years of university in Sheffield; these birds have got a brand new terraced house refurbished to the highest standards. They're classy, wealthy, and very hospitable. Me and Marshy have both pulled but the birds aren't in the mood for partying late; we're all going to sleep not long after we arrive there. Marshy's on the couch, and I'm sleeping on a giant beanbag on the floor in the living room with the bird I've been kissing. We've got a duvet over the top of us and I'm tryin' to be quiet whilst making my move, but with other people in the room I concede that nothing much is going to happen. She's not reciprocating 'cause her friends are in the room with us, so I give up and go to sleep. It's a far cry from the bunk bed situation at the India House in New Orleans, and a different kind of girl. It's weird being in someone's house after staying in hostels and hotels for the last five weeks; I've got used to bunk beds. Charlie wakes us up early in the morning and drives us back to his house.

Later that evening, we're out on the booze again. Big Mac's organised another night out with one of his friends. We're off to watch the Nashville Predators, the city's ice hockey team, at their stadium – the Gaylord Entertainment Centre. Funny name for a stadium, they'd get abused for that in England! I've seen a few ice hockey games on TV; the atmosphere always sounds good at these American sports so I'm up for this. Sports in the States are completely different to ours – baseball, basketball, American football, and ice hockey. You don't get much of them in England, so this is a good chance to see what it's all about.

We get our tickets and met up with Charlie's friend, Rob.

He's tall and skinny, with a ginger beard. You can tell he's a local 'cause he's got his 'Predators' cap on and he's high-fiving all the other home team fans as he walks past, and faking a high-five to the away fans, pulling out of it at the last second, leaving them hanging. He looks like a bit of a geek but he's funny. He's all pumped up about the game. He's your classic man's man; talking about sports, beer, women, and country and western music, and how those four things make life 'awesome'.

Our seats are near the front, by the Perspex that protects the crowd from taking a puck in the face, so we've got a good view of the action. I haven't got a clue what the rules are, but soon after the game starts, I quickly figure out that fighting is allowed, which is pretty cool. A couple of the players are kicking off with each other and the referees are skating around them, waiting for them to finish. The crowd are going mental, baying for blood, like it's some sort of gladiator showdown; they appear to enjoy the fighting more than anything else in the game. Rob's trying to teach us the rules, as we watch. There is a code amongst the players and referees that determines when they're allowed to fight and when to stop. Four big screens hang above the middle of the ice rink, high up in the air, showing the scores, and replays of players getting smashed into the protective barriers at the sides. They show pictures of fans in the crowd, dancing, making stupid faces, and waving. The Americans certainly do know how to put on a show. After the game, Rob's deliberating over which bar to take us to. He looks across the road and spots his target – Tootsies!

Tootsies Orchid Lounge is a famous honky-tonk bar where country and western stars perform and drink. It's been around since the sixties and the walls are covered with pictures of some of the famous bands and artists that have played there over the years. The bar is set out on two floors, which are both filled to the brim. We get a beer and go upstairs. There's live music on both floors, but the upstairs bar is much bigger and the better-known band is up there, according to Rob. He takes us to the front of the crowd, to get the best view. There's a large gap between the crowd and the band. We drink our beers and watch the performance. When the band finish their song, Rob walks boldly towards the lead singer, to speak to her. He must be making a request for a song.

The lead singer counts the band in, to start playing the next tune, and she's speaking over the top of the music.

"Thanks, y'all, for coming out to see us tonight; we really appreciate y'all being here."

The crowd go wild. There are quite a few wolf-whistles for the singer; she's pretty hot.

"Now, what about this, y'all? I hear we got some guys from England visitin' us, and my friends over here tell me they wanna come up and have a little dance; show us how they do it across the pond. What do y'all say about that?"

The crowd obviously fancy a laugh, so they're going mental to get us up there. Me and Marshy get pushed up, with resistance, on to the stage, and we're thrown right into the spotlight, in the space in front of the band. I'm going beetroot red, completely embarrassed. The closest thing to Country and Western music that I've ever heard is 'Cotton Eye Joe' by Rednex; I haven't got a clue how to dance to this. I'm hopping around, pumping my leg on the floor and slapping my thigh. Now Marshy's starting the classic 'Dosey Doe', so we're linking arms and swinging round. Everyone's pissing themselves with laughter at how bad we are. Marshy drags Rob up onto the stage with us. At least two hundred people are watching the three of us make complete idiots of ourselves.

We're starting to like Nashville and we've got a sweet set up with the flat, so we've decided to stay a bit longer than the three days we thought we would. As good as the place is, there is one thing about America in general that I'm not happy with – 'light' beers. A lot of the bars we've been to sell Bud Light and Miller Light – two percent alcohol. It's not right. If you're going to drink, get pissed for fuck's sake! It's a waste of money otherwise.

Flashing Neon Lights

We've been spending a lot of our daytimes playing pool. By this point, the score between me and Marshy is something ridiculous like fifty-eight to sixty-one, in my favour. We're looking around the centre of town for a new pool bar. We find a massive place, behind the main strip. Outside is a well-dressed promoter offering deals to people as they walk past. As we contemplate going in, he immediately takes a few steps towards us, and starts his pitch.

"Hey there, guys, whereabouts you from?"

"England, mate."

"You wanna come shoot some pool? We got beer on draught and some hot chicks upstairs, man!"

"Really?! Sounds good, mate. How much's it for a hour?"

"It's usually twenty bucks an hour, man, but I tell you what, 'cause I like English guys, I'll give you two hours and two free drinks each on top of that, for twenty bucks each. You can't get better than that, in the whole of Nashville, man, for real."

Compared to the other prices in the area, this is a pretty good deal. We've looked around for a while and this is the best we've seen.

"That sounds like a good deal, Marshy, reckon we should go for it?"

"Yeah, why not, man, let's do it."

The promoter shows us into the building. We go up a long, wide flight of stairs and walk through a set of doors into the large pool room; there are fifty tables here, at least.

"Okay, guys, you got your twenty bucks?"

"Here you go mate, here's forty."

"Alright, wait there while I get the table ready. What do you wanna drink?

"Two pints of Coors please, mate."

"No problem. Just wait here and I'll get your table number, and I'll get the barmaid to bring the drinks to your table. Have a great time, guys."

He walks over to a counter, where a bird's standing behind a till, about fifteen metres away from us. After a minute, he walks back over.

"Okay, you're on table number seventeen, over there. The tables have got numbers hangin' over the top of them. Can you see it?"

"Yeah, I see it."

"Grab yourself some cues and I'll have your drinks sent over."

"Okay, cheers, mate."

"They'll start your time as soon as you start playin'. You guys need anythin' else?"

"Nah, we're okay, mate. Thank you."

We walk over to the table and begin playing. After three or four games, we still haven't got our drinks, so I go over to the bird behind the till.

"Excuse me, hi. We paid for the deal, with two free drinks about thirty minutes ago, and the promoter said he'd have our drinks sent over, but we don't have them yet. Could someone bring them over please?"

"Um, deal?" She's raising her eyebrows, looking puzzled. "We sure don't have any deal like that here, sir, who did you order that from?"

"The promoter, from outside, yeah? We came in with him; he paid for us about thirty minutes ago."

"Promoter? Uhhhh, we don't have any promoters here, sir, or

any deals; it's a flat rate per hour, sir."

"We came in with him, the promoter who stands outside offerin' deals, you know?"

"I spoke to a gentleman about thirty minutes ago, when you came in, and…he just asked if he could use the toilets here. He said he was with you guys."

"What, so you're tellin' me he doesn't even work here?"

"No sir, not at all."

"And he didn't give you any money? The forty dollars we gave to him?"

"No, sir, he didn't give me any money. You pay for your drinks at the bar and you pay for your table here when you're finished. I'm sorry, sir."

Fucking stitched up, again. That fucking thieving cunt. Me and Marshy are arguing about it in front of her.

"Oh, for fuck's sake, well done, Bill. I knew there was somethin' dodgy about him."

"You think this is my fault? If you're so fuckin' on the ball, why didn't you say anythin'? Anyway, what the fuck are you on about? You lost our money for the weed from that guy in Miami…don't be such a prick."

This is the fifth time we've been hustled or robbed and every time it's something different. Just like in Miami, the hustler's long gone before we've even noticed. He must have walked straight out, and legged it down the road. He probably saw us coming a mile away, like we've got a big fucking neon light flashing over our heads – 'Over here! Come and fuckin' mug me, come take my money. Here, you can fuckin' have it!'

It's all about fucking money. Anywhere you find naive tourists, there'll be hustlers, ready and waiting.

Me and Marshy don't usually argue, but if I spend long enough with anyone, they'll eventually start to piss me off. Something little that doesn't usually bother me will get on my nerves. I've known Marshy for ten years and only ever argued with him once, when I told his parents, by mistake, he was going to a party at my house; he'd told them something different. We were sixteen years old; I let it slip by accident and we argued on the way to my house. It wasn't a big deal, his parents didn't really care, but he didn't want them to know he was getting pissed. Within minutes, it was over and forgotten about. He got me back by hanging a porn magazine on my parents' washing line, with clothes pegs; it was open at the centrefold picture. When my Dad went out into the garden, to read the morning paper, he found a big, hairy beaver staring at him. Funny, looking back at it – my Dad never mentioned it, but I'm sure he probably thought it was quite funny too. Never mind laughing now though, 'cause Marshy's starting to piss me off.

In the end, we have to pay for the table again – the manager of the pool bar tells us we could be trying to hustle them, for all they know. I wonder if the bird on the counter has an arrangement with the hustler? Maybe they've figured out a scam together – like something out of 'Dirty Rotten Scoundrels'. That fucking cheeky little twat. If we see him, he's going to get a fucking kicking. We were going to get a taxi back to Charlie's house with the money we've just lost, but we can't now. Instead, we have to walk. For fuck's sake, it's freezing outside. We walk down the stairs towards the exit, arguing.

"Well you gave him the money, that's all I'm sayin', Bill."

"Well you didn't exactly see it comin', did you, Marshy, otherwise you would've stopped me givin' him the money. Anyway, shut up, I'm the one who's gonna be payin' for this. It's not like you've got any money on you. At least I didn't leave my card in a cash point, on the second day out here."

"Oh fuck off, you know I'll pay you that money back."

"Yeah, right. Anyway, where you going? Charlie's house is down here."

"No it isn't, it's down here."

"I'm tellin' you, it's this way."

"No it isn't, Bill, it's down here."

"Fine, you go that way. I'm going this way."

"Okay then, Bill. See you later. But you're walkin' the wrong way."

"No mate, you're walkin' the wrong way."

"Fine then, go back the wrong way."

"Fine then, but I'll get back before you, fuckin' bell-end!"

"Fuck off, knob-head!"

Both of us can be stubborn bastards. I haven't really got a clue where I'm going but we both want to be right so we go our separate ways. It's a race to get back now. I think I remember the interstate road number that Charlie's house is next to, so if I can find someone and ask for directions, I should be okay. Marshy's already set off, down a different road.

My blood's boiling after being hustled, arguing, and now ending up walking back on my own when I haven't got a clue where I'm going, thousands of miles away from home. The streets are desolate; not a single person around. I'm in the middle of some residential street that I don't recognise 'cause it's pitch black, and to cap it all off, it's fucking freezing. All I've got to keep my torso warm is a t-shirt and a thin tracksuit top, so I'm stomping down the road, as fast as I can, with my arms folded, lost. There's this little voice in my head.

'You've gotta make it home first – then you're right, then you win.'

I know Marshy's thinking exactly the same thing, just so the winner can be smug. This is about bragging rights.

I walk on for a few minutes and I can see a taxi in the distance, coming towards me. Get in there! You fucking beauty! I can tell it's a taxi, 'cause it's got that extra bit on the top of the car that lights up. I've got a vague idea of which direction to go but I'm not a hundred percent sure. As it gets closer, I flag it down.

"Hello, mate."

"Hey there. Where d'ya wanna go?"

"I dunno of the name of the road; I'm not from round here."

"Okay, do you know anywhere close by? Or can you describe where you need to go?"

"Yeah, my mate's house's next to an interstate road, a few miles down the road."

"I think I know where you mean – there's an interstate road a few miles back, where I've just come from."

"Yeah, and there's a Shell petrol station alongside the interstate road and there are houses on either side."

"We can have a look when we get down there."

"Can we get to a cashpoint too?"

"You mean ATM, right? If it's the gas station I think you're talkin' about, there's one there."

I jump in the taxi and out of the cold, knowing that I'm stealing a march on Marshy. He hasn't got any money on him and he hasn't got a cash card either, so I should definitely beat him now. As we approach the interstate, I recognise the road and the layout of the buildings. I don't know the name of Charlie's road, so the driver drops me off at the petrol station, which I recognise. I'm sure I've been here during the day, so I can't be far away. I pay the driver and get out. I look around but I'm not sure which way Charlie's house is. I'm fairly drunk, but I know it must be around here somewhere, so I begin walking. It all looks familiar but I can't find the right house. I walk for a couple of miles but still no sign. It must be well into the minus degrees; I'm shivering uncontrollably and my teeth are clattering together rapidly, as I storm down the road. My blood certainly isn't boiling anymore.

After walking for thirty minutes, the scenery is becoming unfamiliar; I'm sure I've fucked this up now. I've been to that Shell garage before; it must be back the other way. I bite the bullet, turn around, and go all the way back. I'm so confused; I'm starting to doubt if I'm even on the right road. I reach the petrol station, where I started from, and carry on in the other direction. The houses this way don't look right either; I can't fucking suss it out. I'm so cold, I can't think straight, my brain isn't working properly. It's frustrating. I just want to be inside somewhere; this is starting to take the piss. Marshy's probably made it back by now, too.

All that time I saved in the taxi has been fucking wasted now; surely it must be around here somewhere?

After a few minutes, I see a tunnel leading underneath the interstate road to the other side. It's all flooding back to me – I've had an epiphany – it's on the other side of the fucking road. What a fucking donut. I've been so preoccupied looking for the house on this side, I didn't even stop to think I could be on the wrong side of the road. And it's even more annoying when I get to the other side, and Charlie's house is two minutes away – I find it pretty much straight away. I pick up the key from under the bin and walk in. The light isn't on so Marshy's either in bed already, or he's not there. I switch the lights and heater on to thaw out. Marshy isn't here and Charlie's lights are off, so, on the plus side, I've won the argument; on the down side, it looks like he's having even more of a nightmare getting back than I did.

I'm starting to get a little worried about Marshy. He's been out in that cold for more than two hours. I'll stay up and wait until he gets back, but there's no way of contacting him. I was freezing my tits off after an hour of walking, and Marshy's been out there for double that. Where the fuck is he? I hope nothing bad has happened to him.

Forty-five minutes have passed. I hear a faint thud of shoes coming up the stairs outside and the door opens. It's Marshy. He looks frozen to the bone, blue in the face. He's pissed off and doesn't say anything to me. He's only got a T-shirt on. He's been out there all that time, with a T-shirt on; unbelievable. I've warmed up, so I give him a blanket and he stands by the heater. The argument's forgotten; we don't need to apologise to each other; we're both just glad to be back inside in the warm. And I'm amazed he's still alive!

"What happened to you, man?"

He's still shivering.

"I've had a fuckin' nightmare, mate. I walked down that road and took a turnin' off and must've got lost."

"You've been out there for about two hours. I was startin' to get worried, mate. You must be fuckin' freezin'. Where did you get to then?"

"Uhhhhhhhh. Fuck knows, mate. At one point I was about to try and sleep in a phone box, I was that cold."

"You fuckin' nutcase! Well you're here now, mate."

After Party

It's a midweek evening and we're having some beers at a few bars, before heading to a club called 'Sixty-Five'. We've spent most of our time in the centre of Nashville, so we're buzzing 'cause we're going to some new places, out of town, where the locals go. Having Charlie here is an advantage 'cause we've got a source of local knowledge; someone who knows the area inside out. He can show us the places that other tourists may never hear about. As the city is spread out over a large area, it takes a long time to get anywhere; you need a car, really. Most people we meet drink and drive so they don't have to shell out for taxis, which means more money for booze. If Charlie is driving, he doesn't drink – he's responsible like that. I would find it hard to go out without drinking. On the outskirts of the city, the buildings are rarely above three stories. Some of the old, disused warehouses have been turned into clubs, and 'Sixty-Five' is one of them.

We pull into the gravel car park, directly outside the club. It's mostly full, but we find a space and queue up outside, chatting as we wait. As we pass the doormen, I catch one of their eyes for a split second and it induces a flashback in my mind.

"Marshy, did you see the doormen, outside?"

"Er, no, mate, I wasn't payin' attention. I was chattin' to those people behind us. Why's that?"

"I just had a flashback; it was weird, mate."

"Flashback from what?"

"New Year's Eve."

"Oh really! I'm surprised you even remember your own name after that, mate!"

"Haha! Whatever! I know I don't remember much, but

I could swear one of the bouncers outside is the bloke that I punched in the face."

"Really? I doubt it, mate. He had a skinhead; loads of bouncers have skinheads. Could be though. If it is, you best not fall asleep in here!"

"Probably isn't him. Weird though, havin' a flashback from a night out that long ago!"

I best keep out of that bloke's way, in case it's him!

The club is well done-up inside; a mixture of old and new. The bar and seating areas are all modern, and the bricks are left exposed, keeping the warehouse feel. It makes for a raw, party atmosphere. Its remote location means the music can be turned right up; it's the type of place where you need to shout to have a conversation with the person next to you. It's packed inside and the lights are dimmed; the DJ's are playing old-skool hip hop which is a welcome change to the cheesy dance music and endless use of Def Leppard's 'Pour Some Sugar on me', that they play in most of the other bars we've been in, New Orleans excluded. The drinks are expensive and everyone's dressed up. It's Saturday night so there are more people out than during the week, ready to let off some steam after their week at work.

We force our way through the crowds and up the stairs to the mezzanine floor, which looks down onto the dance floor. Charlie introduces us to some birds he knows from his university. Perfect. I get talking to a bird called Natasha. She's got big curly blonde hair and she's a bit of an extravert, which I like. We're getting on well and there's an obvious spark. At the end of the night, we're all smashed and Natasha invites us all back to her flat, to continue the party. We jump into an SUV with one of Charlie's friends. He's probably well over the limit – we've been doing shots all night. I don't really think twice about it, he seems alright to me.

Natasha's hosting and she's supplying us all with red wine. I'm standing in her living room, chatting to some bloke, and she accidentally nudges me as she walks past, spilling red wine all over my white jumper. I'm gutted 'cause that's one less item of clothing I've got to keep me warm. She apologises, holding her hand up to her mouth. I walk into her bedroom to take it off. She brings a cloth and dabs the stain, to try to soak up the wine. We're on our own now. I look her in the eye and kiss her. Looks like this little accident has worked in my favour! I joke with her that she spilt the wine over me on purpose, to get me alone in her room. When we go back into the living room, we're talking to everyone else and dancing around, but staring at each other. I know we're going to get it on later, when everyone else leaves.

It's morning and Natasha has dropped me off at Charlie's. I've got a big smile on my face and a spring in my step, as I bounce up the stairs to the flat. No numbers are exchanged and she drives off. I'll probably never see her again. How strange we are.

It's Sunday night and Charlie's planned to take us to another club; it's just the three of us this evening. It's another old warehouse, this time a long, thin building, that looks like a large Scouts hut. We walk up a set of steel stairs to the entrance; ten dollars to get in. It's a live music venue with ten unsigned bands playing rock 'n' roll. The crowd has almost subconsciously organised itself into rows, like in a church, which I find a little weird. No-one's dancing or singing, as they don't know any of the tunes, but I like seeing live performances; you never know when the next big band might show up.

It's two o'clock in the morning and we're leaving, pissed again, stumbling out the door.

"Lads, d'ya wanna go somewhere else?"

"Why's that, Big Mac? Is anywhere open at this time?"

"Yeah, there's a place I know, stays open twenty-four hours; it's really nearby. We can check it out if you want?"

Me and Marshy are loving the idea of a twenty-four hour bar.

"I'll have some of that, mate, let's go!"

"Sweet, I'm in too."

Charlie takes us to an old diner called 'Café Coco'. It's open twenty-four hours and it's got a licence to serve alcohol until five o'clock in the morning, which is ideal. There's a small car park outside and two rooms inside. It's not very big, but it's popular enough for all of the tables to be full. We get a beer and go to the conservatory at the back of the building, where all the smokers are. We find an old, ropey table and some chairs going spare, and start talking to the people on the table next to us; We're the only foreigners here so we're getting a lot of attention. There's a mad mix of people around – goths, metallers, townies, students – all drunk and here for the laughs. It's a meeting place for the stragglers to go, when all the different clubs have shut – the hardcore from nights of the various genres of music – all in one place. It's a mishmash of clothing styles, hair styles, body piercings, and outlooks on life, all under one roof, giving it a unique, diverse atmosphere. Initially, I'm expecting there to be some fights kicking off, with such a range of different people, and particularly 'cause everyone's wasted, but it's exactly the opposite – they couldn't be nicer to each other. It's pretty fucking cool; a sign of the times, perhaps. The coolest people I meet on a night out are the ones that are happy to talk and laugh with anyone. There's no bad attitude here. It reminds me of a pub I used to work in whilst at university in Sheffield, called 'The Howard'. All the clubbers used to get high together – a big mash-up every Sunday afternoon, after the nightclubs finished at midday, and everyone was too high to go home.

We pull our chairs over to a different table. Two birds in goth clothes are sitting there, so we ask if they mind us perching on the end. No problem. They're sound birds – one's called Annabelle and the other one's called Rachel. My short term memory's pretty bad and I'm fairly pissed; I've forgotten which one is which and I'm waiting for someone to use their names again; They've both got thick eyeliner in exactly the same style, like they've got ready together and agreed it looks cool. They're both in long black dresses and they've got some crazy jewellery on. These birds have definitely got a different attitude to the kind of birds I'm used to hanging around with – much more mysterious. You can tell these birds don't give a fuck what other people think about them; the type of birds that don't conform to what's in the girly magazines. They tell us they're leaving to go and smoke some weed back at their house. Marshy asks them if we can join them and they say 'sure'. Charlie's going home 'cause he's got to work, and besides, smoking weed isn't his scene, so he bails and leaves us to it.

We get into their car, outside the bar, and they drive us to their house; it's fucking miles away, right out in the suburbs, nowhere near Charlie's gaff and nowhere near the city centre. Where the fuck are we going? I haven't got the foggiest clue where we are. We pull up at a row of terraced houses. It's pitch black and there aren't any street lights; I can't see what my surroundings look like. We're out on a whim here but the party's carrying on, so fuck it.

The birds rent this house together; they've got free reign to do what they want. They put some goth music on as soon as we walk in. We're sitting in a large living room, which stretches ten metres, all the way to the back of the house; they've got sofas all around the edges – it's a perfect place for house parties. One of the birds is rolling a joint and the other one's loading up a bong that she's brought in from her room. These birds aren't messing about. The bong looks pretty expensive – it's heavily decorated with hand-carved gargoyles all over the surface. It looks like an instrument used by a cult for sacrifices. Me and Marshy are sat on the opposite side of the room, keeping our distance – we've only just met these birds for a few hours and now we're back at their house. They're totally different birds to Natasha and her friends; I feel awkward around them; I'm certainly not getting any vibes that we'll be pulling them, but you never know. I can smell the weed from where I'm sitting and they haven't even started smoking any of it yet; that's a sign of fucking strong weed.

The sweet, potent scent of the skunk is filling up my nostrils and I know it's going to fuck me up. I ask to look at the weed and I can tell it's the good shit 'cause I can see all the lovely crystals between the buds, winking at me as I examine it closer. They're saying 'We're gonna fuck you up!' From my dealing days at university, I know strong weed when I see and smell it. I've been drinking all night too, so when I add this weed to the mix it's going to get interesting. There's only one way to find out. The girls take their hits, holding the smoke down like seasoned pros. Neither of them coughs, even mildly. Now it's my turn. I take my hit whilst Rachel – well, I think she's called Rachel – is lighting a spliff. I pass the bong to Marshy and he takes his pull. Afterwards, me and Marshy are coughing heavily, for five minutes, non-stop. The back of my throat's tickling like it does when you're ill and you've got a bad cough. I know the effects of the bong aren't going to hit me properly for a few minutes, but I also know that when they do, I'm going to be a total mess.

The spliff's being passed round. I don't want to back down; even though I can't focus on anything. I'm smoking it and so is Marshy. I'm sure this stuff is laced with something; I've never been this fucked from a bong. The birds seem fine though, like it's normal to them. I can't concentrate; the room's spinning round and flipping back like a typewriter. Although I can't focus on them, I can sense tension from the birds now 'cause me and Marshy are absolutely fucked and we've both gone silent. I'm so high, I can't keep my eyes open, I'm starting to fall asleep. It feels amazing but it's so intense that I need to lie down. I get up, without saying anything to the birds, and go to lie down on a sofa. I can hear Marshy lying down on the sofa at a right angle to the one I'm on. I'm closing my eyes and trying to drift off to sleep. I'm too fucked, I've got no control over my speech or my body. When I close my eyes, it feels like my whole body's spinning round. I'm thinking some mad shit and I'm hallucinating. I've been stoned many times before so I'm experienced enough to ride the high; I'm not panicking. I'm as fucked as I've ever been right now. In thirty minutes, I'll be fine.

I can feel my heartbeat increase, the blood pump around my body faster, the thud of every pulse as it surges through my neck. I can hear the birds whispering and giggling as I'm tripping out, seeing shapes merge into each other and change colour, and then I'm flying over the ocean, like Superman.

I hear the sound of a doorbell and it takes me a minute or two before I realise I've been asleep; well, more like passed out. I don't know how long I've been here but I'm awake now. It could've been ten minutes; it could've been two hours. I'm keeping my eyes closed 'cause I can't talk – I can't think straight for long enough to remember how to speak properly. I reckon if I try to speak, I'm going to make strange sounds like 'hhhhrrrrr' and 'naaaaaaah'. The birds are still here but they're at the other end of the room from where I'm lying. My head's still spinning and my eyes are heavy. I want to sleep but by the sounds of things, that's not going to happen. I'm listening intently to what's going on. One of the birds gets up to answer the door and a bloke walks in the room. I open my eyes, very slightly, to see who this guy is. He's about five foot eight, stocky, with freckles and short, spiky hair. He's got an angry look on his face; his eyebrows squashed down, screwing his face up, his mouth frowning. He's got a puffer jacket on and he's sticking his chest out. Both of his hands are hidden in his jacket pockets.

"I got here as soon as I could. It's okay, you don't have to worry now."

I reckon these birds have called him round for protection. He's got something in his jacket pocket and he's moving it around. I can't tell what it is. The noise it's making sounds like two pieces of metal clanging together. What the fuck is going on? It sounds to me like it's a weapon, possibly a chain or a gun. Whatever it is, he wants us to know about it. Fearing for my safety, I open my eyes so I can watch what he's up to and so he can see I'm awake. We catch eye contact for a split second but he turns his head immediately, and sits down on the floor with the birds. He's making hostile hints about us outstaying our welcome.

Marshy hasn't moved or said anything. I can't tell if he's awake. He's only a metre away from me and I'm lying the right way to reach him, without having to get up. I shake his shoulder to wake him up and he stirs, opens his eyes, but stays lying down. Even moving that much is a fucking effort; I'm only doing it 'cause I'm worried this guy's about to fucking kill us. What if these birds have got us back here to spike us with that weed and then start some fucked up goth ritual on us, like fucking sacrificing us, or chopping us up and burying us in their back garden? If they're going to do anything like that, I'm in no state to try and defend myself; I can barely move. What if more people are on their way round? Fuck! But surely they wouldn't do that. Surely they don't want to kill us. Or do they? I really don't know.

I'm hoping nothing weird is going to happen to us. I know this guy doesn't want us here, but we're both paralysed on the sofa and vulnerable. I still can't compose myself to put a sentence together. I'm trying to get my thoughts straight enough to be able to explain what's happened, but I'm so fucked I can barely talk; the fact he's got a weapon on him is making me scared to say anything, just in case he loses it and goes fucking mental on us.

The freckly twat is continuing to aim his snide comments at us. He's speaking loudly to make sure we can hear him.

"Don't you hate it when two assholes invite themselves round your house and think they own the place?" and "Pass the joint, Rachel, or maybe I shouldn't have any of this in case I pass out round someone's house, someone that I don't even know? How fuckin' rude is that?"

The birds aren't actually saying anything to join in with him, they're just looking at the floor, giggling, embarrassed by the whole situation but at the same time validating him, 'cause they feel safe now he's there to protect them. In a way, it's fair enough – for all they know, we could be a pair of dodgy bastards – I can understand them not wanting to leave us asleep on their sofa whilst they go to bed – they don't know us well enough to trust us. And in their eyes, we could be capable of anything. I'm sitting in silence, listening to their conversation. They haven't said anything to us, they haven't told us to go, they've just left us here.

This chubby little twat is starting to wind me up now. He hasn't even tried to speak to us. I can tell the birds are happy he's made his point now, 'cause they're telling him to calm down and stop. All the while he's making sure we can hear the metal clanging together. We've outstayed our welcome, I get it, mate. My head has come round a bit now with all this drama – a mountain out of a fucking molehill, if you ask me. The weed's wearing off and I can feel my powers of speech and thought coming back – I reckon I can attempt to string a sentence together again now. Looks like these birds have turned out to be a pair of fucking drama queens.

"Marshy, come on, we need to get out of here."

"Yeah, alright, man." Marshy's letting out a big sigh as he realises he has to move, but this twat's getting under my skin now, carrying on like we're some kind of predators. I'm speaking to him with my slow, stoned voice, being wary, as I don't want to come across confrontational in case he loses it and tries to stab me.

"Sorry, mate, can I just say somethin'?"

He doesn't reply, so I carry on regardless.

"I'm sorry if there's been a misunderstandin' here, mate, but your friends said it was okay for us to come back with them for a smoke...and then...we just got really stoned and fell asleep... cause that weed's really strong!" I've been rehearsing that in my head for the last ten minutes. No-one says anything and the room's completely silent, so I carry on." Look, we don't get weed like that back home...that stuff just knocked us out – hands up, we can't handle it!"

Still no-one says anything and the twat won't make eye contact. He's staring ahead towards the birds. I've been polite now and explained it. What a rude, horrible cunt. It's as awkward as it can possibly be – like we've committed some horrendous crime.

"Look, we're not tryin' to use this as a place to crash either; we're stayin' with a mate…the girls met him earlier." As I'm getting no response from this jumped-up prick, I try speaking to the birds instead. "Look, ladies, I'm sorry, I dunno what the fuck happened there. We just needed to lay down for a bit to sober up."

One of them replies. I'm still not sure which one is which.

"You guys are fuckin' weird."

"I'm really sorry, we never meant to cause any trouble or scare you. We should get a taxi. Can you order one for us, please?"

"No, it's okay; you guys just freaked us out a little. We don't even know you."

"Fair enough."

"We can drive you back. Your friend gave us his address, so we'll take you back."

So we get up and leave and it's fucking odd 'cause now they're telling the fat ginger cunt to chill.

"It's okay, they're alright."

"Call me if you get any problems."

And now they're alright with us again and they're going to drive us back at five am in the morning, by themselves. What the fuck?

As me and Marshy are leaving, the chubby, speckly dickhead is standing up by the front door, refusing to acknowledge us. I'm picturing myself battering the cunt. What a fucking twat!

It's starting to get light now and the birds drive us straight back to Charlie's house, which takes half an hour. I'm in the back of the car with Marshy and the birds are in the front. We're chatting with them normally now and having a laugh about what's just happened. It's all a bit surreal, like the last few hours back at their house didn't actually happen at all. I can understand these birds feeling vulnerable after some of the scare stories you hear in the American news – murders, shootings, burglaries, etc. But then again, they could've been the nutcases. They could've drugged us, strung us up, and eaten us for all we'd known. I'm glad to be out of that house, away from that little knob-head. Another potentially dangerous situation avoided. We're so fucking lucky right now.

Marshy still needs his replacement bankcard after losing it in Miami in the first few days. We've been here nearly two weeks and Charlie says we can stay a bit longer if we want to. As we've got a set address, Marshy's parents can send his new card here by registered mail. Up until now, he's been getting money transferred into my account and I withdraw it for him. He's called his parents and they've told him that they had a call from Autodriveaway when we didn't deliver the car on time in Memphis. Apparently, Autodriveaway got suspicious of us, thinking we might have robbed the car, so they called the police. We were driving around Memphis with the police looking for us! When I speak to my parents they tell me the same thing – they've had a call from them too. The pigs were trying to find out where we were so they could come and hunt us down! The bloke's got his fucking car now – it was only a day or two late for fuck's sake. It's like the bloke at the passport checks, or the twat with the weapon at the girl's house, assuming we're fucking criminals. They're all paranoid!

We've decided to wait in Nashville until the substitute bank-card arrives; whatever morning the card arrives, we'll leave. We're spending every day in Nashville like it's our last – a leaving do every night. Bring on the booze.

Charlie's brought us to another bar, out of the city centre. On the other side of the room, I notice the bird I was with the other night, Natasha. She's with a few of her friends, playing pool, so we join them. After the bar kicks out, we drive to Wendy's, to get some food. It seems everyone comes here at the end of the night. It's two in the morning and there's a queue leading out of the restaurant and around the corner. We have to wait thirty minutes to get served.

Marshy's fucked, which means anything can happen and I know this more than anyone. He's in one of his mischievous moods where he's hellbent on causing trouble, ripping the piss out of random people, and generally acting like a fucking bellend. I find him hilarious when he's like this, but Charlie doesn't share the same perspective. When we finally get served, we go over to Charlie, as he's got a table for us. I sit down with my straightforward burger meal. Marshy comes over, swaying all over the place, with two trays worth of food that he's bought from the Dollar Menu. He's got salads, onion rings, beef burgers, chicken burgers, four portions of fries, etc. There's no way he's going to eat all the food by himself, it's enough to feed a whole family. I think I know where this is going. When we were teenagers and we went to house parties at our friends' houses, we would always get drunk and start pissing around with the food. At one birthday party for our mate Kelly, Marshy started throwing food at the wall and crushing up biscuits on the floor; he even head-butted her birthday cake. She wasn't too happy, but I was keeled over on the floor with my stomach hurting from laughing so much. Whenever there was a buffet at one of these house parties, we used play the 'stuff-your-face' competition. We both pick up all the different snacks and cram in as much as we can possibly get into our mouths, and look at each other as we're doing it. As we both find this absolutely hilarious, we're laughing at the same time, so bits of the food are flying out of our mouths, which makes us laugh even more. I have never understood why no-one else finds this as funny as we do.

So we're sat at the table in Wendy's with all this food and it's pretty obvious there's nothing better to do with it than stuff our faces! So we do, and it's still as funny as it was when we were teenagers. We're making quite a lot of noise in the process though, and some of the Yanks around us are starting to get annoyed. Natasha's laughing at us and Charlie's trying to pretend he finds it funny. He's keen to get us out of the restaurant as soon as we've finished acting like fifteen-year-olds. Charlie wants to go home now, but I'm going back to Natasha's. I'm surprised she's still here after watching us do that!

Bikini Competition

Another party night and Charlie's taking us to a club in Murfreesboro, a small town just a few miles south of Nashville. There's a keg party in one of the clubs – twenty dollars to get in then drink as much as we want – this time, we fill our cups from a massive keg, which is free-standing in the middle of the club. We don't have to worry about tipping this time, as we're serving ourselves. And it gets even better as there's another surprise in store.

Mid-way through the night, the DJ gets on the microphone and announces the start of the 'Bikini Competition' on stage. Charlie didn't mention this. There's a raised up stage at the back of the club, next to the DJ booth. Each bird in the competition selects a song and they take it in turns to strip down from their scantily clad selves, to their bikinis; some of them go further. The judges are the audience – the bird that gets the loudest cheer at the end of the competition is the winner. This is fucking cool. The birds in the audience are as excited as the boys. I really think England can take a leaf out of America's book here. It's not one of those weightlifters' bikini competitions, where the women have six-packs; the birds in the competition have all got incredible, curvaceous bodies; it's made our night. After experiencing some of the bars we've been to in the different cities in the USA, I want to open a bar in England with a laundrette, a load of pool tables, a keg party, a souvenir shop, live music, and a bikini competition every Saturday night.

We're on a high after the keg party. Me and Marshy are hammered and Charlie's sober 'cause he's driving. Marshy's sat in the passenger seat in the front of the car, annoying Charlie.

There's nothing more irritating than a really drunk person when you're sober. I'm used to Marshy annoying me whilst I'm driving, screaming like I've hit something or poking me in the ribs repeatedly. This time Charlie is his victim and his patience is wearing thin. At first Charlie warns Marshy not to piss him off, and he's laughing it off, but Marshy gradually wears him down. He's holding a big mouthful of phlegm and pretending to spit it out inside the car. He pretends to spit a few times, just blowing air out. On the third time he does it, he accidentally lets out a massive grennie, all over the inside of the windscreen. He bursts out laughing but apologises at the same time. Charlie's going mental and he's shouting. He pulls the car over and disciplines Marshy like he's a child. There's an uncomfortable silence in the car but Marshy's trying to stop himself from laughing. He's got his mouth closed and he's trying to hold it back, but the air builds up in his mouth and he can't stop himself. It's setting me off too but I know Charlie's getting mad so I'm caught between trying to shut Marshy up and laughing myself. Charlie's warned him that if he doesn't buck his ideas up then he'll be kicking him out of the car, and that kills the atmosphere.

It's approaching three weeks in Nashville now. It's about time we moved on but we haven't decided where to go next. It's the end of January so we've got about five weeks to get to LA. We're considering using an Autodriveaway car to get over towards the West as we want to go to Austin, Texas, but it depends on where the cars are going.

We meet up with Charlie's university rugby team and go out on the beers with them.. Their next game is tomorrow, in Atlanta. We've told them that we know Charlie as we played in the same team together at school, and Charlie's bigging us up, telling them all that me and Marshy are both good players. They ask us if we fancy a road trip to watch the game and maybe even play for them. Even though we're not exactly in the condition of our lives, it makes sense to get a lift with them – it's almost like fate; part of the adventure. We're going wherever the wind takes us. We agree to go with them, but we don't commit to playing a full game – that would be suicide. We settle on half of a game and a lift; any more than that and we'll probably pass out and have to pay an American ambulance for a call out! Our decision has been made, we've got a plan for the next step. With our minds made up, we proceed to get absolutely shit-faced with the rugby team, and get some sleep for an early start in the morning.

As we wake in the morning, I realise our time in Nashville has come to an end. We pack our bags and say our goodbyes to Charlie and his family, thanking them for putting us up, and putting up with us. I've seen a side to this city that I never would have if it wasn't for him.

Atlanta, Georgia

Rolling Stoned

Charlie's taking us to a petrol station, where we're meeting his rugby team. Marshy looks a fucking wreck! The dark rings and droopy bags around his half-cut eyes, coupled with a heavy frown, are a warning sign to leave him well alone. Fuck knows how bad I look; I feel rough but I haven't even bothered to check myself in the mirror this morning; I'm past the point of caring. We've been drinking almost every day for the best part of eight weeks, and I'm pretty sure it shows.

"Look at the face on you, sphincter lips!" I laugh.

"Yeah, cheers, Bill, you look like a donkey's scrote."

The trip from Nashville to Atlanta is about two hundred and fifty miles and it'll take us four hours. At least we don't need to travel through the night or use the Autodriveaway cars this time. We're fairly sure the police aren't looking for us and there's no need to sleep in a dodgy service station car park, where we could potentially be arse-raped at gun point by some cross-eyed, mentally deranged, trailer-trash nutcase, like Marshy nearly was in Fort Lauderdale. We haven't used Autodriveaway since New Orleans, and they're still holding my deposit, so hopefully we can still get a car from one of their other offices if we need to. I wonder if they'll let us have another car after being two days late with the last one, in Memphis; we haven't even been in contact with them yet to find out. I hope we haven't been banned! It's hard to tell without speaking to them, but I won't be surprised if we are. They'll probably try and use the late car as an excuse to hustle us out of our deposit money; these Yanks will find any way to get your money off you.

As we've taken the rugby team up on their offer of a lift to Atlanta, to watch the rugby game, we might as well stay for a few nights and see what the city's got to offer. Then we'll try to get an Autodriveaway car going west. We still want to go to Austin, the Grand Canyon, and Las Vegas, before ending up in Los Angeles. There's no point going any further north; it was baltic enough in Nashville and we're told it's going to be cold in Atlanta. I want to go to New York and Chicago, but that's even further north and there's no way I'm going to freeze my bollocks off anymore. It's cold enough in England for most of the year, so we might as well try and get some warmer weather whilst we can. We're at the end of January now, and there's a month left to fit everything in. Atlanta isn't really that far away from Miami, where we started off. LA is fucking miles away. We've spent quite a lot of our money and we don't want to waste what we've got left on plane fares, if we can avoid it. We'll be going by Autodriveaway from here, or, failing that, the Greyhound coaches.

We leave at nine o'clock in the morning, set to arrive in Atlanta at one o'clock in the afternoon, ready for the game, which kicks off at two. I'm in a car with one of Charlie's mates. My eyes want to shut, my brain is hazy, and I'm not really paying much attention to what's going on around me; I've barely woken up but I can feel my brain telling me I want a cigarette after becoming accustomed to at least twenty-a-day. I'm looking out the window of the car, at my new surroundings. We're in the suburbs of Atlanta, surrounded by vast amounts of grey concrete, interstate roads, slipways veering off in multiple different directions, bridges and flyovers strategically placed every couple of hundred metres along the road. It's got the same kind of feel as most of the other cities we've seen in North America, with all the thousands of buildings spread out over a vast area and the skyscrapers concentrated in the centre. Once we're off the interstate, all the roads are arranged in square blocks and the land's very flat. It's fairly boring, seen all this before. I'm eager to get this rugby game out of the way so we can get to a bar. My lungs are begging for mercy and making threats: 'Don't do it Billy, we'll be fucked! We'll make you pay for it!'

I know my lungs are going to hurt; I've smoked so much, I won't be able to take in the oxygen I need after running around, but it's probably a good idea for me to go through the pain and get some exercise. I'm sure I've put on a stone after all the beer I've drunk and the junk food I've eaten.

Atlanta's another one of these places I haven't really heard much about except for the time it hosted the Olympic Games in the nineties; I don't know what to expect, but if it's half as good as New Orleans or Nashville, we'll be sorted. The lads from the Nashville rugby team are all telling us it's a party city, so I'm keen to get stuck into some local drinking holes and sample the banter and hopefully find some more birds. I'm preparing myself mentally for another North American city to chew us up and spit us out at the next place, as we drink their bars dry again – do your worst, Atlanta! It doesn't matter where we go – Me and Marshy will drink all these Yanks under the table – that I'm sure of.

We're at the rugby club – there are a few pitches and a clubhouse; it's the first time I've seen a rugby pitch anywhere we've been. The Yanks aren't really interested in this sport; it's right down the bottom of their list, probably 'cause they can't wear any pads to protect themselves! Most of them probably haven't got a clue what a rugby ball looks like. Charlie's friend is telling me some American football players don't make it to the NFL so they end up converting to rugby, to try and make it into the national team.

We don't know if we're going to get a game, and we're standing on the sidelines, watching the first half. It's a close game; Nashville are edging it with a five point lead at half-time. The coach asks us if we both want to play the second half, so we get changed, on the pitch, into some spare kit. We play the second forty minutes, I score with my first touch of the ball and Marshy makes a try saving tackle, but we don't contribute a great deal else. We win the game comfortably but I'm fucked at the end of it, like I knew I would be. Every time I inhale, the back of my throat stings with a sharp pain and my lungs feels restricted. I'm wincing every time I take a breath and I can feel my lungs struggling to expand enough to take in the oxygen I need. I'm sweating too; it's probably all alcohol coming out of my pores; someone will probably get pissed from the fumes if they stand close enough. Even though it was only forty minutes, I need to collapse and get showered so I can go and sink some more beers. That'll sort us out.

After the game, as is customary with all rugby clubs around the world, both teams meet up at a bar of the host's choice. The Atlanta team's arranged for some food to be brought out to us all, which goes down a treat. We're in a diner on a wide strip on the outskirts of the city. It's lined with bars, restaurants, and fast food outlets. This'll be useful for me and Marshy 'cause we can come back here once we're settled in at the next hostel. I'm looking around, making a mental note of the area; although it's quiet now, I can see this place will be filled with people later on and will probably be a good place to find some fit birds.

It's evening by the time everyone starts to leave and the sun has set. The guys from the Nashville rugby team aren't staying overnight; most of them have gone already, but two of the guys who are still around want to go and smoke a joint so that they're stoned for the journey home. They tell us they'll help us find our hostel in exchange for skinning up for them, which is a fair deal. We jump at the chance, especially considering that we've got absolutely no idea of where we are or where to go. It's good of them to help us out; some of the Yanks are pretty sound.

We drive into the centre of the city and find a multi-storey car park for some cover, to skin-up. It's mostly empty, besides a few stray cars dotted around. We stay in the car to build the joint, which I roll using my skills learnt whilst I was at university. The windows are closed to hotbox the car and the inside fills with the smoke. We're toking on the reefa and inhaling all the secondary smoke back in, getting higher with every breath. The weed doesn't take its full effect for a good fifteen minutes, but when it does, it's a heavy, mellow feeling in my brain. My eyes are half-cut and bloodshot, my mouth and lips are dry, and I'm constantly trying to muster up saliva to moisten them. All the buildings, streets, and lights look so much cooler when you're stoned like this. Thank fuck this weed's nowhere near as strong as the stuff we had in Nashville, otherwise we'd probably pass out again and they wouldn't let us anywhere near the hostel. I'm much more relaxed around the rugby lads, instead of having two freaked out birds and a psycho with a weapon in his pocket in the near vicinity. I'm comforted by the fact the people in the car are good friends with Charlie and they're going out of their way to help us out. It's nice being driven around the centre of this city, somewhere new to me, as I stare out the window and drift off into my own world. I'm too introverted to hold a conversation or concentrate on anything for more than five seconds.

I'm entertaining myself looking at the patterns being made by the condensation on the inside of the car window. All the muscles in my body have lost their tension; I'm slumped against the side and I'm bouncing on the back seat in tune with the bumps in the road, not giving a fuck about anything, smiling to myself in my blurry paradise.

We know the name of the hostel we need to get to but not the name of the road. None of us know where we we're supposed to be going and I'm too busy being side-tracked by the Dunkin Donuts, McDonald's, Wendy's, KFC, and Burger King fast food outlets densely populating every street we turn down. No wonder Western countries have got an obesity problem. After fifteen minutes of driving around without a clue where we're going, someone comes up with the genius idea of asking for directions. A random on the sidewalk tells us we need to get to 'Ponce De Leon Street'. The word 'Ponce' being in the name of the street cracks us up with laughter and by the time we drive away, we've forgotten which way we've been told to go. After a further six times of asking for directions, we find the street, but it takes us a few more attempts, driving up and down the road, to find the hostel. Being as stoned as he is, the driver isn't going fast enough to be a danger to anyone, but I am wondering – if it's taken us this long to find a hostel, how the fuck are these guys going to get all the way back to Nashville!?

The main entrance of the hostel is down a side road, off the main street, so we can be forgiven for taking so long to find it in the dark, being stoned and all. It doesn't really look like a hostel either; it's part of a large building that anyone could easily mistake for a business premises or block of flats. We get out, ready for the next stage of our trip to begin.

The hostel is called 'The Atlanta International'. It's part of the 'American Hostel Association' chain, so we know it's going to be pretty straight-laced, 'cause it's owned by the same bunch of boring muppets as the place we were condemned to in New Orleans, after I pissed behind the TV set on the air conditioning unit. Hopefully they won't have heard about us already, unless a big warning has been sent around the States to watch out for us. Surely not? This time we haven't done anything wrong, but it's the only place in Atlanta that's a reasonable price and close to the centre of town. We sure as hell don't know anywhere else to go, so we're heading in.

The entrance to the hostel has a canvas hood over the top of the doors, stretching out onto the side street, and there's a small block of grey concrete steps leading up to the doors. As we walk in, the TV area is on our left, in an open plan room that looks onto the main street, Ponce De Leon. There are chairs and sofas along the sides of the room which don't look particularly comfortable; they're plain and boring – you can't really slouch on them – the type that make you sit bolt upright. It looks like a waiting room in a dentist's or doctor's surgery. Directly in front of us is a pool table and on the right is a hatch in the wall where the receptionist's head is poking out. Past that, there are corridors and stairs leading off in different directions, to the rooms. There's an old golden retriever wearily walking around with an innocent gaze, probably looking for food. This place has an eerie atmosphere, very quiet, no-one talking or having fun, no laughter or buzz. The same rules as the Marquette House Hostel in New Orleans – no alcohol is allowed to be consumed on the premises, lights out at midnight. It's like all the rules have crushed the spirit of the people here. Either that or they're a bunch of boring bastards. Maybe we've caught it at the wrong time, but on first impressions, the people in here aren't very welcoming or interesting. I'll reserve judgement though, 'cause I haven't actually spoken to anyone yet and it might improve as I get to know the people staying here.

We check in at the reception, where a resigned, down-beat lady tells us there are still rooms available, which's a relief 'cause we haven't got a plan B. We try a few small-talk jokes with her and she manages to raise a tiny split-second smile before we're shown to our room.

One of the corridors near to the reception leads directly to a cluster of rooms on the ground floor, about twenty metres away from the living room. We're given the room at the end of the corridor on the left-hand side. The room is large, with two sets of bunk beds and two large wardrobes; it's definitely the nicest room we've had so far. The furniture and beds are new, along with all the fixtures and fittings. It's not lavish luxury, but it's good quality. We drop our bags and go to the TV room to see if we can meet some new partners in crime. There are seven or eight other people around. We sit down and no-one's talking. With the TV on it's difficult to strike up conversations without talking over the programme, so when the adverts come on, I start speaking to the bird next to me.

"Alright! How's it going? I'm Billy. Nice to meet you."

"Yeah, hi," she responds, totally uninterested, as if I've disturbed her. She looks at me for a second but turns straight back to the TV. I try to persevere.

"What's your name?"

"What? Oh, Beth."

"You travellin' at the moment or you from around here?"

She doesn't respond, shrugging her shoulders and sighing deeply, blowing air out of her mouth like my attempt at conversation has been an ordeal to sit through. There's no more chat between us, just uncomfortable tension. Cheers for the conversation, you fucking arrogant retard. I know small talk can be boring but you've got to start somewhere! You quickly move on to the banter once you establish some basic information about each other, no need to be so fucking rude about it. Now I'm a little self-conscious because this bird won't talk to me and I've pretty much failed in front of everyone. I'm looking around the room for other possible mates, but no-one seems even the slightest bit interested that we've shown up; it's actually the opposite – they seem annoyed, like we're invading their space. Has someone tattooed 'wanker' on my face when I wasn't looking? Maybe we've been lucky up until now, with the other hostels, but then again, maybe this lot are all just twats. I'm getting bored now 'cause there's some shit programme on TV that I've got no interest in and my head's still buzzing from the weed we smoked; I need to chat shit to someone, have a laugh for fuck's sake; isn't that what people our age are supposed to do?

Two quite large blokes come in through the main doors. They're English and in their mid-twenties. Beth springs up with a big smile on her face and runs over to hug them both. They come and sit down next to where I am. I'm trying to work my way into the conversation but I'm being totally ignored again. The men are laughing and joking loudly with Beth and another bird, keeping the conversation to themselves. I'm trying to figure out the dynamics of the group, going off on one in my head again, being stoned. It's like we're animals in the wild and these English blokes think we've come to invade their territory where they've got the 'Alpha Male' status. Beth is probably shagging one of them so she doesn't want to be seen talking to us in case the blokes see her and get jealous, so she's ignoring me to show her loyalty to them. She probably won't pay me any attention until I get some validation from the men. I might be over-analysing this; I'm stoned after all. I'm not put off completely, I'm hatching a plan to make other friends in the hostel or get these English guys on their own, to try and find some common ground with them. Once they let their guard down and chat to me, they'll realise I'm alright and we'll all get along. In the meantime, I'm looking at the TV and eavesdropping on their conversation. The lads tell the birds they're on their way to wrestling practice which makes sense 'cause of their size and build. This also explains the macho bullshit towards any other blokes trying to get involved with 'their' birds – the whole caveman mentality. Maybe I'm just overthinking this.

We're too stoned to go out so we chill for the rest of the evening and get some much-needed sleep. From what I've seen of Atlanta so far, I want to know more.

I'm hearing a lot of talk about the Super Bowl final this morning; it's all over the TV too. It's on TV tonight and it's a big thing out here, probably the biggest sporting event of the year. The hostel has livened up and there are some more interesting people about that weren't here last night. I get talking to a bloke from Brazil called Mikel. He speaks fairly decent English with a Latino twang. He's looking at my eyes and he notices they're half-cut and bloodshot. He asks me quietly, with a big grin on his face, making circles round his eye with his fingers.

"Haf you, errrr bin smoking, errrrr, di hash?"

I'm nodding my head and smiling at the same time.

"Can you errrr, make for me?" He's making the spliff-rolling action with both of his hands.

"Yeah. No problem. Where?"

"Come to my room, we put di, errrr, towel on di floor and we, errrrr, haf out di window."

I'm not planning to go anywhere this afternoon, so smoking another joint is probably the best use of my time. We're going out later on to watch the Super Bowl final, so I might as well get stoned and chill at the hostel. Marshy's not up for getting stoned again so he stays in the living room, watching TV. He's probably scared of anyone from that part of the world, after his abduction in the car back in Fort Lauderdale! From what I can tell, Mikel seems like an alright bloke, and if he's got weed, he must be a good lad.

We go through the corridor and up one floor to Mikel's room. He opens the door and we walk in. It's a much smaller room than mine; there isn't much space to manoeuvre. There are two sets of bunk beds on either side of the room as you walk in. The gap between them leaves just enough room to pass through without turning your body sideways. There's an open space at the end of the room, past the bunk beds, with a small table and two chairs, and a large window looking out the back of the hostel, into a courtyard. There's enough distance between his room and the reception to get away with smoking a joint. Mikel puts a towel on the floor, to cover the gap at the bottom of the door. People will go to all sorts of lengths to smoke a joint and not get caught. This reminds me of when me and Marshy used to roll joints at boarding school and find places to smoke them. Once, we nearly got caught smoking a joint up a tree when the Royal

Marines Band was playing a concert there. Two security guards with sniffer dogs walked underneath us. We stayed dead silent and still. The dogs went crazy but the guards didn't think to look up in the trees and notice the stream of red-hot hashish rocks, falling like fireworks from our poorly rolled joint. We would've been expelled on the spot if we were caught. In the States, we would probably be arrested and jailed for years if we got caught with drugs, especially being in one of these 'No Fun Allowed' hostels – the staff would be fighting each other to be the one to grass on you.

I sit down at the table and roll the joint. My new Brazilian friend is weary of the strong smell of the skunk; he keeps checking the towel is covering as much of the gap as possible so no smoke will get out into the corridor. Although I'm shitting myself that we might get busted, Mikel's putting my mind to rest 'cause he's so worried himself; I'm pretty sure he isn't trying to set me up. We both stand at the window, which is opened as far as it'll go. The windows have blocks on the sides to stop them from opening all the way. Whenever we take a toke of the joint we have to make sure we don't blow any smoke back into the room. When we're holding the joint, in between tokes, we need to keep the lit part of the reefa outside, holding it at an angle to stop any smoke blowing inside. If anyone walks past the door and smells the weed from outside we're fucked; and this is skunk – the smelliest kind of weed you can get.

After the joint, Mikel's showing me a book that he's written. He's had it printed himself, and he designed the front cover. He's trying to sell it to people as he travels around the world. He asks me to read a few pages, but in my hazy state, I can't concentrate long enough to read; I'm so stoned that my eyes won't focus on the small words, so I tell him I'll read it later. He laughs and we're both totally caned. I ask him if he can get me some weed – after smoking a joint together I'm pretty sure I can trust him. He tells me forty dollars a bag and I give him the money on the spot. I ask him if he wants to go watch the Super Bowl later but he's too stoned to go out. I can get the weed off him later or tomorrow – assuming I haven't just been hustled again!

Chatting Shit

We find a pub, ten minutes' walk from the hostel, towards the centre of town. It's not very busy, but we've still got two or three hours before the game kicks off. We settle on a couple of stools at the bar with a decent view of a large TV screen, directly behind us. We haven't got Charlie introducing us to people anymore, so we need to make our own luck now. This is as good a place as any to meet some new people.

A couple of hours pass as we sink some beers and chat whilst watching the build-up to the big game. I'm starting to get tipsy, reaching the point where my confidence level is high enough to start chatting to strangers. I'm looking around for suitable targets but there isn't much to be going on with. There's a ropey-looking, skinny man standing next to me at the bar, on his own. He's in his late sixties, grey stringy hair, centre parted, down to his ears; a wrinkly, weathered face, permanent frown and scruffy clothes. He's been there a while and hasn't spoken to anyone. This reminds me of home a bit; it's not unusual to see people drinking on their own in English pubs. He's looking into thin air towards the ground. I'm aware of him but it doesn't occur to me to speak to him as we're looking out for birds and people our age; he doesn't look like much fun in any case. A few moments go by and he turns towards us.

"Where are you two from then?"

"Portsmouth on the south coast of England. Are you English too then?"

"Oh, right!" A spark of recognition hits his face and his eyebrows raise, "I'm from Fareham! I've got a son about your age. I don't see him anymore though."

The comment about his son seems like an obscure thing to tell a stranger in your first few sentences, but I put it down to him being lonely. Fareham's only three or four miles away from Portsmouth so it seems a little strange that all these thousands of miles away from home, having met a total of four English people so far, there's an old man on his own, in a random bar, who's from a small town down the road from where we're from, with a son our age – of all the places in England. It's a small world.

This old geezer moves towards us, parking his beer closer to where we're sat. For fuck's sake, he's going to start babbling on at us now; he probably thinks we're his new best mates just 'cause we're English. I don't mind him talking to us 'cause we're not talking to anyone else. I chat to him for a bit to see if he's got anything interesting to say and he's telling us about his son.

"I haven't seen my son for ten years. I wish I had done."

"Why not?"

"I split up with his mother and haven't seen him since. I was going to meet up with him but then I came over to America and haven't been back since."

We're talking about the USA when he starts getting political. I don't really know a great deal about politics and I'm out of my depth very quickly. Marshy's got out of the conversation and turned his attention towards the TV. This guy's views are quite strong.

"It's the Americans' foreign policy that alienates them from the rest of the world; If you go back to…"

And he goes on. He comes across fairly intelligent and knowledgeable about all the history of the world and how he thinks everything fits into place. He's gone from not saying anything to anyone to ranting about the apparent failure of America's foreign policy in the middle of an American bar. It's making me a bit uncomfortable 'cause I know how proud the Yanks are about their country – they're always banging on about how they reckon the USA is the best country in the world, blah blah blah. I'm entertaining his conversation, neither agreeing or disagreeing. I'm not into all this political bollocks; I just want to get pissed. Even if I wanted to speak though, I couldn't get a word in 'cause he's having a proper rant.

I'm starting to wonder, with all this negativity about America's politics, it doesn't add up that he's moved to the States. If he dislikes the place so much, why has he emigrated here? Then again, he is English and old and all they do is moan about shit. I'm still a bit stoned from the afternoon spliff and my head's ticking over again; I'm becoming suspicious of him. Does this guy actually believe in what he's saying or is it something more sinister? Is he trying to see if I agree with him to see if I'm some kind of activist? Is he testing me? Or am I thinking too deeply again? Paranoia? Maybe this guy is a spy. I can't figure this place out – Atlanta is fucking weird, so far. First the hostel and now this! Maybe he's a lonely old guy who wanted someone to listen to him whinge 'cause he doesn't have anyone to listen to him. I can't get rid of him so I'm just going to sit here and pretend I'm listening.

The scenario becomes even more peculiar when another man appears on his own at the bar, and stands next to the English bloke. He's eavesdropping on the old man's rant and wants to get involved. He's poking his head around and it doesn't take him long to start giving his ten pence worth, once he hears one of the English geezer's controversial opinions. I'm starting to think this could get interesting now, but I don't want to be involved. As soon as he speaks I know he's American. He's a large, shady-looking character with a flaky scalp and receding, thinned hair on the verge of turning grey. He's got thick jam-jar glasses and a blazer with a shirt underneath. He butts in.

"I'm sorry to interrupt ya there, guys, but I couldn't help overhearin' what ya talkin' about. Do ya mind if I join in?" He enters into a full-blown discussion, introducing himself and asking our names. This American's got some quite strong opinions of his own, opposing the English bloke's, and they're trying to coax some opinions out of me, but I'm not going to be drawn into this. Marshy's always said you shouldn't discuss politics and religion with randoms – there's too much difference in opinion and you end up kicking-off with each other. It's such a personal thing, you never know who you might upset. Every time I'm asked what I think, I just say I don't know enough about the topic to have an opinion.

The bar's filling up and the game's about to start. I turn my attention to the TV 'cause these two old farts are still banging on and I'm starting to get bored. I've heard enough now. I'm hoping they'll fuck off soon.

Marshy's started chatting to some people next to him, closer to our age. As he's got his back to me though, I'm cut off and I can't really join the conversation from where I'm sitting. It's a group of five people of different ages ranging between twenty and forty. I could move round to join in with Marshy but I'm intrigued to hear what these old gits are talking about. As the beers are taking effect they're getting animated and deeper into disagreement with each other's opinions. The Americans have been asking us about our political opinions all the way around. I guess we're supposed to be their allies and they want assurance that we think the same things they do. In England, there aren't that many people I know that are bothered about politics, not our age, at least; and if they are, they don't show it. We don't really talk about it, especially on the kind of level these guys are going into; certainly not in my circle of friends anyway. I'm freaked out by these weirdos. The American gets my attention.

"I'm interested to carry on this discussion with you both; can we meet for breakfast tomorrow morning? I'll buy you both breakfast."

Why is this guy inviting me? I've got nothing to do with this conversation.

"Eeerrrrr, I don't think so, I dunno if I'll be up for breakfast. Sorry, mate." I'm trying to be polite, but at the same time, I'm concerned what the fuck this flaky weirdo wants from me. No fucking way am I going to breakfast with this fucking nut-job; he probably drugs teenagers and locks them up in his cellar. He might be some dodgy paedo for all I know. The English fella doesn't reply, he just stares across the bar into thin air, as he was doing when he first arrived, with the same grumpy look on his face. The American doesn't wait for him to reply; he takes a pen and paper out of his inside coat pocket.

"I tell you what; here's my number. Give me a call tomorrow morning and we can all meet up, my shout."

Something doesn't feel right here; this is all too bizarre for me – I don't know anything about these wankers – who they are, what they do, why they're so interested in me. The whole situation seems contrived; is it some kind of set-up? Maybe I'm being paranoid, maybe it's all innocent, but I've got a gut feeling something's wrong with those two. I decide to move away from them and round to the people Marshy's talking with; two of whom are fit birds.

I can always tell when Marshy's having fun because I can hear his distinctive laugh a mile away. He's always cackling with his loud high-pitched laugh; he loves to be the centre of attention, but he is a funny bastard. Not wanting to be stuck on my Jack Jones, I move around next to Marshy and introduce myself to the group. They're all airline crew – stewardesses and pilots. They've just finished their flight and come straight to the pub to get pissed; they're a good bunch. I'm relieved to be away from the old bastards and their fucked-up conversation. Instead of talking serious politics, this lot are talking shit about who would win in a fight between a piranha and a hedgehog, seeing how many fingers you can fit in your mouth, doing party tricks, telling jokes and taking the piss out of each other; these are our type of people.

By the time the Super Bowl game finishes, which's about three hours later, I'm starting to feel smashed and I'm slurring my words, but I'm good to carry on. The airline crew finish their drinks and invite us back to their hotel room, to carry on the session. We jump at the chance and down the rest of our drinks. You can't beat a random adventure! I wave goodbye to the old farts and walk out, happy to be rid of them. We stop at a convenience store, stock up on beers, and continue on our way to a massive multi-storey hotel. Their rooms are on the twentieth floor and there are still another ten floors above us. The room has several floor-to-ceiling windows looking out over the city, but it's dark and I can only see the buildings in front of me and the lights in the distance. One of the crew suggests we play a drinking game. We write the name of a famous person we want to shag on a Rizla. We lick the back and stick it on someone else's forehead. Then, by asking questions, we have to figure out which person is on our foreheads. We take it in turns to ask a question like 'Is it a movie star?' and if we get the question right then we get another go. After the game finishes, it becomes obvious the air stewardesses and pilots are shagging each other, so we take the hint and fuck off. There's nothing worse than having to spell out to someone that they need to leave 'cause you want to get laid!

Now we're at a loose end. We're not ready to go to sleep; we've only just reached a decent level of booze in our bloodstreams. We need to find some more bars or maybe even a club. None of the airline crew know Atlanta well enough to help us out. We leave the hotel and look around but can't find anything – I thought Atlanta was supposed to be a fucking party city! It's only one am and we're surrounded by office blocks. The bar we were in earlier has closed. We must be in the wrong part of town 'cause there's no strip of bars like Bourbon Street in New Orleans or Ocean Boulevard in Miami. There's the place we went to yesterday, after the rugby game, but we don't know the name of the street and there aren't any cars around, let alone taxis. We just need any old place – somewhere that's open, serves alcohol and has got nice birds – that's not too much to ask in a 'party city', is it? For fuck's sake, this place is shit!

Crystals & Angels

The streets are dead and we haven't got a clue where to look. We're stuck for ideas, so we resort to asking random strangers if they can direct us to somewhere that'll be open. A few passers-by are walking alone, with their heads to the ground, trying not to make eye contact, as if we might try to mug them. We're not having much luck, until we find one man who tells us there's a club fifteen minutes' walk away. He says it's situated behind an office block and we have to walk through a car park to find it. Sounds like the adventure we need – we might as well give it a go 'cause there isn't anything else to do around here.

As expected, it's difficult to find and I'm starting to get agitated. We're surveying the area, looking down all the little back alleyways and side roads, going back on ourselves. The booze is starting to wear off and we're both getting tetchy. I can feel another argument coming on, as we disagree on which way to go. Eventually, after thirty minutes of searching, we find the club – it's got to be here 'cause there's no other fucking place around! Let's get in quick and get a fucking beer before we kick-off with each other. There's no queue, but three bouncers are standing at the door. We get searched and pay ten dollars each to get in. We descend a long flight of wide stairs and walk through a long corridor with a set of double doors at the end, which leads into the main room below ground level. I can hear the dance music pumping out and the doors are rattling with vibrations as we get closer.

Through the doors there's a seating area and a long bar on the right. Further in, the room opens right up, on to a large dance floor. It's a mad venue – an old office block converted into a club.

The ceiling stretches right up to the top of the building. There are three floors, all with balconies looking down on to the dance floor, which is surrounded by a wire fence – it's like being in a big cage. There are spaces on the left of the dance floor where people are loitering around, as well as several different staircases leading up to the other floors and the balconies. The club is fairly empty for its size but there are at least three hundred people in here and that's as busy as it's going to get – we're already in the peak hours of the night. We get a drink and the barman tells us the club's open until six o'clock in the morning, which is ideal for us considering we aren't tired and we want to continue our night. We take our drinks and wander around. As we walk around the different floors, I notice there are a lot more blokes than there are birds; probably eighty per cent blokes and twenty per cent birds. Some of the blokes have also taken off their t-shirts and are dancing with each other very close – then the penny drops…fuck! We're in a gay club! I grab Marshy, shaking him by the shoulder, asking him what kind of club he thinks we're in, pointing out the clientele to him, and he's sussed it out. No big deal though, just got to be careful in the toilets, that's all! They've got booze here and that's all that matters.

After a couple of beers the tetchiness has disappeared and we're back on it. The DJ is playing house music and I'm drunkenly dancing around. As usual in these late night clubs, I start thinking I could do with something to add to the booze, something extra to complement the music. I'm getting the urge for a couple of E's. When I used to go clubbing in Sheffield, whilst at university, I'd have a few of the 'little fella's' to liven things up. The music and the energy you get from the 'disco biscuits' go hand-in-hand, and you can dance away all fucking night. Normally, I'd order some pills in beforehand, to avoid any disappointment, but we don't know anyone to get them from here and we weren't even thinking about going clubbing earlier on. Otherwise I would've asked that Mikel to see if he could've sorted us out. We're a bit wary of asking people for drugs in the club. We don't know who we might be talking to – we could end up trying to buy some E's from an undercover pig. Being in a foreign country does put the shits up you a bit – what if you get caught? It's a big risk, but we hedge our bets and back ourselves to make an educated guess by looking at the state of the people we're asking – if they look off their faces themselves, they probably aren't pigs – an undercover pig on ecstasy would probably be too loved up to arrest you anyway!

We split up and walk around, asking people who fit the bill. I'm pretty sure I don't look like police to a potential seller, being twenty-two years old and English, but it's hard to trust someone enough to sell drugs to them, in a club, when you don't know them or you've never seen them before. There's always going to be an element of doubt and the drugs themselves can make people a bit paranoid anyway. I ask about ten different people and get mixed responses. Some give me suspicious looks, some flatly turn me down, saying they've only got enough for themselves, and the others just say 'sorry, I don't take drugs', when it's blatant from the sweat dripping down their faces and their gurning chins that they've been climbing the walls and licking the windows for the last five hours; but I understand why they're cautious. I can't find anything so I'm going to find Marshy and see if he's done any better.

After looking around the different floors of the club, I see him chatting to a bloke a few years older than us. I wait for them to finish their conversation before approaching. He has to shout at me so I can hear what he's saying over the loud house music.

"How did it go, Marshy? Did you get anythin'?"

"Yeah, I've got it in my pocket now. I've already paid for it. Did you?"

"Sweet, you fuckin' legend! I couldn't find anythin'. Asked loadsa people. What did you get?"

"I dunno what it is, he wouldn't say."

"He wouldn't say? What d'ya mean he wouldn't say?"

"I asked him if he had anythin' to sell and he said 'yeah', but he wouldn't tell me what it is."

"Why not?"

"I kept askin' him but he all he would say is 'you'll have a wicked night on that'."

"Alright, fuck it – I'm sure we can figure it out. How much was it?"

"Fifty dollars."

"Fifty dollars? That's not bad. D'ya want half the money now?"

"Nah, just buy the drinks."

"Alright, mate, no bother. What the fuck d'ya reckon it is then?"

"I dunno mate, could be anythin', could be fuckin' chalk dust for all I know!"

"Well, let's have a taste and see if we can figure it out. I doubt he'd fuck us over if he's still in the club. Look – he's still over there."

"Tell you what, let's go get a drink first and then figure out what it is."

I've taken quite a varied cocktail of different drugs on nights out – ecstasy, skunk, speed, charlie, LSD, GHB, on top of smoking cigarettes and drinking booze, of course; and I've taken them loads of times. I'm pretty well-rehearsed in the consumption of drugs, and the different effects they have on me. I'm also used to mixing two or three of these drugs at the same time – that's come through a great deal of experience. Marshy's the same – he's been there and done it all before too so we know we can handle most things on the market and we know what our limits are. I draw the line at crack and heroin and I've vowed to myself never to take them – from what I've heard and seen, they're much more addictive – they'll fuck you up. I've seen films like 'Basketball Diaries', and read the horror stories about people spending all their money to get their next fix, losing their job, rotting all their teeth away and fucking their lives up. That isn't for me, that wouldn't happen to me – I know what I'm doing and I know I can handle myself.

We're pretty sure we'll be able to figure out exactly what Marshy's bought by tasting it, so we find a remote corner and try to be discrete as possible. I'm leaning against a pillar, looking out onto the dance floor, sipping on my beer whilst Marshy gets the paper wrap out. He opens it up, being careful not to spill any of the contents. It's a standard wrap made out of a rectangle cut from a magazine page and folded so the powder sits nicely in the middle. It's dark inside the club, besides the intermittent flashing of strobe lights; there aren't many people around, and specifically no bouncers patrolling the spaces. I'm keeping an eye on what's going on around us, just in case. The powder in the wrap is finely chopped up, no rocks or lumps at all – like it's been ground down. That says to me it's been cut with something.

"What d'ya reckon it is then, Marshy?"

"I dunno. It's powder but I can't really tell what colour it is, in this light."

"Here y'are, let's taste a bit."

We both lick our fingers and dab the powder, look at each other, and taste it at the same time. Our faces mirror the joint disgust at the flavour. It's not like anything I've had before.

Marshy's trying to narrow it down.

"That's definitely not coke, Bill."

"No, it isn't. I dunno what it is. I don't think it's speed either. It might be a crushed up E?"

"Well, you know what I reckon? Let's just have it all now and hope for the best."

I pause for a second in hesitation to think. At first I'm a little worried but then I let myself go.

"Yeah, fuck it. We're here now and we've paid for it. Let's do it."

"That's the spirit! How often d'ya get the chance to get smashed in a club in the middle of America?"

Marshy divides the powder into two piles in the palms of our hands. I know we're good to go when he screws up the empty wrap and puts it back in his pocket. Then we count down from three and lick our hands clean of the powder.

"Urgghhh, that's fuckin' rancid."

I quickly down a gulp of my beer to get rid of the taste and wash the powder down.

"Doesn't matter now. Let's fuckin' 'av it!"

And we're straight back on to the dance floor. From my experience with drugs, the stuff we've taken is okay, it's not great – it's not like cocaine, which makes me wide awake and completely alert; I'm not loved up like I am on a good E; I don't have a moment where the drug takes a hold of me and I 'come up' from it and my mood's completely altered; but I am high and I know it's had some kind of effect on me. It's not intense, it's mellow. My eyes are half-cut, my head's pulsing with a nice buzz, and I've got a smile on my face. I'm enjoying the music and having a dance but I'm not speaking to many people, like I do when I'm on other drugs – talking the largest amount of bullshit possible; but I'm having a good time.

As the night goes on, more and more people leave and the club empties out. I've got no idea what the time is, but when the place's practically empty, me and Marshy move to the bar to finish our beers. We're the last people in here. A middle-aged lady is looking around all the nooks and crannies of the club, checking behind the pillars, picking up glasses. As she walks past, Marshy asks if it's alright to finish our drinks and we start speaking to her. She's the owner and quickly picks up on our accents. We're invited upstairs to her office to continue our chat and look around other parts of the club that aren't being used.

She takes us to the top floor, which has been decked out as a cabaret suite – the walls are covered with pictures of drag acts that have performed here, past and present. She tells us, if it was ten years ago we could've stayed as long as we wanted and the place would've been packed out, but all the licensing laws were changed in the mid-late nineties. Apparently, Atlanta was previously a twenty-four hour party city where people used to go out all day and stay out for hours on end, but there was a change in the law when they had the Olympics, which restricted the licences for clubs to stay open all hours. Nowadays, they have to shut at six o'clock in the morning. Since then, the whole culture has changed and the crowds have started to dwindle. I ask her why the laws were changed and she tells me it's because the locals complained about the noise and the type of things going on in the clubs, i.e. drug taking. It's a shame really 'cause the majority of clubbers aren't committing any real crime in my eyes; they're just people having fun. All some people need's to hear's the word 'Drugs' and they shit themselves and get on their high horse. I'd love to give them an E and then ask them about it. Load of fucking bollocks. It pisses me off 'cause a similar sort of thing happened in Sheffield when someone complained about the parties we were having at the pub I used to work in called 'The Howard'. It was a similar scene – people getting off their faces and enjoying themselves – but oh no, some twat can't have that, so let's complain and get it all banned.

After our chat with the owner of the club, we're told we have to leave. It's close to seven am and it's light outside. My eyes sting as they adjust to the sunlight and my ears are ringing. It's fucking freezing so we get some directions and take a brisk walk back to the hostel. It's strange to be walking back at the end of our night out, when there are all these other people around us, on their way to work or out on a run – people walking past each other, living in two completely different worlds. We're still high and, all-in-all, it's been a quality night, an adventure.

The Evil Eyes

As we return to the hostel, there are a couple of people already on their way out, but the receptionist isn't there. Good job really, 'cause she shouldn't see us in this state! It must be obvious to other people that we've been up to no good, when we walk into a place at this time of the morning, looking like we do – clammy, pale-skinned, the same clothes on from the previous evening; and of course, people talk. We're still high and not quite ready to sleep, so we stop for a game of pool. My body wants to sleep but my brain's still active; the drugs aren't going to let me sleep, whatever they are. After the game I send myself to bed to try and switch off, but I know it's going to be hard to fall asleep; I've been like this on drugs many times before. We've still got time to try and get a few hours kip before completely scrambling our body clocks, so I set the alarm for midday. I lay down and close my eyes but all I can hear is a ringing in my head, like tinnitus. I don't know if I'll actually sleep, but at least I'll give my eyes and body a few hours rest.

I come round to the sound of my alarm. I'm still high and my head's heavy; I feel sketchy, twitchy. My body's quivering and my hands are shaking. It's a mixture of a comedown from the drugs and a hangover from the booze. It's not a nice feeling, but if you're going to get high, you've got to accept the consequences. I don't usually mind comedowns 'cause I start thinking loads of mad shit and let my imagination go off on one. I'm still really tired. People are going to know I've been up to something 'cause I look like a shipwreck. I can't get comfortable lying in bed, so I get up and go to the living room to occupy my brain with some crap TV programmes; I'm keeping myself to myself, not making any effort to make conversation with anyone. I get some funny looks from the other people in the living room – they're probably wondering what I've been up to, coming up with their own conclusions. Fuck them, the boring bastards. But surely they won't know what I was doing, will they?

They might figure out I was taking drugs. Shit. Don't say anything to them just in case they start asking questions. Luckily, there aren't any conversations happening and no-one's making any effort to speak to me; I'm happy about it this time. I'm thinking, maybe they're all on drugs in here and that's why no-one speaks to each other. There isn't anyone sat near me, which is allowing me to relax a little bit more; I can feel my neck, torso, legs, and hands twitching every ten or fifteen seconds, a different muscle every time, sometimes my eye. I'm getting self-conscious about it; it happens to me when I smoke skunk too. The last thing I want is someone sat next to me, watching me twitch. Just fucking leave me here to myself. I'm tired and grumpy and this TV's what I need right now, to take my mind off things. Marshy's awake but he's staying in bed – he isn't feeling too good either.

As people potter about the living room, I'm taking sharp looks around to see who's about. I'm sure that guy opposite keeps looking at me. I turn my head across his line of vision to check. What the fuck does he keep looking at me for? Fucking weirdo. My heart stops for a second as I catch a glimpse of someone I recognise. My brain takes a few seconds to start working but surely it can't be…I have to double take but I'm sure that man sitting by the window, looking out onto the street, is the old English fucker that was in the pub last night. I can't fucking believe it. What the fuck is he doing here? This is freaking me out a bit. I'm completely shocked 'cause most of the people you see staying at hostels are all between eighteen and thirty-five, and there's only been one or two I've seen in their thirties. I've got to try and keep calm now. This old geezer must be in his late fifties, maybe even early sixties, and he's standing by one of the windows. He said he's been in the States for years – then what the fuck is he doing in a hostel? I was suspicious of him last night and now my head is doing cartwheels. What's he up to? I need to find out so I gather myself together and walk up to him.

"Hello, mate. I recognise you from the bar last night."

He turns around and recognises me instantly. His answers are all short and abrupt, like he's trying not to give anything away.

"Oh, alright."

"Did you stay here last night?" I ask.

"Yeah."

"Oh, that's strange. I didn't realise, I was around most of the day yesterday and didn't see you here. You should've mentioned it. What a coincidence!"

He doesn't reply, so I carry on.

"So did you go and meet that American guy for breakfast then?"

"Nah."

"Fair enough." I'm trying to figure this guy out. Maybe I shouldn't ask too many questions in case I alarm him into thinking I'm suspicious of him; play it cool. He's a lot quieter than he was in the pub.

I watch TV for an hour, thinking how odd it is for him to show up. I'm trying to think of reasons why he's here. I didn't see him in the hostel at all yesterday, only in the bar in the evening. I suppose it's one of the cheaper places to stay in the area, so maybe he's just skint, but at that age, why would you want to be staying in a hostel with a load of youngsters? Is he that lonely? If he did move out to America years ago like he says he did, surely he should have his own place by now? All these questions are running through my head. I've got to put this to rest. Maybe I'm overreacting to this but with last night's weird conversation, the fact he's from a town down the road from where I grew up in England, that he says he has a son my age who he hasn't seen for years, and the other weirdo that turned up trying to get me to go to breakfast with him, the situation is getting more and more bizarre. He walks over to me and asks nonchalantly:

"You hungry then?"

First, the old fat paedo American asks to take me out for breakfast and now this weirdo. I'm actually hungry though and was planning on getting some food soon anyway, so as Marshy's still in bed I might as well go with him. Maybe I can get to the bottom of this and find out a bit more about him, to quell my suspicions. And in any case, he might know somewhere decent to get some food 'cause I sure as hell don't and I'm fucking starving – I haven't eaten anything since yesterday evening and it's mid-afternoon now. Everyone else in this place is boring too, so I might as well follow up on my curiosity about this character.

There's no way he's going to be tough; if he tries to make me go somewhere I don't want to, I'll leg it.

"Sure. D'ya know anywhere?"

"Yeah, I know a place."

"Alright. Give me five minutes and I'll meet you back out here."

He's standing by the main doors, waiting. This guy obviously knows his way around Atlanta, and it's adding to my concerns. How long has he been staying in this hostel? We leave and start walking down the road. I don't know where we're going but he's walking like a man possessed and I'm struggling to keep pace with him, even though he's shorter and much older than me. My brain hasn't kicked into action and my body's resisting the exercise; my lungs are taking a while to get used to the pace. I still need to rest but I need to eat first. It's raining lightly, that annoying rain that gets all over your face and sticks to it; it's the last thing I need right now.

We walk to a 'MARTA' station, Atlanta's transport system, similar to the London underground. We take a train heading out of the city centre. The journey takes half an hour and when we get off, I recognise the surroundings 'cause it's the same road with the strip of bars and restaurants that I went to with the rugby team, after the game. We go into the restaurant next to the bar I went to a few days ago. It's all a bit strange; all the way throughout the journey, I'm trying to start conversations with this old grumpy old git, but he doesn't reply; just ignores me totally. I don't even know his name, and I'm trying to make small talk to find out about him, but there's nothing coming back and it's frustrating me; it's putting me on edge. Why won't he reply? Say something, you fucking waste of space! It's hard to read a situation when the other person gives absolutely nothing away.

It's one big uncomfortable silence the whole way through, even in the restaurant whilst we're eating our food. It's awkward and I'm not enjoying it. Is he doing this on purpose? Is he enjoying winding me up? Is he playing some kind of mind trick game with me, waiting to see what I say to him? He's trying to make me lose it; waiting for me to react. Fuck this. He's not bothered by it at all. During the silences, my suspicious mind starts ticking over again. Why come all the way up here? Take all this time to get here? We could've gone anywhere in the centre of town. The man turns up in the bar last night, talking all that shit, and now I'm sat here with him in a restaurant and he isn't saying anything. Did he want me to come out with him so he can pretend I'm his son? So people look at him and think 'ahhhh, that's nice, that fella's taking his son out for some dinner'. Is he known around here as some kind of weird loner and he thinks if he walks around with me, it looks like he's got family? Maybe he's a spy? Everything that's happened since we arrived at the hostel has been fucking odd and disturbing. And Marshy isn't here to confirm it for me so I can't tell if I'm being paranoid or if the fears I'm having are real.

We finish our food, pay, and go back to the hostel the same way we came. The shops are open but the streets are quiet, with hardly a person in sight. The roads are busier and it's still raining. The cars roll past slowly, spitting water into the air. Still no chat from the old tosser and I've given up trying to make conversation, so we sit in silence the whole way back, both looking out the windows as if we're strangers. When we get back to the hostel, I breathe a sigh of relief 'cause I can get away from this nutjob. From the entrance of the hostel, I go straight to my room to find Marshy, and he's lying down on his bed. I stay quiet at first, in case he's asleep, but he pipes up and catches me by surprise, just when I'm hoping to relax for a minute.

"Where the fuck have you been, man?"

"I went to get some food. You'll never fuckin' guess who with."

"Why? Who did you go with?"

"You know that old guy that was in the bar last night?"

"What, the American or the English guy?"

"The English one. Well guess what…he's only showed up here, at this hostel. He says he's stayin' here. He's about fuckin' sixty, mate. What's he doing here?"

"Mate, that's fucked up. Why did you go with him?"

"I was hungry and I wanted to try to suss him out. He was fuckin' weird though, mate, he barely said two words the whole time. He's fuckin' sketched me out. How you feelin'?"

"Bill. This place's fuckin' weird, man."

"You what? What're you on about? Somethin' happen whilst I was out?"

"It's fucked up in here, man, they've got little robotic cameras hidden in here, in this room; they're fuckin' watchin' us, mate."

I'm laughing at Marshy. "Naahhhh. Don't be silly, man!"

"No, I'm being serious, mate. And earlier, right, I tried to have a chat with one of the guys stayin' here. He was all fuckin' lairy with me, sayin' we'd come in, played pool and woke everyone up. I apologised to him but he got up and fucked off without sayin' anythin' to me."

"Have you been outside yet, mate?"

"No, man, I didn't wanna go outside on my own 'cause we're being watched. This is seriously fucked up, mate!"

Initially, I'm concerned about Marshy's mental state, 'cause usually, he's level-headed and on the ball. I haven't had a great deal of sleep so I get into my bed and lay down for a while, to rest my eyes. I'm so tired but I can't switch off. All these things happening at once, my head can't cope. We're both silent for a few moments and then I hear a noise. The door is closed most of the way, but there's a small opening to the outside so I know the sound definitely came from inside the room and it's the same kind of sound that Marshy described – an electronic movement like a CCTV camera turning or some kind of robotic arm. I become alarmed. I start looking around the room for anything that might be making the sound – under the bed, in the drawers, along the sides of the walls. I can't see all the way under the bed, as the mattress is blocking the light from getting through. If I was on my own I'd be questioning myself, but me and Marshy are both hearing the same noises at the same times. There are no CCTV cameras on the walls.

"There it was. Did you hear that?"

"Yeah, I heard it. Fuck, mate, that's weird…I've never heard that sound in a hotel room. D'ya reckon there's somethin' in the wiring?"

"If you say so, man, but I'm sure we're being watched. I think they've got some kind of little gadget out there, that they can control."

"What, you reckon it's the people stayin' here? Like they've been planted here to fuck with our heads?"

We stop talking for a moment and hear sounds of laughter coming from the living room. Marshy is certain it's them.

"Mate, you can hear them outside, they're listenin' to us and laughin' every time we finish speakin'."

"Fuck. That's weird."

We can hear them laughing in the TV room about fifteen metres outside our room, just as Marshy says – whenever we finish talking. They're silent whilst we speak.

"Maybe we're just being paranoid, Marshy? You know, from the drugs?"

"I don't know, maybe we are, but what if we're not?"

"You need to get up and get some food. Come on, mate, I'll go with you."

Now, I'm becoming wary of the other people in the hostel, which is putting me on edge even more. Marshy gets dressed and we go for a walk to find the nearest place to get some food. It's too far to go back to where I've just been so we stick to the area nearby. We walk along Ponce De Leon, away from the city centre; it's around nine pm and it's dark. My mind is spinning with thoughts of what's happening. We walk up the road, not knowing where we're going, but searching for a Wendy's or a KFC. I didn't think it would be hard to find one in this land of junk food, but after walking for fifteen minutes, all we've seen is a Dunkin Donuts. We turn around, walk back past the hostel and up the other way, where we see a petrol station. I go in to buy some cigarettes whilst Marshy waits outside on the forecourt. When I step outside, Marshy's spotted something and he's whispering to me.

"Walk with me down here, I wanna check somethin'." He's acting like some kind of detective, but he looks worried. We cross the road and carry on, further away from the hostel.

"Don't look back right now, but did you see that black four--by-four with the tinted windows, outside the petrol station?"

I'm looking straight ahead.

"Oh yeah, parked up against the wall. What about it?"

"Yeah, well the same fuckin' four-by-four was parked outside the hostel when we walked out half an hour ago. No shit, Bill. The engine was runnin' when we walked out. It followed us up to Dunkin Donuts and turned around in the car park, and now it's followed us here. We're being followed."

"Are you serious? Marshy, you better not be jokin'. That's some mad shit if it's true."

"Look, I'll prove it you, let's go down here and see if it follows us again."

I don't want to believe him, but he's got no reason to lie to me, of all people. We take a left turn, which leads us down a slope and into a large, half-full supermarket car park. As we walk down the steps, towards the entrance of the supermarket, the same black four-by-four takes a left turn, from the main road, and enters the car park. Maybe we aren't being paranoid! We smoke a ciggie at the entrance, waiting to see if anyone gets out, but there's no sign of movement and the vehicle is sitting there, stationary, with the lights turned off. So we go inside. I'm beginning to lose any sense of rationality now. I can't find any other reasons to explain this besides being followed. All my fears about the old guy are being confirmed by what's happened to Marshy whilst I was out and now both of us being tailed. I'm starting to lose my grip on reality and we're both panicking.

We walk to the freezer section of the supermarket to look for some pizzas, but we're both distracted by the thought of being followed. On the inside, I'm shitting myself, but I'm trying to act as if nothing's wrong. We don't know what they look like, so everyone in the supermarket is a potential culprit. A man with a large dark coat on walks past us; he's talking on his mobile phone. He walks behind us as we're facing the freezers and continues ten metres past us; then he stops. Marshy whispers under his breath.

"Did you hear what he's sayin'?"

"Yeah, I heard him say 'They're in here'."

"See, I told you, man!"

"Fuck!"

"What're we gonna do, Bill?"

"We need to get back to the hostel. D'ya wanna get some food first?"

"No, man, let's just go. This isn't right."

"You haven't eaten anythin' though. You need to eat somethin' mate."

"I'll be alright. Let's keep calm and act as if nothin's wrong. We don't want them to know we've sussed them out."

We walk out, trying our best to remain in control of ourselves, or look as if we are, at least. We go back to the hostel, then straight to our room. There's no privacy 'cause of the camera devices they've put in our room. Wherever we go we can't get away from these people – we've been set up, it's a trap, there's no escaping them. We're both starting to panic.

We can hear people talking in the living room again and we're both quiet, listening intently to what is being said. The two English wrestlers, who haven't said a word to us since we arrived, are talking about us, and the birds are laughing along at what they're saying.

"I'm gonna smash their heads in. I'm gonna pick them both up by the throat and slam their heads on the floor."

"Can you hear them out there, Marshy?"

"Yeah, I can hear them talkin' about us. They're plannin' on comin' after us."

"They must be working with the people followin' us and watchin' us on those cameras, they're all workin' together."

Scarper

We take a ten minute breather to assess what's happening and make a decision on what to do next. We're sat down on the bottom bunk beds, looking at each other. There's an awkward tension between us. We don't need to tell each other, as we both know; we're in deep shit and we're stranded. We take it in turns to come up with ideas, but brush them off, and then there's a silence again.

Our door isn't closed properly. The old English man from the bar is out there. The Brazilian guy, Mikel, who I got the weed from, is talking with them all. He's the only one I thought was normal, but he's laughing and joking with the wrestlers. He must be in on this as well; he must have got me stoned to fuck with my head. I can see it now, they're all working together. It's all planned; they've all got their roles to play.

I feel threatened; I can't think straight; I don't know what to do with myself. Marshy's the same. We're pacing around the room. Initially, we think about staying the night and leaving in the morning, but knowing we're being followed and those wrestlers are planning to attack us, we decide to get out straight away, in case something bad happens during the night. We pack our bags. I go to the receptionist and ask her to call us a taxi; she's sorted one to arrive in fifteen minutes. I go back to the room with Marshy. After a few minutes, we start panicking again – now they know we're leaving, they might try to get us before we go; we need to get out of the room. We head towards the exit door to go and wait outside for the taxi.

As I walk out, I see Mikel sitting on a ledge by the exit door. He must have been trying to be my mate to get close to us, find things out about us, and pass the information on. I rush towards the door, hindered by the size and weight of my bag. Everyone in the room stops talking and turns towards us. Mikel stops me.

"Hey man, where you going?"

I'm trying to keep my composure on the surface 'cause underneath I'm a pile of nerves.

"Going to the next place, man."

"Ah, man! Don't go, man – you only arrive di other day!"

"Sorry, mate, I've gotta go."

"Why you go so soon?"

"I've just gotta be somewhere. Sorry, man."

He lowers his voice and whispers to me, whilst making the hand actions of smoking a joint at the same time. "But what about di, errr…you know…the money? For di smoke?" He's trying to stall me.

"Don't worry about it, you can keep it."

He was probably trying to set me up – he'll get me the weed and then I'll get busted. Fuck that – he can have it. I need to get out of this room; I don't want to be standing around, waiting for the taxi whilst everyone from the hostel is standing there watching us, asking questions; it's doing my head in. We're in a bad place and we need to get away as soon as possible; neither of us know where we're going, but I'll go anywhere to get away from this place and these people.

I say goodbye to Mikel and he tries to make us stay. You're not going to fool me, you cheeky cunt, I know what you're up to. I shake him by the hand, say goodbye. We exit the building, no goodbyes from anyone else. Five minutes later, the taxi pulls up, so we throw our bags in the boot and get in the car. Thank fuck that's over; now we can relax. We need this driver to get us out of here.

"Hi there, folks. Where can I take you today?"

"D'ya know any other hostels around here?"

"Uh, no, not really, this here is the main place to stay for travellers."

"D'ya know any other hotels or motels you could take us to?"

"Uh, yeah I know a few places. What kinda place you lookin' for?"

"Anywhere, mate; anywhere you think's alright."

"Uhhh, okay, I think I know a place…" The taxi driver radios his destination to his office. As we leave, Marshy's checking behind and around us, to see if anyone is following us. We're whispering to each other, trying not to alarm the taxi driver.

"Marshy, d'ya see anyone?"

"I dunno, I can't tell from here, I'll check in a few minutes."

We're silent in the taxi, looking out for cars or four-by-four's like the one that followed us to the supermarket. The ride to the next hotel takes twenty minutes. We must be on the outskirts of the city; the space around us has become darker, as there are fewer streetlights and fewer buildings. It's hard to make out exactly what our surroundings look like. There isn't anyone immediately behind us, so it looks like we might be okay. Maybe those guys just wanted us out of the hostel. But why?

As we approach the turning for the hotel, the taxi driver tells us it's at the top of the hill. We can see a large building in the distance and there's a long driveway leading up a hill, to the car park and the entrance. The driveway's lit up on either side and there are flags and plants all the way up. When we get halfway up the hill, we see a row of four black SUV's with tinted windows, parked bumper to bumper, blocking off the entrance to the car park. We can see it in the distance about fifty metres away. I push

Marshy's shoulder to get his attention.

"Shit! Mate, can you see that up there?"

Marshy jolts his head, quickly looking out the windscreen. "What?"

"Look at all those SUV's blockin' the entrance."

"You've gotta be fuckin' kiddin' me. What the fuck?"

They're exactly the same kind of vehicles as the one that followed us to the supermarket. I change the plan.

"Um, excuse me, Mr driver, can we go to a different place please, not this one."

"Er, okay; it looks like we can't get in here anyway. There's another place up the road but it ain't as nice as this place. It's probably cheaper actually. Do you wanna give that place a go?"

"Yes, mate, that's fine, take us there, please."

Just when we think we're safe. This is fucking ridiculous. It can't only be the people at the hostel following us; it's some fucking gang with a fuckload of blacked-out vehicles. What the fuck have we done to deserve this? What do this bunch of cunts want?

The driver does a three point turn in the middle of the driveway; every second of hesitation adds to our anxiety. He must have picked up on the panic in our voices by now; I think he knows from our whispering and nervous behaviour that something's wrong. He's driving faster and speeding up his actions; he probably wants to dump us, get his money and fuck off… unless…unless he's part of this too and he's been told where to take us? Where the fuck are we going now?

He drives back on to the main road, carries on another half--mile and turns up a driveway to a much smaller motel. It's a budget motel, old and run down; a small and eerie place. The paint on the surface of the building is starting to flake off. It's a shithole. As we approach the entrance, there's a short tunnel in the side of one of the motel walls, which leads through to a courtyard; that's the car park. There aren't any cars blocking the entrance this time. The motel has three floors and the doors to the rooms all look out onto the car park in the middle. There are grey concrete stairways at intermittent points around the courtyard that lead up to the first and second floors; but no lifts. It's a no-frills motel, as cheap as it gets without having to share bunk beds or dormitories, like you do in a hostel. The reception is in the tunnel on our right-hand side as we drive through, and it's lit up inside. The taxi drives into the courtyard, turns around, and stops in the tunnel to drop us off. We might as well chance our luck here; at least we'll have our own room where we can lock ourselves in and get away from those twats that are chasing us.

I'm wondering how those four-by-four's knew where we were going. Did the taxi driver take us there on purpose? If it wasn't him, was his radio transmission intercepted? If that's the case, it would take some pretty sophisticated gang to have the money to buy all this expensive technology; pay all the men and buy all those black SUV's with the tinted windows – they aren't cheap! Whoever's putting us through this has obviously got a shitload of money and a network of employees. Surely it can't be the CIA or FBI? What the fuck would they want with us? I know America's paranoid right now, after nine-eleven, but what the fuck would they think we're doing?

We pay the taxi driver, get out of the car quickly, and get our bags. I say thank you to him through gritted teeth 'cause I suspect he's part of this setup. He speeds off, happy to be rid of us. We go to the reception to see if we can get a room. There's a white, middle-aged man behind the desk and a large black security guard, peering round from a separate adjoining room. I'm hurrying my words uncontrollably.

"Um, er, excuse me, have you got any spare rooms, please?"

"Just a minute, sir…I think you're in luck. Twin room is it, sir?"

"Yes, yes, we'll take a twin room please."

"That'll be sixty dollars for the night. Just the one night is it, sir?"

"Yeah, just one night. Thank you." I pay him and I'm ready with my hand out, waiting for the key. Come on, you fucking loser, we haven't got all day. Those fucking SUV's might be coming any fucking second. I need to get in that room, now!

"Okay, sir, your room number is one-one-four and breakfast starts at seven am. Enjoy your stay, sir."

Red Alert

Even though the motel costs the same as two nights at the hostel, I don't give a fuck. I've also lost forty dollars on the weed and the taxi has cost us another twenty dollars, but right now, any concept of the value of money has flown out the window; we're fearing for our lives here and we just want to be in a room with a lock, by ourselves. We can only trust each other now. The only thing that's stopping me from completely losing it is that Marshy's here; if this was happening to me on my own, fuck knows what I'd do.

The receptionist points to our room; it's on the ground floor. We're directly opposite the security guard's office. I make brief eye contact with him and wave the key in the air, so he can see it. We walk briskly over the courtyard, weaving in and out of the stationary cars, towards our door. The car park is half full and it's around midnight. The lights on the walls are giving off a dim orange glow, creating shadows at different angles. I'm alert to any movements and sounds, preparing myself to react if anyone attacks us.

As we get closer to our room, a middle-aged black lady storms out of the door next to the left of ours. There are two children with her, about two and five years old. She's carrying the youngest and the other one is standing next to her. The mother is rushing frenetically to get her bags and close the door to the room. They all look worried. The standing child is looking up at her mother.

"Why are we going, Mommy?"

The mother ignores the question. "Come on, get your bag. Let's go, please."

She hurries into her car, making no eye contact with us, not even acknowledging us. This gets me thinking – why would a mum be leaving a hotel room at midnight with her two young kids, just as we're arriving? That's not right; they must have paid for the room. Why would you pay for a room and then leave at midnight? They must have been told to get out. But by who? The receptionist? Is he in on this as well? Has he been told to get them out of that room by the people chasing us? No-one else is leaving, just the people in the room next to ours. It's fucking weird. We enter our room. Half the way down the adjoining wall, there's a door that leads to the room the lady and her kids have vacated. Is it a coincidence she was leaving, when there's another door to get into our room in hers? I don't think it is.

We throw our bags down near the window at the front of the room and lock the door behind us. It's got three locks on it – a bolt lock at the top, a bolt lock at the bottom, and a big catch lock in the middle which you can double lock. I check the door to the room next door and it's locked, but you could unlock it if you've got the right key. This isn't ideal but we've already paid for it so we're going to have to stick with our choice; we've got nowhere else to go. The window is covered with white netting and we can see directly into the car park. We don't want anyone looking in, so Marshy draws the curtains.

There are two double beds against the wall, on the right-hand side. The furniture is old and the air smells of old cigarettes, like the grotty place we had in Miami. At the back of the room, on the right, is a bathroom, boxed off by two walls. Against the back wall, next to the bathroom, there's a big round mirror with a worktop. We sit down on our beds. I'm holding my hands around the back of my head and looking towards the ceiling;

Marshy's got his head in his hands, rubbing his face.

"This is seriously fucked up, Marshy."

"Why was that woman leavin' with her kids at this time of night?"

"I dunno. It's fuckin' weird."

Marshy gets up and starts looking around the room. "Are there phones in these rooms?"

"Yeah, here, look. On the bedside table, between the beds."

"They must have phoned her up and told her to get out. What d'ya reckon, Bill?"

"D'ya think the motel staff know what's going on, too?"

"Yeah, maybe. Every other fucker seems to be in on this."

"Maybe they've set this room up for us on purpose; they've forced us here. Think about it; the other motel was blocked off and this is the next one along. The taxi driver was made to take us here and that woman, with the kids, was told to leave so they can get to us through that room next door."

"We need to listen out and see if anyone else goes in that room. They could've paid the receptionist off with a bit of cash to let them box us in this room, don't you think?"

"I don't fuckin' know, man. I dunno what the fuck's going on. I dunno if I can take much more of this."

As we're talking, there's a noise in the room next door. We're whispering to each other so no-one else can hear us.

"I just heard someone in that room."

"What? That bird only left a few minutes ago!"

"Come over here; listen a second…"

We creep over to the door between the rooms and press our ears up against it; we're facing each other.

"See? Can you hear them?"

"Yeah, I can hear them. I can't make out what they're sayin' though." Marshy's distracted by something in the courtyard. He walks over towards the window and peers through a gap between the curtains. "Bill, cars are comin' in!"

"What? Those SUV's?"

"One four-by-four and three other cars. They've parked up."

"Turn off the lights, quick!"

We're sitting on our beds, trembling with fear. There are people in the room next door, and people in cars outside. We're surrounded; we're trapped; we've been backed into a corner and we've got nowhere left to run. We've barely slept and we're hungover. The situation is going from bad to worse. This is turning into a nightmare. What the fuck do these people want from us? How much longer can this go for?

As we sit inside the dark room with all the lights off, we're watching the shadows of people walking past our room, outside. We're sitting in unbearable silence, pointing out shadows to each other when we see them, to confirm we're both seeing the same thing. They're walking past our door and stopping by the staircase outside. We can hear the sounds of male voices; it sounds like they're trying to coordinate a plan. I walk over to the main door, intently watching the locks and light coming through the gaps in the doorframe. By the floor, I can see shadows cast from people standing outside, moving around slowly. They're going to try and break in by picking the locks, and probably through the side door, leading to the room next to us. The suspense is increasing and I'm breathing heavily. It's becoming too much for me to handle. I feel like I'm going to explode with anger and shout something out. I pace around for a few minutes but enough's enough.

"Right, this has gone too far. I'm gonna go and speak to them." I bound over to the main door. Marshy tries to stop me.

"No, Bill, don't go out there, you dunno what'll happen to you!"

"I can't take this anymore, man. I wanna know what they want." As I get closer to the door, I see the shadows of the people outside scurry away. I stand at the door for a few minutes to listen for any movement outside, but there's no sound, so I open it, slowly and carefully.

I poke my head out without stepping out of the room. If they're going to get us, then now's their chance. I'm preparing myself to fight. There's no-one in sight. They must be hiding behind the cars and the staircases. At first, all I can hear is the sound of the wind blowing around the courtyard. Then a tapping sound starts. It sounds like it's coming from the first floor. It's the noise of a heavy metal object being hit against the hollow metal barriers, which stretch around the perimeter of the corridors on the floors above us. I can't see who's doing it; they must be directly above me. It's a distinct, regular, three-tap pattern followed by a pause: tink, tink, tink...tink, tink, tink.

I'm shitting myself and I don't want to go out any further. I just want to stay inside the room. They're toying with us, mentally torturing us. They're doing this to fuck with our heads 'cause they know we've got nowhere else to run and we're boxed in. I go back inside and close the door, making sure I lock all of the locks. Marshy's sitting on his bed, closest to the door. I tell him what I've just heard and he's shaking his head in disbelief.

We're both restless and we can't sit in one place for more than a few minutes.

Marshy's seen something. He grabs my shoulder and points

to the window.

"What is it?"

"Bill, look at the fuckin' window. Look at those fuckin' red lasers!"

Two single red beams of light are shining through the window. They must be from laser guided guns. They're searching around the room, trying to focus on us, one each. If they get fixed on us, they can shoot us. We're fucked.

"Oh fuck! Fuck! We're gonna be fuckin' shot, Bill! They're gonna fuckin' kill us!"

I can see the full length of the lasers stretching across the room and the red dots they're making on the walls, where the beams finish. We're trying to evade them by crouching down behind the beds. I can only think the worst – if those beams get focused on either one of us for long enough, we're going to be shot and there's no way for us to get out of here. It's inevitable; they're going to get us; this could be the end for both of us. My heart's beating frantically; I can feel the thudding inside my chest, my neck, and the back of my head as I anticipate the sound of a gun firing. Is this really happening? Are we both really seeing these laser beams? They must be there, if Marshy can see them too? We move to the back of the room, in the alcove next to the bathroom entrance, as far away from the window as we can get. We're standing opposite each other, with our backs against the walls. I'm standing by the entrance to the bathroom; the laser that is searching for me can't get me here. Marshy's opposite me, next to the door that leads to the neighbouring room. If we can evade the lasers, they can't shoot us. We agree not to go in the bathroom as we won't know if someone's trying to break in.

I've lost all concept of time. I don't know how long we've

been standing here – five minutes? An hour? I can see the thin red laser beams moving around the area where we're standing, still searching for us. They're close, just missing me but targeting Marshy every few seconds.

"It's on me now, I can see it."

When it focuses on him, he turns his head sideways and tilts it up, with a petrified look on his face, like these seconds are going to be his last, like he's staring death in the face.

The laser that was searching for me has disappeared, but just when I think I'm safe, another one appears from a gap in the doorframe to the neighbouring room. It's pointing up from near the floor towards my head. Marshy tells me it's plumb on my forehead. It flashes in my eye for a split second, so I move my head around to get away from it. We're both shivering, nervous wrecks. I'm looking at the floor by the door and I can see insects crawling through the gaps and moving towards me. I think they're spiders. Are the people outside doing this? They're only coming towards me, none of them are going to Marshy. How are they doing this? It's paralysing me; I can't move my body. I'm rooted to the floor with fear. I can only feel my head; everything from the neck down is paralysed. They're getting closer, they're crawling up my shoes and up the inside of my trousers, all over my body; but I can't feel anything; my body has shut down. I must be hallucinating, but I can't stop to focus on the insects – I'm too worried about the laser getting a target on me. I break out of the paralysis; the trance. I wipe my body down and shake my legs to get the spiders off me, and I move around into the bathroom doorway to escape the clutches of the laser. I see a red dot on the back wall; it moves downwards and flickers on the surface of a plastic water bottle. This is real, this is happening.

We're panting, out of breath; the expressions on our faces are mirrored. Our eyebrows are raised up as far as they can go, our eyes wide open, nostrils flared and jaws dropped.

"This is it, Bill. They're gonna shoot us! I know it!"

"Surely, if they were gonna shoot us, they would've done it by now?"

When we realise the lasers have disappeared, we're able to breathe a sigh of relief; a precious few minutes to allow our bodies to recover. It feels like I've just run a long race; I'm trying to regulate my breathing. But it's not long before they're at it again.

Outside our room we can see the lights of a car. It's reversing into the parking space directly outside our room. It stops moving, but the engine is still running.

"What's that noise, Marshy? Can you hear it?"

"It's comin' from the air vent above the front door, up there."

"What d'ya think they're tryin' to do? Hang on…can you smell somethin'?"

We walk to the main door together and sniff the air.

"Shit, Marshy. I can smell fumes."

"They must be tryin' to gas us out."

"Oh shit, man, they're tryin' to poison us."

"Those fuckin' cunts. They're using the fumes from their car's exhaust."

"They've probably put some kind of pipe up through that vent."

Marshy looks around the room. He picks up the clean towels on our beds. "Quick! Get this over your face and breathe through it."

"Let's get into the bathroom. Come on!"

We take it in turns to wet the towels under the cold tap.

We're holding them over our mouths and noses, still able to see. This is our last option. We're backed as far into the corner as possible. Nowhere left to run. Are we both going to die in a shitty motel bathroom? I peer out the door, with the towel still covering half of my face, and I look up at the vent. Next to it is a plastic lever that closes and open the curtains; it's melting. The fumes are so powerful, they're melting the plastic lever. That can't be real, can it? Are we really smelling these fumes? Am I just hallucinating the lever melting? We can't risk it, we might die. I go back inside the bathroom, hoping the gas won't reach back far enough to intoxicate us. If we inhale it we're as good as dead.

"Marshy, has this room got air conditionin'?"

"Yeah, I think it has."

"Let's turn it on to get rid of those fumes."

We both leave the bathroom and start looking for the control panel on the wall. Marshy finds it and starts the fans.

We're outside the bathroom again, in the same places as before, but holding the towels to our faces. The sound of the fumes coming through the vent has stopped, but the red lasers are coming through the window again. We're not as scared of the lasers this time. We're more concerned with keeping the towels to our faces until the smell of the fumes is gone. We can't bring ourselves to open the curtains to see where the lasers are coming from; we're too scared to see what might be out there. I wanna check the smell in the air by the vent, so I tiptoe over to the main door. My eyes have adapted to the darkness and there's enough light from outside to make out the fixtures and fittings in the room. I catch a glimpse of movement on one of the locks on the main door. Looking closer, I notice that the screws in the middle lock are starting to turn, one at a time. This is it. They're making their move to get in. They're breaking down our last defences. We thought we were safe, but if the screws come out, the locks will just fall to the floor. How are they doing this? They must be using some kind of magnet. The screws are turning around slowly, loosening. My mind's frozen; I can't think straight. I don't want to go outside 'cause I might get shot. We put a table in front of the door and go to our places at the back of the room.

I've had enough now. I've reached saturation point. They haven't killed us, they're just trying all kinds of different tricks to fuck with our heads. Well, it's fucking worked. We've been shitting ourselves all night and I can't take any more of this. I need to find out what the fuck is going on and what these cunts want. I'm going out there to face up to them. As I walk towards the door, I see the shadows running away. I pull the table out of the way and Marshy's behind me. We step outside and it's starting to get light. I've got the key for the room in my hand, in case the door shuts on us. This ordeal must have lasted four or five hours; our bodies on high alert the whole time; it's exhausted us. The daylight is helping to calm us down; we can see all around us now. The car park seems emptier than when we arrived. Our stalkers must have left for the night, but we can't be sure. Marshy storms out of the room into the middle of the car park and puts his hands in the air. He's looking up and down the balconies, calling out.

"Come on! Come out and show us who you are." He thinks they might still be hiding there.

"Marshy, get back inside, man. Marshy, the fuckin' security guard's over there."

"I can't take this anymore, man."

It looks like they've gone. The tricks they were playing have stopped. It's light now so they've fucked off; the other guests will be getting up for breakfast soon, and they'd look suspicious sat in their cars at this time of the morning. I try to convince Marshy they've gone, at least for the time being. I'm dealing with the situation better than Marshy is and I'm trying to calm him down. He hasn't eaten anything for more than twenty-four hours now, so that can't help his mental state; he needs some food.

We sit in silence on our beds for a few minutes whilst we try to compose ourselves, sort our heads out, and get a grip on reality. Whilst I don't think I'm going to die right now, I'm still trying to come to terms with the fact that we're being chased and neither of us have got the slightest clue why. We're not at the point where we can even have that conversation though; we need to figure out what to do next. There's an unexpected knock at the door. We both spring up from our beds. Is this it? Is this them? I walk over to the door, apprehensively.

"Who is it?"

"Can you open the door please?"

I look at Marshy on his bed and he shrugs his shoulders like he's ready to accept his fate.

"Might as well see what he's gotta say."

I open the door with the chain lock on, just enough to see who's there. It's the security guard.

"Hello," I say.

"Hey, man. I need to speak to y'all a second, let me come in there a minute."

He closes the door behind him, leaning against the wall by the door. I stand back a few metres with my arms folded. Marshy stays lying down on the bed with his eyes closed.

"Now what y'all doing in here?"

"Oh, there's no problem, my friend can't sleep, that's all."

"Now look, man, I just saw him come outside and I heard him shoutin' some crazy ass shit about come out here, show yourself, or some shit. What's been going on in here?"

"There's no problem, honestly, mate, he's just tired."

"Aight, whatever. Look, man, maybe you should get the guy some beer or somethin', help calm his ass down. I can't have people shoutin' around like that, y'all. Somebody gonna call the police up in here. D'ya feel me?"

"Oh shit, yeah, sorry about that, mate. I hope we didn't wake anyone up."

"Now look, why don't y'all take a walk wid me up to the gas station and we'll get some beers."

"Marshy, do you want a beer?"

"Yeah, that would be good, man."

"Aight. There's a place just up the road. It's open twenty-four hours and, errr, I need some food anyway so let's go."

I want the beer but I'm worried that if I walk up there with him, I'm going to get bundled into a car and taken off somewhere.

"Errrr, I dunno; can you just give me some directions and I'll go up there myself?"

Now instead of being all laid back, he's getting all assertive.

"Look, I need you to come out here 'cause I need to talk to you. Now come on; the gas station's two minutes' walk."

If I don't go with him, I reckon he might grass us up to the police, so I take the plunge and start walking. I recognise him from when we first arrived so I've convinced myself it'll be okay; he's quite fat anyway, so I fancy myself to outrun him if I need to. The idea of having a beer, to take the edge off the nerves, appeals

223

to me, and I think Marshy really needs it too. I feel so vulnerable right now; I'm open to any ideas that might help my state of mind. I tell Marshy I'll be back in ten minutes. I'm worried to leave him there on his own but I haven't got a choice. I can get him some food too. He's lying on the bed, looking at the ceiling with both hands on his forehead, palms facing upwards. It seems like the main threat has gone now and the security guard seems alright. I wonder if he's seen anything during the night, but I don't want to ask him, in case he's part of it all.

I walk up to the gas station and I'm chatting to this security guard – the normal small talk about where we're from and how old we are. When we get into the shop, the guard picks up some snacks, while I get some beers, cigarettes, and crisps. I pay for it all. As we're walking back, I find out what the guard has really been wanting to ask.

"Look, man, I need to set somethin' straight with y'all. Now I dunno what the hell's bin going on in ya room, and to be honest wit' ya, I don't really care too much either but…part of my job's to report anythin' suspicious I see to the police. Understand what I'm sayin'?"

"Uh well, what d'ya mean by–"

"Look I'll spell it out for ya. I'm gonna give you a choice: I can either call the police and get them to deal with this or…well, you know, you can make it worth my while not to."

"Okay then. How much d'ya want?"

"Let's not do this here. Wait till we get back to my office."

We arrive back to the motel reception and walk into his office.

"Come inside here a minute, man," he says.

"Alright, how much d'ya want?"

"Tell me how much ya got and I'll tell ya if it's enough."

"Look, I've got forty dollars on me." I empty my pockets to show him forty dollars is all I have, except for a few coins. "Look, I'm young and I haven't got much. Please don't call the police, please!" I'm begging. The power of money is right there in his hands. He's laughing at me.

"Shiiiit! You want me to risk my job for forty bucks?!"

"It's all I've got, I promise you!"

"What about ya friend in there?"

"He hasn't got a cash card – he left it in an ATM, back in Miami."

I don't actually know if Marshy has got any money on him, so this is a massive risk.

"Damn. Aight, but not a word of this gets out. You didn't speak to me about this and I didn't take no money from you, gat it?"

"Sure. Of course. And thank you…I guess."

Hustled again. I've lost count how many times it's happened now. Everywhere we go, there are fucking cunts trying to make a quick buck from us. But given the circumstances, I couldn't give a fuck right now. We're alive when we thought we were going to get killed. The fresh air and conversation with a level-headed person has done me good; it's helped me calm down, but my mind and body are still stressed. I walk back to the motel room and open the door to find Marshy lying down on his bed with the TV on, but he's not in a good way. I set the beers down on the side table.

"Mate, are you okay?"

"There's somethin' moving under my bed, man, I can feel it."

"There's nothin' under your bed, mate."

"There is, I can feel it moving, listen…I can still hear them talkin' next door as well. Look, my foot's twitchin' and whenever it twitches they're laughin', I can hear them!"

I can hear the people next door but I'm pretty sure we're safe for the time being; it's light and the security guard is across the courtyard. I try to take his mind off it.

"Look, mate, I've got us some beers. I think we need 'em. That bloke's right, it'll help calm us down."

"Yeah, okay."

"Here you go." I pass a beer to Marshy and try to change the conversation.

"D'ya know what that cheeky bastard did?"

"No, what?"

"He made me bribe him with all the money I had on me, not to call the police."

"Not to call the police for what?"

"He saw you go outside, in the middle of the car park when you shouted out, and he says he's supposed to report anythin' suspicious to the police."

"How much did you give him?"

"Forty bucks!"

"Forty bucks! The cheeky cunt! Fuckin' hell, I'll pay you back, mate."

"Don't worry about that, mate. He's not callin' the pigs."

"Are you sure about that? He could be callin' them right now."

"Nah. I don't reckon he will. He seemed alright. I was chattin' to him on the way up to the gas station."

"Did you ask him if he saw anyone outside durin' the night?"

"No, I didn't wanna get into any of that. He was in that office though, so he must have fallen asleep."

"Or they paid him to turn a blind eye – he's obviously open to bribes!"

"That's a good point. Maybe that's why he came knockin' on our door. He knew what was going on and he knew he could make some extra money out of it."

"I think we need to get out of here soon as, mate."

"Yeah, definitely. They know where we are. We're sittin' ducks at the moment. I reckon we need to get to the airport and go somewhere else. Have you got any money for a taxi?"

"Yeah, I think I've got thirty or forty dollars in my bag."

"Sweet. That should do it."

Good job that security officer didn't check Marshy too.

Shake

We drink our beers and check the time; it's close to seven am. We're ready to get out of this place. I'd rather top myself than stay here another night. Whoever's chasing us wants us out of Atlanta. Fuck the budget restraints; we're getting a flight out of Atlanta to the next place – Austin, Texas. We could get an Autodriveaway car but we'll be easy targets.

There'll be a lot more people in the airport, so we'll be less likely to run into trouble. As soon as it hits seven o'clock, we pick up our bags and head straight to the reception. The car park seems like a different place now. We eat some doughnuts and drink some coffee, whilst waiting for a taxi to arrive. Hopefully the food will sort our heads out. We're calming down with the thought of getting out of Atlanta. The taxi arrives.

"Can you take us to the airport, please?"

"No problem, sir."

The taxi makes its way down the driveway towards the main road and turns right. We're driving down the road, gaining speed. A white van with blacked-out windows comes flying out from one of the side roads. It skids as it turns the corner sharply, and latches onto our tail. It's following us – every turn we make, every lane we go into; it's five metres behind us. Here we go again. I feel my brain descend straight back into a state of panic and fear.

"Marshy, did you see that white van come flyin' out? D'ya think that's them?"

"Yeah, that's definitely them again. I don't believe this."

"We need to lose them."

Marshy leans forwards between the seats, to speak to the driver.

"Excuse me, mate, but we're being followed by that white van behind us, can you try and lose them, please?"

"Err, right, okay, I'll go as fast as I can."

We're in the middle lane of an interstate road that leads to Atlanta airport. The van's getting closer to us, switching lanes and driving up alongside us, on our right. I take a quick glimpse out the window at the van but can't see the people inside, as the windows are tinted. Part of me is glad I can't see them; I'm so frightened. I can't stand them being alongside us 'cause I think they're going to ram us off the road. I just want to be out of this taxi and in the airport, so we can get out of this fucked-up place.

The taxi driver knows the van is following us. He says he knows a back route to the airport. As we approach a slip road, he waits until the last second, presses the brakes down firmly, and the van goes straight past us. He turns sharply to his right, cutting across the slow lane and off the interstate, onto the slip road.

"I shouldn't really be doing that sort of thing."

I could swear this taxi driver is enjoying the chase. The van carries on along the interstate.

We think we've lost them and we're buzzing from the stunt the taxi driver has just pulled off. We turn into the airport and the taxi pulls in at the drop-off area. The same white van, with the blacked-out windows, comes flying past us at high speed.

"Oh no, Bill, there's that van again."

"Shit! Quick! Get the money for the taxi, now!"

The white van pulls up fifty metres ahead of us. I see the back of the van tip forwards, as they slam the brakes on. Back to panic stations. Marshy gets his money and pays the driver. We hurry out of the taxi, take our bags from the boot, and run into the airport through a set of rotating doors.

The airport building's like a huge warehouse with windows. There are hundreds of people walking in different directions, bumping into each other, changing their course randomly, as they struggle towards their check-in points with their luggage. It's organised chaos. All the activity around us is making me nervous. We've got no idea what our pursuers look like; they could be everywhere. As we delve further into the crowd of people, everyone we walk past becomes a suspect. We get our bearings inside the airport, looking around to find the ticket desks, well aware that the people from the van will be in here, looking for us. Marshy's on edge.

"Be careful who you walk past. They might try and stab us now, before we get on the plane."

"Yeah, we need to face different directions to cover each other's backs."

We're nervous; we know this may be their last chance to get us before we get a ticket to Austin and go through to the departure lounge. We're constantly checking around ourselves and trying to keep out of everyone's way, especially people walking directly towards us.

"There's no way I'm gonna be stabbed in an airport, Bill, I think we should tell a policeman we're being chased."

"Okay then, yeah, if they see us to talkin' to the police, it'll put them off."

"Look, there's one over there, let's go."

I don't want to get the police involved, but in this situation, we've got to. This is fucking life or death and we'll do whatever it takes to stay safe. We'll feel a lot safer if the police are involved. We walk over to the policeman, who's in full uniform. Initially, I feel a great sense of relief, 'cause we'll be safe with him. I'm hurrying to get my words out.

"Excuse me, officer; we need your help."

"Okay, I need you to calm down." He's pushing his hands towards the floor repeatedly, to accentuate his words. "Now, tell me what the problem is."

"We're being chased by a gang. They've been chasin' us for a day now."

"Are you sure about this?"

"Yeah, their white van just pulled up outside, it's followed us from our motel."

"Okay. Did you get a look at any of them? Can you give me a description of what they look like?"

"We dunno what they look like or why they're chasin' us. They were in a white van with black tinted windows, so we couldn't see them. Someone in a large, black SUV is followin' us too. We ran into the airport here as soon as we got out of the taxi so we didn't see any of them."

"Alright. Can you tell me why you think they're chasin' you?"

"We dunno. We haven't done anythin' to them."

"Right." The policeman is looking at both of us as if we're guilty of something; he's suspicious of us. "Give me your passports."

We hand them over to him. He opens them up to examine the personal details at the back.

"What are your names?"

"I'm Billy Walker."

"And I'm Andrew Marsh."

"In the same order, what are your dates of birth?"

We both tell him.

"What hand do you write with?"

I stop for a second, knocked back by the question, and then respond.

"My…errrr…left."

"Your left?"

"Yeah, I'm left-handed."

"Okay. I want you to remain calm and wait right here. Don't move from this spot. I'll be back in five minutes with your passports. Just stay here."

So this is fucking great. Now, we're left waiting in the middle of an open space; we're a sitting target. People around us have seen us talking to the policeman; some of them are giving us funny looks, turning their heads back as they walk past us; they want to know what the fuss is about. The policeman returns.

"Right. I've alerted the security guards to keep their eyes out for anythin' suspicious."

"Thank you, officer."

"Now, are you both flyin' from here?"

"Yeah, we are. We're gonna go to Austin, Texas."

"Right. I want you both gone and out of this airport within the next three hours. If you're not, then I'm gonna arrest you both and you'll be locked up overnight in the cells. Do you understand?"

We're startled by his response, but we don't question him out of fear that we'll anger him.

"Errrrm, okay, officer."

What a fucking bell-end. We go and ask this guy for help, thinking we'll be safe, but now, as if we haven't got enough to worry about, we've got a time limit on getting out of the airport or we'll be arrested! That's the last fucking thing we need! What a fucking load of bollocks that is. He hands our passports back and walks off. I'm fucked-off at the way he's spoken to us, like we're criminals. What a prick. Talk about kicking you whilst you're down. The fucking lazy, useless bastard just wanted to wash his hands of us.

We find a ticket desk. I want to get out now. Maybe having a time limit will force us to get an earlier flight. We've been told good things about Austin and some of the travellers we've met have advised us to go there. We purchase our tickets; our flight is departing in two hours. Perfect. That should keep that twat policeman satisfied. It's eight am and the flight is at ten am, so we go to check our bags in and head to the departure lounge.

At the security checks, the staff are hostile and curious, like they were in Miami. I walk through the metal detectors and my hand luggage is scanned. All the other people in front of us went straight through. I look back and Marshy's being stopped.

"Could you step aside please, sir?"

He looks annoyed. The staff are putting plastic gloves on. For a second, it looks like they're going to take him away for a full internal cavity search.

"Can you take off your shoes and socks please, sir?"

Marshy must be wondering, 'Why me? Why now?' But to be fair, we're a fucking mess. We're tired and we haven't showered for a few days now, so we probably stink pretty bad.

Every cunt is against us right now. After a thorough search, they let him go.

"Enjoy your trip, sir!"

Marshy puts his shoes back on and walks over to me.

"Fuckin' hell, mate, we must look like two fuckin' hobos right now…and I'm sure that twat was being sarcastic to me."

We walk up a big spiral staircase, to the departure lounge.

All the gates to board the planes are in the same area; it's a big open plan room. We're surrounded by enormous glass windows, which are letting the daylight stream in. We find a bar and order a beer. It's busy and all the tables are taken, so we have to stand. People are constantly coming and going. Maybe now we've made it to the other side, we can relax. We're close to getting away from this nightmare; we can start from scratch in Austin. I'm sure the people will be nicer there. But wait, Marshy's caught a glimpse of someone he recognises and points him out. He's over the other side of the bar and he's reading a paper; the way he's holding it is obscuring my view, so I can't get a proper look. As soon as he lowers the paper, to turn his next page, I see him. Lo and fucking behold, it's one of the English wrestlers from the hostel; I recognise his face and, in particular, his beard.

"No way, Marshy, fuckin' hell! We can't get away from these cunts! D'ya reckon it's them followin' us? Is the other one with him too?"

"I dunno. I haven't seen him yet."

"Let's wait and see if he's with anyone else."

"It must be them; they must be followin' us to Austin."

We wait a few minutes, trying not to stare at him. He doesn't look over at us at all, making me think he knows we're here; he doesn't want to make eye contact. No-one else joins him. He's obviously paid for a ticket to keep on our tail. It makes sense now – all the hostility started with them at the hostel – the camera devices in our room; being followed to the supermarket; the threats of attacking us. They must have followed us to the motel and he must have been in the van that followed us to the airport. I thought it was something to do with those two old fellas from the bar, during the Super Bowl, but maybe they're all in this together?

"We're gonna have to wait and see if that dickhead gets on our plane, Marshy."

"Yeah. Why don't we move away from here and see if he follows us?"

We leave our drinks and go to the smoking room. It's fucking horrific in here, one of the most rancid places I've ever had the displeasure of being. There are too many people; I'm getting claustrophobic. The ventilation is poor and the room is filled with everyone's second-hand smoke; you can't even see people's faces. Just walking in here and breathing for a few seconds is like smoking a whole pack of cigarettes. The smell is disgusting, like a gigantic, old ashtray. No-one is talking to each other. It's like death's waiting room. I never want to go in one of these rooms again. I've got to get out of here.

At our departure gate, we sit and wait for the plane to start boarding. I'm trying to figure out how different situations will pan out, depending on what happens next. It's like a game of chess – if they make this move then what will we do? If the wrestler gets on our plane, shall we stay on it? Do we change our flights? Do we leave the airport and get an Autodriveaway car? There's an office in Atlanta so we could get a car and drive to another city. But what if it goes wrong? What if that policeman sees us leave and arrests us? Or the chasers follow us and wait till we're on a long stretch of road with no-one around? They could run us off the road and shoot us. We've driven on the interstates out here and the stretches of road between cities are too long; we'd be vulnerable. We could end up being buried in a field, in the middle of nowhere. No way. We've got to stay in the airport and get a flight out of here.

Marshy's trying to distract himself from everything, by reading a paper he's found on the seats, but he can't stop himself from looking around. He leans towards me and whispers.

"Bill, you see that guy sat over there, to my right, with the hat on?"

I turn my head slightly, look out the corner of my eye, and spot him.

"What, that guy with the briefcase, readin' the paper?"

"Yeah."

"What about him?"

"He's got one of those red lasers. He's shining it at me. He's got it in his left hand...look."

"You're jokin'."

"Honestly, look..."

Marshy lifts his newspaper up and holds it wide open in front of him. A beam of red light hits the page.

"Fuckin' hell, first the guy from the hostel and now this bloke! They're in here too. How many of these fuckers are there?"

"The wrestler, he's at our gate as well. He's probably getting on our plane."

"We need to do somethin', Marshy."

"Like what?"

"I dunno, change our flight or somethin'."

"You think we should change our flight? Where are we gonna go?"

"I dunno...but if we go to Austin and they follow us out there, we're even further away from home. They've followed us here and it looks like they're getting on the plane too. Don't you think they'll follow us wherever we go?"

"Yeah, you're probably right, but I don't wanna go home yet, man."

"I know, I don't either. But they're gonna follow us every-where. Can you really put up with this for much longer?"

"This is fucked up. You're right."

"Maybe we should go back to Miami."

"Why Miami?"

"We can see if they follow us there. If they do, maybe we should just go home, and if they don't then we can go somewhere else."

"I dunno, man."

"Look, on top of being able to change our flights, we know the place already. We know the hotel where we stayed when we first came here, and we know the manager there."

"Alright then, Bill, but I think we should wait till the last minute and then go and change our flights."

"What about that policeman, though?"

"We've still got an hour and a half left; we should be alright. There must be a flight going to Miami from here."

"Let's go look at the departures screen; I wanna call my parents as well."

"Okay, I need to do that too."

We wait for the plane to start boarding and get up to stand in the queue. The man with the briefcase, who was shining the laser at Marshy, gets up, and joins the queue too. He's standing a few places behind us. When we get close to the stewardesses, we look at each other and make the gesture, with our heads, to leave the queue.

Walking back to the main entrance, I see a pay phone on the wall. I use my charge card to make a call to my parents, back in England. There's no answer so I leave a message on the answer-phone.

"Mum, Dad, it's Billy. I'm in Atlanta airport and I think a gang's chasin' us and I dunno why. I just wanted to tell you so you know where we are and what's going on. We're gonna fly back to Miami and call the British Embassy when we get there. Love you both and I'll call again soon. Bye."

I know the message will scare them and I'm sorry to do it to them, but at least they'll hear from me and at least I've told them I love them. I'm in a dangerous country thousands of miles away, where guns are legal and I'm being chased by a gang. I imagine they'll probably feel quite helpless and worried. But there isn't really much they can do right now.

We're back at the same desk where we bought our tickets to Austin. I ask if we can change our flight, to go to Miami instead. The attendant takes our tickets through a door at the back of the kiosk and we wait for twenty minutes. Why are they taking so long? What are they doing back there? Luckily, they allow us to change them, for no extra cost, and we're told to wait while they print off the new tickets. As we're waiting, a tall black man approaches the desk next to us and asks for fifteen tickets on the next plane to Miami – the same flight as ours. When asked how he would like to pay, he replies, "Cash", and pulls out his wallet. He's got a large wad of brand new notes and he's counting them out on the worktop. I'm nudging Marshy and whispering to him.

"Did you just hear that bloke buy fifteen tickets to Miami?"

"Yeah, I clocked him. He must be with the gang chasin' us. What shall we do?"

"We're fucked whatever we do…fuck it. We've just gotta get on the plane and go. Wherever we go they're gonna go to the same place and we can't stay here 'cause we'll get arrested, so we've gotta fly somewhere…and Miami's the best place to get home from so let's just stick to the plan."

They must have followed us out of the departure lounge, or maybe they've got people at the entrances as well. The ticket attendant took twenty minutes – maybe she's involved with this too? Maybe she was calling them up to tell them where we were changing our flights to? We can't tell. This gang, whoever they are, have got people of all different ages, races, and nationalities working for them. Everything that's happening to us is too contrived to be a coincidence; this is a set-up. The attendant comes back out.

"Okay, sir, I've changed your tickets for you. If you hurry you will just about make it – the plane's boardin' now."

We take our tickets and run back through the security checks. It's just dawned on me that our other luggage is already on the plane to Austin, which has boarded and is about to take off. From this point onwards, we're stuck with the clothes on our backs and what we've got in our hand luggage. We're left with the bare essentials – passport and bankcard. We get through the security checks again, run up the stairs and over to the correct gate. They're closing the doors.

"Excuse me, excuse me, can we get on please?"

"Sorry, sir, boarding is finished. You've just missed it."

We stand there, dumbfounded. Not only have we lost our luggage, but we're going to get arrested now, too.

"Only kiddin', sir! Can we see your boardin' passes please?"

Any other time and that would be funny, but right now I could slap that smarmy bastard. We board the pain with a massive sigh of relief.

We get on the plane and look for our seats. It's a small plane with capacity for about one hundred people. The first six rows at the front are full but the rest of the plane is empty. We find our seats but they're right near the back of the plane, about eight rows back from everyone else. On top of this, there is a well-built white man sat in one of the seats in the row directly behind us. This is making me nervous; it's obvious they've done this on purpose. We can't see the guy behind us or what he's doing. We're being treated like terrorists.

As if things can't get any more absurd, the English wrestler we saw in the airport bar, the same guy from the hostel, gets on the plane and sits down at the very front, by the aisle. There's an air stewardess standing up at the front, facing everyone, talking and laughing with him, as if they're good mates. She passes a huge knife to him, the size of a sword. He's holding it up in the centre of the aisle, twisting it round in his hand, reflecting the light off it. No-one else on the plane budges an inch. Any normal person, if they see someone with a sword on a plane, particularly after nine-eleven, would go fucking crazy! What the fuck's going on? The only thing this can mean is that everyone on this plane, bar us, has been planted here. We're helpless against almost a hundred people. Are we going to get stabbed on a plane? Even the airplane crew are in on this – how the fuck is this possible?

Marshy's got the window seat and I'm sitting in the middle chair. The seat on my right is empty. Marshy can't bear to sit on the outside. We both still think we're going to die but I'm starting to build up some defiance inside me now; I've accepted that if it's going to happen, it's going to happen, but I'm not going to be killed without putting up a fight. I'm ready to pounce on anyone that tries anything. Just fucking try it, you cunts. I'll go fucking mental. If either of me and Marshy are going be stabbed, it's going to be me first, unless that bloke behind us reaches over and slits our throats; he could get either one of us first; we can't see him or what he's doing.

"This is it, Bill. They're gonna kill us now and throw us off the plane."

"Don't say shit like that, Marshy."

"I know it, man. If you make it out alive, tell my Mum and Dad I love them."

"We're gonna be alright, the flight's not long, if we make it to Miami, we'll be alright."

We're waiting for the plane to take off and the air stewardess is handing out plastic disposable rubber gloves to everyone at the front of the plane. Do they need these to stop them from getting blood on their hands? Several of the passengers are taking it in turns to go to the toilet, and they have to walk past us to get there. Every time one of them goes by, they put their hand in their pocket and pull it out, right at the very moment they pass us, as if they're going to pull out a knife and attack us. I tense up, gripping the armrests every time someone walks past, preparing myself to react to any sudden movements; watching each one of them carefully, until they're out of harm's reach. They don't make eye contact with us; they're all trying to tease us. We're communicating with each other using hand gestures and facial expressions, to confirm we're seeing the same things, as they happen. We need to be on guard at all times; we can't lose our concentration for one second, otherwise that might be it – the end. This twat behind us is sitting there in silence, trying to listen in to what we're saying; watching our every move. People in the seats at the front are taking it in turns to raise their arms, making stabbing motions. I hear one of them.

"When are we gonna do it?"

Marshy alerts me to another noise.

"Bill, can you hear that behind us? It's a fuckin' drill."

"A drill?"

"He's got a drill, behind us. We're gonna be fuckin' tortured and chopped into pieces! This is it!"

I need to get a hold of myself again. We're getting carried away. After everything that happened in the motel room, all the times we thought we were going to die, we got out okay. They were trying to destabilise us; to make us think we're going to die. It was mental torture but nothing actually happened to us. This is what they're trying to do now, on the plane with the sword; seating us back here, eight rows away from everyone else with someone behind, to make us feel paranoid. They've planned all this – they want to make us think we're losing the plot, like we're going crazy. It's psychological warfare – I've sussed them out. If they wanted to harm us, surely they would've done something by now? It all makes sense now – everything they've been doing. They're trying to get us out of the States. But what've we done to deserve this? Was it all the drinking? Are we guinea pigs in some sick test? How could all this be possible? Who else can organise people like this? Have the money to employ them all? Have all these expensive vehicles? And be able to get knives on planes?! I'm on to them now, I know what they're trying to do and I'm not going to let them get to me anymore. Marshy isn't in a good state; he's still shitting himself, but I'm going to see him through this. Now, when people walk past I don't flinch, I don't tense up, I'm not taking the bait anymore.

We stay awake during the flight; we're too scared to close our eyes. The stream of people walking past us slows down but we can't relax. As soon as anyone moves, I peer over the top of the chairs so I can see what's going on, but there's no danger. Marshy's curled up on his seat, leaning against the inside of the plane with his hands between his legs, staring into thin air. He looks cold. The occasional movement from the person sat behind unsettles us. I'm too frightened to turn around and look him in the eye though. An hour later, when we've landed, one of the air stewardesses makes an announcement over the speaker system.

"Welcome to Miami, everyone, but not Billy and Marshy. We hope you have enjoyed your flight with us and we hope you have a tremendous stay in Miami – except for Billy and Marshy. Please remain seated until the seatbelts lights go off. We would like to thank you for travellin' with…"

"Did you hear her, Marshy? Sayin' our names at the end of the sentences, lowerin' her voice?"

"Yeah, mate, I heard her."

I see it now. I can see that they're doing this so we think we're going to be killed. They're using fear to get to us. We've got three choices – we can either give up, fight, or run. We aren't giving up, and there are too many of them to fight, so we're fucking running. That's what they want us to do, so they can play their sick games; they're toying with us like it's a game of cat and mouse.

No-one on the plane reacts to the air stewardess mentioning our names in the welcome message. It's like a play that has been rehearsed; they all know how to play their parts, what to do, what to say, how to react. It's like they're all trained. Their mission is to fuck with our heads. The sick fucking cunts, all of them. This is some fucked up target practice game for them. I know they're going to be following us around Miami as well, but we've just got to see it out and get back on that plane to Heathrow, as soon as we can.

Luck's Tether

When we get off the plane, I'm relieved that we're still in one piece. We haven't been stabbed, or murdered, or thrown out of the plane mid-flight. We both look shell-shocked and pale. We haven't slept for two days, which has fucked with our mental state. They've been keeping us awake; not allowing us to rest. It's all part of their tactics to keep us weak, so they can instil fear in us. We don't know why this is happening, but what we do know is that they want us out.

Miami, Florida

Ducking & Diving

It's early afternoon, just past midday. We get out of the airport quickly, as we don't have to hang around waiting for our luggage; that's gone to Austin without us. It's comforting to be back on familiar soil, where we started the trip, and that little bit closer to home. We've done this bit before; we know where the taxi rank is and where to ask the taxi driver to take us. If we went to Austin, we would be in the unknown, exactly where they want us. We can change our plane ticket going home, from Los Angeles to Miami. I'm not even considering completing the trip via LA now; there's only one place I'm going and that's home, as soon as I can.

Marshy's gone to use the phone. He's phoning his parents but he doesn't want to tell them anything is wrong. He tells them he's in Miami again and that he loves them. I'm on my own and I can't stand still. I'm tapping my foot and rocking backwards and forwards. Everyone around me is a suspect. I'm trying to make mental notes of people's faces in case I see them elsewhere. It's the hottest part of the day and it feels safe 'cause the sun is shining. There are a lot of people around, looking normal, but we're both running on empty. Is anyone following us? I'm looking all around, turning my head in every direction, slowly scanning the area. Where are those people from the plane? They're all part of the same group. I can't see them anywhere; maybe we can lose them for a bit.

We get a taxi from the front of the airport and tell him to take us to South Beach. After what happened in that motel room, at Atlanta airport, and on the plane, it's obvious that this group, whoever they are, have a whole network of connections working for them all over the country. If they're able to get people onto planes with swords, buy a shitload of plane tickets with cash, follow us in surveillance vans; and co-ordinate psychological torment in motel rooms with lasers, then they've probably got people operating in Miami as well. As soon as the taxi starts moving, we realise things are not about to let up, either.

The driver gets a call on his radio. We can't quite hear the exact words of the conversation, but the caller is asking where the driver is going. Our stalkers, with their powers and connections, must be able to get this information from the taxi company, just like they did in Atlanta, when they were waiting for us at that hotel in their blacked-out SUV's.

When we get back to South Beach, we decide it's best to go and stay in the same hotel we started at, 'cause we know the manager; the familiarity will help us settle down. They've also got private rooms you can lock, so we don't have to share with anyone else. Going back to the hostel isn't an option – we would have to share a room; if we get stuck with one of our stalkers, that could be the end of us.

The taxi driver stops a few hundred metres away from the entrance of the 'San Juan' hotel. This doesn't bother us at first, as we know it's only a few minutes' walk, but as we get out, there's a large group of people standing on the opposite side of the road. A woman from the group comes running across the road, signalling to the rest of them to follow her. Marshy's pointing at them.

"That must be them as well."

"Yeah, they're comin' to get a good look at us. They're straight onto us again."

The whole group cross the road. The taxi driver's been told to drop us off here, so they can all get a good look at our faces, so they know who to follow. They're watching our every step; more tactics to keep us scared. We walk the opposite way to the hotel, cross the road and walk back, to try and shake them off our tail and to see if they follow us; but they've seen us already. We march back to the hotel to see if we can get a room for the night.

As we enter, the same manager is behind the reception desk. He recognises us and we have a brief conversation about the other places we've been to, keeping our cards close to our chests. Our room is on the second floor, overlooking the main road. There are rooms either side of us. We rest on our beds. My body is drained of energy but my brain still won't let me switch off; the adrenaline is still pumping through my veins. The last twenty--four hours have been surreal, but being back in Miami is like seeing a glimpse of the light at the end of the tunnel.

Innocent people around South Beach are carrying on with their daily lives as normal, but little do they know two English tourists are on the run, locked away in a hotel room. They're walking past our window and they haven't got the slightest idea what's going on. Last night's panic has subsided. We can regroup and think about who we need to look out for.

It's easy enough to spot the people that will be following us. They'll be using mobile phones to communicate our whereabouts when we walk past them. We'll hear them talking and we'll catch them looking at us. We need to be aware of the red lasers; any suspicious-looking vans or SUVs with tinted windows, parked up with their engines running. They can be people of all ages, but it's the younger ones we need to be wary of; they're the most dangerous – quick, strong, and maybe carrying weapons. If there are more people like those wrestlers, they could overpower us – they're the ones who could physically hurt us or throw us into a van. They'll try to psychologically torment us to keep us panicking. We know how they operate and we know their tactics. We need to be on our guard. We need to listen carefully to what people around us are saying; they might let something slip; they might give the game away. We've got to think carefully about our next move, think two or three moves ahead. We've got to be ready to react quickly and change our plans if we're getting backed into a corner; vary our movements so we're not in the same place for too long. Tire them out, keep moving, don't stay still. These people have got a mission to follow us, scare us; they won't stop. I've had enough; I've reached my limits. I'm starting to overcome this psychological cage they're trying to put us in; I'm fighting back now. They're not going to get to me anymore. This is a game, a test of my mental strength; they're not going to beat me. They'll have to kill me; I'm not going to take this lying down. Let's come out fighting; let's stand up to them. If I have to fight them, I'll fight them; I'm not going to roll over and let them walk all over us. It's me and Marshy against them all and our mission is to make it out of Miami, alive.

The games begin straight away. We're lying down on our beds, trying to sleep. We've opened the windows to let some fresh air in. We hear someone outside the hotel, shouting up to the windows. Marshy gets up and slowly pulls back the curtain, to see who it is.

"What's going on out there, Marshy?"

"Some geezer's standin' outside, lookin' up at our window."

"What the fuck's he doing?"

"Dunno, I can't hear what he's sayin'. He's talkin' to someone in a car by the side of the road."

"What the fuck, man! Not more people. When the fuck's this thing gonna end?"

"He's going now, but he's seen me so he knows what room we're in."

"Oh fuckin' great!"

We've only been at the hotel for twenty minutes and they're on to us already. As we try to rest, cars drive past, sounding off their horns at the exact moment they pass our room. It isn't a long press of the horn, just a quick tap and it happens every few minutes. There aren't any traffic jams outside the hotel and there aren't any traffic lights close by either. It's another way of letting us know they're watching us; another way of stopping us from getting any sleep; there's no other reason for them to do it. We've got to ignore it; put it to the back of our minds; we can't let them get to us.

We leave our room to find an internet café, to get the number for the British Embassy in Florida. They should be able to help us. We call them from a phone box on one of the main roads.

"Hello. My name's Billy Walker. Me and my friend are in some trouble."

"What's the problem? Can you tell me about the situation?"

I explain the chase and what's happened in Atlanta, on the plane, and now in Miami.

"I need to know if there's anythin' you can do to help us."

"Well, I'm sorry to hear about your situation but there isn't really anything we can do for you."

"Nothin' you can do? Our lives are being threatened and you're sayin' you can't do anythin' about it?"

"I'm very sorry, sir. There's only one flight back to Heathrow today and it leaves in ten minutes, so you've already missed check-in, and I'm pretty sure they won't hold it up for you."

"What, so you're sayin' there's absolutely nothin' you can do? You can't let us into the embassy to be safe?"

"No, I'm afraid not. We finish work at five-thirty and the building's locked overnight. You'll just have to try to change your flights with your airline or tour operator. At the earliest, if you're lucky, you might be able to get tomorrow's flight."

"What're we supposed to do in the meantime?"

"Sit tight and make sure you lock your doors when you go to sleep and just be careful where you go and who you speak to."

I was hoping for a bit more. I can't believe this is all the help they can give us.

"You might be able to get tomorrow's flight if you're lucky."

What the fuck are they actually there for? We call on them for help, as British citizens, when we're in danger, and the fucking idiots tell us what we already know. That means we've got the whole day to kill, being watched everywhere we go. This is going to be a long day.

On every corner we walk past, one of our stalkers is standing there, waiting, talking on a mobile phone; they're tracking our every move. We're pointing at them as we walk past.

"We know you're workin' for them."

They walk away quickly, as soon as they're identified. We go to the beach. As soon as we sit down on the sand, an old couple walks over and sits down about ten metres behind us. Every fifteen minutes, a different couple swaps places with them, and they're all looking at us, constantly. It's obvious they're following us; they could sit anywhere else on the beach; there's no-one else in sight; we can't get away from them. As we walk around the town, there are people behind us who stop when we stop. We turn around to check if they're still there and sure enough, they're standing still, talking on a mobile phone. At one point, we even walk a few miles out of South Beach and the same people are still following us all the way.

We need to try to change our flights before it's too late. We phone our travel agent. Luckily, as it's the middle of February and off-peak season, there are spaces left, and they allow us to change our flights so we can fly back from Miami tomorrow, instead of Los Angeles in three weeks' time. Even though they charge us a fee for this pleasure, it's the first bit of luck we've had in what seems like a fucking eternity. I can't help thinking we should be having fun in Austin right now, where our luggage is, but instead we're in this shitty hotel, being followed and tormented. What the fuck have we done to deserve this?

We're exhausted; I've still not slept. After spending the rest of the afternoon and evening at the hotel room, I'm beginning to get cabin fever. We go for a beer. It's a bold move 'cause we might put ourselves in danger, but we can't cocoon ourselves in that room all day and night. We know we've got to be careful where we walk; if we go down the wrong road, they'll be there waiting for the right opportunity to kidnap us and bundle us into a waiting van. We need to stick to the busy main roads and the tourist areas, in the view of the public; stay on streets that are lit up. That way, they can't use the darkness as their cover; it'll make it harder for them to get us where they want us. I can feel them waiting to strike; I can feel the eyes all over us. We walk along a row of shops into the centre of South Beach, up the main shopping precinct. It's busy with people eating outside. Most of the restaurants are full, so there are too many witnesses for us to be in any danger. As we walk up the precinct, we can see people strategically placed in the doorways of closed shops. They're on their own, talking on mobile phones. They all say 'they've just passed', as we walk by.

At the end of the street is a bar we've been to before. We don't want to go any further, as the street lights stop and there aren't any people. We go inside, get a beer, and start playing pool. From playing so many games during this trip, we had reached quite a good standard, but right now, our nerves are shot to pieces; we're both missing most of our shots. It's a relief to see a ball get potted. My eyes can't focus and my brain won't coordinate my arms how I want them to. I'm a nervous wreck. Having to concentrate on a relatively simple task, like using a pool cue, is highlighting how fucked I am. Halfway into our second game, two American blokes come over to the table and ask to play us, winner-stays-on. Marshy accepts their offer. We look at each other, confirming our joint suspicion; these two Americans are part of the surveillance, posing as friendly guys. As the first guy's preparing to break, he whispers in his friend's ear, putting his hand over his mouth, and they burst out laughing when he finishes talking. It's childish taunting, meant to wind us up; they're using that psychological torment again. We know what's going on and we're copying them, whispering between ourselves, showing them we're not affected by their tactics. Marshy walks around the table to take his shot; he's near the Yanks. He comes back over to me, keeping his back turned to the Americans.

"Mate, have you heard what those blokes are talkin' about?"

"No, what?"

"They're talkin' about us. They've just been talkin' about someone shaggin' a Canadian bird in a Mercedes Benz, which was me, and someone pissin' on an air conditionin' unit in New Orleans. Then they said somethin' about playin' rugby in Atlanta. How the fuck do they know this shit?"

"No way, man, there's no way they should know that stuff. That means we've been followed since New Orleans, at least!"

"Let's finish this game and go back to the hotel room. I can't be arsed with any more of their shit."

The lack of sleep is affecting my ability to function. The beer isn't going down easily and we know we're being followed everywhere we go. I want to try to sleep now; it's been too long.

Back at the hotel, it's time for more drama, and this can't be a coincidence. As we get into the lift, the wrestler, from the hostel back in Atlanta, walks into the hotel with two other guys. This is the same bloke we keep seeing – at the hostel, the airport on the plane back to Miami, and now here. The lift doors close, giving us plenty of time to scurry into our room once we get upstairs, without having to be confronted. I lock our door and press my ear against it, listening intently to the noises in the corridor. The sound of the lift goes; it must be them. I'm trying to figure out what room they're going in. We hear a door close followed by voices and movement in the room next door to us. We're in for another long night. I whisper to Marshy.

"Go in the bathroom."

"Why?"

"To try and listen to them. Look up there…you see that air conditionin' vent?"

"Oh yeah."

"Let's see if we can hear anythin'."

We climb onto the edge of the bath and perch our feet over the edges, to manoeuvre ourselves as close to the air vent as possible. I can hear one of them.

"I'm gonna get that Billy and string him up and cut him into pieces."

That fucking prick. Just try it, you cunt. I'm ready to fucking kick-off; I'm fuming inside, but I know there's nothing I can do. I'm not going to go over there and start swinging, but if they try anything on me, I won't be holding back. I keep telling myself, if they were going to do something, they would've done it by now; they're only doing this to scare us. But I might be wrong. The rage is bubbling up inside of me; I'm ready to do whatever it takes to survive. They're next door and it's unsettled us, again. My bed is closest to the door so I'll be the first person they get to. The possibility of another night of torment is quickly becoming a reality.

Marshy's checking outside again. He leans out of the open window and sees a car parked a few metres down the road. He waves at it and the lights come on. A head appears out of the driver's side of the car and a voice shouts "Fuck you, man". Then the speaker drives off. Another one of the stalkers clocked. Once we identify them, they disappear and leave, then someone else takes their place, parking up somewhere different or standing in a different place. They don't want us to be able to identify them.

It's getting dark now. I can't let my mind rest; I can't let my guard down. I try to sleep but I can't. I can hear people in the corridor and a red laser is coming through the keyhole in the door. This time, the dimensions of the room allow us to stand either side of the door so they can't focus the beams on our bodies. I stand in front of the door and the beam stops. I fill the keyhole up with paper and put a towel down on the floor so the lasers can't get through. We can walk around the room at ease now; We can stand, sit, or lie where we want without having the curse of those red lights on us.

We're both lying on our beds. I think Marshy's asleep but I

can't tell and I don't want to disturb him if he is. I've got to stay awake to keep watch, just in case they storm the room. I sit and wait as each hour goes past. I treat myself to a cigarette every half hour, making it last as long as I can. It's pitch black. Everything is silent. I sit as still as I possibly can, listening out for the slightest noise in the room next door, or outside in the corridor. The only noise I'm making is when I take a toke of my cigarette and tap the ash. I can hear each flake of tobacco burning every time I inhale from the filter.

It's five o'clock in the morning and I've run out of cigarettes. It was around this time when things calmed down last night. I shut my eyes and lie completely still. I've outlasted them; they've gone, but I still can't sleep.

As soon as it's a reasonable time in the morning to leave the hotel, we get a taxi and go straight to the airport. We check in without any issues and find the departure lounge. We're one step away from the plane and our safety. We know Virgin airlines won't allow knives on their planes. I can't wait to step through that gate, away from the madness. But we've got a few hours to kill before the plane starts boarding; it's far from over yet.

I want a ciggie, so I tell Marshy I'm going back outside. I know I've got to go through all the checks again, but as long as I've got my passport and nothing else, it won't take long to get back through. On my way back to the departure lounge, a woman checks my passport. As she passes it back, she puts two fingers to her mouth and crosses her eyes, as if to simulate someone being high from smoking drugs. They're in here too, working in the airport. How does she know this? They can still get to us in here and they know exactly where we are.

Time at the Bar

There's only one hour to go until we board; the finish line is in sight. We're at the bar in the departure lounge and we order a pint of lager each. The bartender says he'll bring our drinks over to us, so we find a table and wait. Marshy's drinking his faster than me; he's had half a pint within five minutes. I've barely had a quarter of mine. I'm chatting to him about getting home. He's called his parents to tell them we've changed our flights. He's told them what's been happening and they've been worrying so much, they've arranged to pick us up from the airport. Whilst we're talking, I notice his face is going bright red.

"Mate, are you alright?"

"No, man, I don't feel so good."

"What's up? D'ya feel sick?"

"No, I just feel really hot; I think I've got a temperature."

He doesn't look good at all; he looks like his face is about to explode and his head is rolling around uncontrollably. He's only had half a pint and he's usually pretty hardcore when it comes to boozing. I've known him for ten years and never seen him react like this to alcohol, especially not from half a pint. I start feeling my face heating up too.

"Is my face going red too?"

He struggles to speak back to me; his eyes are closing as he tries to fight what's happening to him. He opens his eyes, looks at me, and mumbles.

"Yeah, man, you're going red too."

It hits me; our drinks have been spiked with something. It must have been the barman. He's working for them too.

"Quick! Get to the toilets – we need to puke this beer back up."

"In a second, man."

"No, not in a second, man, get up NOW!" I grab Marshy by the arm and hurry us to the toilets, opposite the bar. We're both keeled over a sink and we're sticking our fingers down our throats, forcing ourselves to be sick. It's horrible. As soon as my finger hits the back of my throat, I retch violently and I'm panicking. The beer is coming back up and it's mixed with the acid in my stomach. My throat is burning and the taste is unbearable. I wince with pain. I'm drinking water from the tap and spewing it back up again. I don't know if we've done this in time to get the drugs out of our system before they're absorbed in our stomachs, but there's no way we can go to a doctor; we'll miss the flight and that's exactly what they're trying to make us do. It's their last attempt to fuck us up; we can't let them win.

We wash our faces and walk out to the departure lounge. We don't go back to the bar; instead, we go to the seats by the gate where we'll board the plane. One step closer to home. As we walk past the bar, I hold a hostile stare at the barman, insinuating his guilt, and that I know what he's done. That fucking cunt. I want to smash the prick's face in, but I can't cause a scene in here; I'll get arrested or kicked out.

I'm looking for some spare seats, away from other people, so we don't have to talk to anyone. I don't want anyone to see what a messed-up state we're in; they might grass us up or alert a medic. With half an hour to go until boarding, Marshy's face is still bright red and he's struggling to stay awake. I'm not feeling good but Marshy's had a lot more of the spiked drink than I have. Fuck, just what I don't need – an American family has sat down next to me and the dad is trying to be friendly. He's started talking about the weather in England. I'm trying to be polite, whilst keeping an eye on Marshy to make sure he doesn't pass out. I really can't be arsed with the small talk so I'm short with my responses and he soon takes the hint.

I'm looking around to see if there's any potential danger. Is someone else going to throw another spanner in the works? Everyone looks familiar, like I've seen them all on our travels, from all the different cities we've been to. They're all here now; all the people that we've pissed off, all the people that have been chasing us. They're all part of this. Maybe we've been followed from the start? Who are these people? Why are they chasing us? I'm going through everything that's happened, trying to figure it out. The passport officers, when we first arrived, were so suspicious of us, asking all those questions. They're paranoid of everyone, 'cause of nine-eleven, and maybe they thought we looked shady? They were suspicious of us quitting our jobs to come to the USA. Maybe they were following us right from the start but we didn't realise it until we got to Atlanta.

Or the guy that drank the hot sauce in New Orleans. He was completely humiliated. Marshy shaves his hair and makes him look like an idiot, then he downs that hot sauce and the ambulance and police are called out, then I pull the bird he fancies. He must have hated us. Maybe he's rich and we pissed him off so much, he's paid to have us chased?

Or what about the owner of the India House hostel in New Orleans? I pissed on their air conditioning unit and we were involved in the hot sauce incident when the police turned up, after being kicked out and let back in. That can't have done their reputation any good; it was probably bad for business. Maybe he wanted to teach us a lesson? And if the hostel owners around the States communicate with each other, they could've planted those two English wrestlers in the Atlanta hostel, to get us back.

It could be the bouncer I punched in the bar on Bourbon Street. Maybe he wanted revenge and he's got connections? Maybe he was following us and it was him at the club in Nashville?

What about the Autodriveaway car we delivered late, in Memphis? Was there something in that car the owners thought we knew about? Some drugs they thought we were trying to steal? Or did the Autodriveaway manager's call to the police set alarm bells ringing, so they informed the FBI, who followed us from Memphis onwards? Maybe they thought we were using the cars for dealing drugs or something more sinister?

It could've been the mental bloke in Nashville, at the girls' house. Maybe he fancies one of girls and he thought we were trying to shag them? It would've been easy for him to follow us – the birds drove us back to Charlie's house, so they knew where we were staying and Atlanta isn't far from Nashville.

Maybe there's something fucked up going on in that hostel in Atlanta? Some kind of weird cult? I don't know what we did to piss them off, but that's where it all went mental; and that one wrestler has been showing up, wherever we go. It's definitely got something to do with him.

Maybe we've been guinea pigs for some kind of psychological warfare test, set up by a secret organisation in America. It has been pretty fucked up – all the resources they've had at their disposal – the technology and surveillance they've been capable of, the cameras in the hostel room, the blacked-out SUV's following us and blocking the entrance to the hotel, the lasers at the motel, the white van, the connections in the airports, the knife on the plane, the fact we were sat eight rows back from everyone else on the plane, the lady on the tannoy saying our names, all the people following us around Miami, our drinks being spiked by the barman. All this wouldn't be possible unless it was arranged by a powerful, wealthy agency that operates under the radar, with people employed as secret agents or spies. Who else could have people working for them inside airports, getting swords on planes and spiking people in departure lounge bars? Who else could train people to be able to intimidate us, mentally and physically? They've shepherded us where they want us to go – out of the country.

But maybe all of this is just some fucked up effect from the drugs we took? We don't even know what we took! It could have been crystal meth, angel dust, or LSD. What if it was all just a paranoid hallucination? Me and Marshy could've been planting ideas in each other's heads – our fears. Maybe none of this happened at all and we've experienced some kind of synchronised hallucination, where we can't tell the difference between what is actually happening and what our minds are making up? Marshy says he hears robotic cameras in the room, then I hear them too; if I say I see red lasers, then Marshy sees them too. If Marshy smells gas in the room, I start smelling it; we trust each other to the point where we believe whatever the other one says; so much so that we hallucinate it. Before we know it, we think everyone's following us; everyone's part of this scam to get us, when actually none of it's happening at all. Was anyone actually outside the motel room in Atlanta? We didn't physically see anyone, just shadows. Surely the security guard would've seen something? We didn't get poisoned by any gas. Did we actually see a sword in the guy's hand on the plane? Or were we hallucinating and it was something else? We were eight rows back from everyone else on the plane, but that was probably because we approached the policeman before we boarded, and they thought we could be a danger to other people. Maybe the drugs we took induced a form of psychosis? We believed the people in the hostel were laughing at us when actually, they were just talking amongst themselves. And the group in South Beach that we suspected of following us could've just been crossing the road at the same time we arrived. We could make anything fit into the story that we're being followed; we're just hearing and seeing what we want to believe. We haven't been thinking rationally.

It's been like having a dream that I'm being chased, except I've been awake. The more I think about it, the more it seems like one big episode of paranoia, brought on by the drugs. But then again, it can't just be the drugs – there are things that have happened that can't have been hallucinations, like the black vehicle following us to the supermarket and the white van chasing us to the airport – you don't hallucinate a white van with blacked-out windows; and in any case, the taxi driver saw it too. And the wrestler from the hostel turning up on our plane and at the hotel in Miami – that's no coincidence. How the fuck did it get to this? We can't take the chance that this is all just a hallucination, and anyway, it's too late to change our minds now. My only concern is to make it onto that plane.

So many times when I've been on a night out, me or one of my friends have been turned away for looking too drunk. At least when you're at home, you can go somewhere else, but this time, we've got to get past the cabin crew to get on a plane – there's a lot more at stake. We have to get through so we can get home, five thousand miles away. We can't afford to get stopped for looking too wasted. We haven't exactly done ourselves any favours, though. We've barely slept for three days; our faces are bright red, our eyes are bloodshot and half-cut. I can't help but think the cabin crew are going to pull us aside and stop us from getting on.

I'm tapping Marshy and shaking him every few minutes, to keep him awake. I'm trying to coach him on what he's got to do when we walk over; and I'm going over what I'm going to say, if they ask me any questions.

The gate opens and boarding begins. Most of the other people have got up, to get in the queue, but we've stayed seated until it quiets down. I don't want to stand in line, swaying all over the place. I hand Marshy some chewing gum and have a piece myself, to get rid of any potent smells from when we were sick. I shake Marshy's arm and stand him up. It's time for the defining moment. We walk over to the queue. Everything is happening in slow motion. We approach the stewardess. She looks at me but I dodge her attempt to make eye contact. She asks to see our passports and then the dreaded question comes.

"Is he okay?" She's nodding towards Marshy. My heart's in the back of my throat. I can feel my chest pounding. I swallow the saliva building up in my mouth and respond with a smile.

"He's fine…we just had a heavy night and we're a bit tired. Looking forward to some sleep on the plane!"

"Okay…through you go then, please." And she waves us on. I've never felt a feeling of relief like I do when I get on the plane.

I put our hand luggage in the compartments above the seats and we sit down. I do my seatbelt up straight away. We've made it. I feel safe now. I inhale and exhale one large breath and my body lets out a long and thankful sigh. I close my eyes and drift, instantly, into a deep, deep sleep.

I open my eyes. The Panic is over.